T0043883

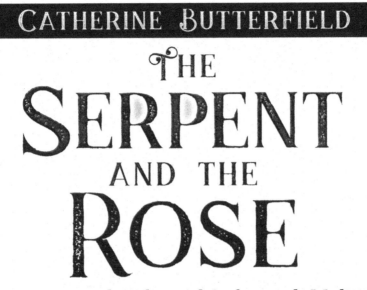

CATHERINE BUTTERFIELD

THE SERPENT AND THE ROSE

Marguerite de Valois and Catherine de Medici
A mother-daughter battle for the ages

Print ISBN: 979-8-35092-801-3
eBook ISBN: 979-8-35092-802-0

For my mother, who bears no resemblance.

HISTORICAL NOTE

The French Wars of Religion raged between the years of 1562 and 1589. Millions of people died, directly or through the disease and starvation that resulted from displacement and violence. It threatened the power of the monarchy and took an enormous toll on France's standing in Europe. When Frances II died in 1560, his mother Catherine de Medici cleverly pitted two powerful factions against one another and rose above the fray to become regent for her second son Charles. The extreme actions taken in the name of saving France have caused her name to go down in history, perhaps unfairly, as "The Serpent Queen."

Marguerite de Valois was Catherine's youngest daughter and was, unlike her other children, favored with unusual beauty, intelligence, and wit. Catherine's attempts to exploit her daughter's gifts and make use of her as a political pawn caused Marguerite to become the object of deep resentment on both sides of the religious conflict. A political pamphlet published in 1660 entitled "The Satiric Divorce" depicted Marguerite as a deranged sexual deviant whose unnatural number of lovers included a couple of her brothers. Her reputation never really recovered.

The author of the pamphlet was never identified, but one can speculate.

PRIMARY PERSONAE

Marguerite de Valois, Princess of France

Catherine de Medici, mother to Marguerite

King Charles of France, brother to Marguerite

Henri de Bourbon, Prince of Navarre

Henri, Duke of Guise

Duke of Alencon, brother to Marguerite

Jeanne d'Albret, Queen of Navarre

Jean d'Aubiac, First Equerry to the Crown

Duke of Anjou, later King Henri III of France, brother to Marguerite

Adrienne, Countess de Lalaing

Princess de Roche-sur-Yon

Don John of Spain

Cardinal Lenoncourt, advisor to Marguerite

Rosalind, Maria, and Agatha - Ladies in Waiting

Incidental Characters of Note

William Shakespeare, poet and playwright

Queen Elizabeth of England

1.

"There is no stronger test of a person's character than power and authority, exciting as they do every passion, and discovering every latent vice."

– Plutarch

1581

5 May, 1581 – Perigord

Our journey must be cursed. First, the rain; buckets of it for three days even though Nostradamus assured Mother the skies would be clear, and when the rains finally stopped it became so hot that one of our bishops collapsed whilst carrying his saintly relic. I suppose walking for a hundred miles next to a royal procession isn't easy, but do they not practice? Perhaps they should have found a younger bishop. From the window of my litter, I can see Mother pacing back and forth impatiently as they attempt to revive the old fellow. It's against all protocol for her to leave her litter unmasked, but that's Mother. She probably thinks it will attract God's attention to the situation if Catherine de Medici displays her face to the heavens.

Plutarch, my favorite author, writes, "What we achieve inwardly will change outward reality." I am very attracted to that notion and am desperately trying to achieve an inner calm to alter the fact that Mother is screeching orders outside my litter. Why is she so excitable? I have heard people suggest (behind closed doors, of course) that Mother is a witch, and it's true that she does make it easy to draw such unpleasant conclusions. Her unruly hair, piercing black eyes, and hooked nose terrified me as a child. Add to that the fact that she frequently mutters dark imprecations in Italian, a language few at court have bothered to learn, and it's no wonder they connect her to the dark arts. I shall attempt to rise above the commotion taking place outside my litter, to reflect on the circumstances that have brought me to this point.

The seeds of our journey were planted over a month ago. It was a rainy day, but my ladies and I were having the loveliest afternoon inside the Louvre Palace. Madame de Tournon was braiding and bejeweling my hair for the ball that night, and Lady Agatha was singing a sweet *chanson* whilst Ladies Rosalind and Maria practiced dance steps together. The room was filled with fresh roses, the scent of which rendered me slightly drowsy and filled me with a sense of well-being. Does any other flower have that delicious effect? I think not. There was much to look forward to, with the promise of an evening's entertainment lying ahead.

Suddenly, the doors were thrown open, and my mother marched furiously into the room accompanied by Charles, who should have entered first as he is king, but Mother was too angry to remember that. My ladies jumped up and curtsied, but Mother pushed past them and placed herself face to face with me, fairly quivering with rage. Charles turned to my ladies and bellowed as best he could in a voice that had only recently broken with adolescence.

"Leave us!" They all rushed from the room, but I'm quite sure they stood by the door to listen to the humiliation that was about to unfold. Mother grabbed me by the arm. She's small, but she has a fierce grip.

"What is this I hear about you and Henri of Guise? How dare you go behind my back?" She slapped me hard. It took me a moment to recover from the shock; Mother hadn't slapped me since childhood.

"Mother, I don't know what you've heard. It's nothing! A flirtation only."

"Don't lie to me, whore!" She pulled me up by the hair and rained down a series of blows upon my person, causing me to fall to the floor. I screamed, more in injured pride than in pain. Charles clapped his hands with enjoyment and offered a few kicks to my person himself; those hurt.

"You will not! Form an alliance! With that man!" Mother screamed, ripping at my lovely new gown. She and Charles issued a thousand threats about the repercussions that would unfold if I allied myself with any member of the Guise line, then left me alone to sob in humiliation. My ladies tiptoed back in with sympathetic expressions, but I couldn't face them and rushed to my bedchamber to weep alone. How could they treat me so viciously, when all I ever do is march to the step they set? I am a princess of France; should not be permitted to choose with whom I have flirtations?

Impossible to go to the ball now, with scratches on my face. How hideous my life was! I spent about an hour more on wrenching self-pity and then, because I consider myself to be a rational individual, composed myself and tried to take a clear-eyed look at the facts that led to this dire moment.

Mother hates the Guise family. During the short time when my oldest brother Francis was king, Henri's father François practically ruled France as his regent. Mother strongly felt that she should be regent, so she cultivated my brother Charles and awaited her moment. When Francis suddenly died – no, Mother did not kill him! Why do horrible rumors like this persist, he was her son! – When he died, Charles took the throne, and Mother managed to get herself named as regent this time. It was not taken well by the Guise clan.

When whispers about my dalliance with the Duke of Guise reached her ears, I should have known Mother would be angry. And I did, of course, I should be honest about that. I didn't, however, anticipate the extent of her fury, and I was completely unprepared for what happened next.

About a week later, I was summoned to the King's chambers. Charles and Mother were both there, and so was Henri of Guise, looking enormously uncomfortable. Although he customarily stood quite near to the throne, he was now relegated to the back row with a couple of bishops. Henri normally bears himself proudly and even arrogantly, but that day he looked small and covert, with his nose twitching occasionally like a field mouse. His gaze was fixed as I entered, apparently fascinated by something on the far wall. I curtseyed to Charles and my mother, then waited to hear the reason for my presence there, deeply hoping it was not to be a public upbraiding.

"Daughter," said my mother, "we bring you joyous news. A match has been arranged between you and the Prince of Navarre. His mother, Jeanne d'Albret, has agreed in principle to this felicitous union, and a royal procession is being arranged to take you to Nérac in a fortnight to meet Prince

Henri. The King has commanded that I accompany you, which I am most happy to do. *Félicitations!*"

I stared at my mother in confusion. "But, Moth- Your Majesty, the Prince of Navarre is a Huguenot."

"Yes. The King feels that a union between our two religions will send a signal to the country that the wars between Catholics and Protestants must cease."

I looked to my brother, who managed somehow to appear both fat and gangly splayed out on his throne like a frog. Realizing something was required of him, he pounded the arm of his throne. "These wars must cease!" he croaked.

"If I may," I ventured, "will not a marriage such as the one described have the reverse effect? The people of France –"

"Silence!" my mother snapped. "The people of France will accept the marriage when we inform them of it. Resolve yourself to this fate, Marguerite. We live in difficult times."

Charles waved me away with a flick of his wrist.

I curtseyed again and made my way out, trying to catch Henri's eye, but his gaze was still committed elsewhere.

I, marry a Huguenot? I understood that they were angry with me, but to punish me in this way! What honest citizen of France wants to see his devout Catholic princess auctioned off to a heretic? Protestants don't view the Virgin Mary as the queen of heaven; they don't worship her in any way. What good is a religion that offers only men to pray to? And Henri of Navarre, of all people, the leading Huguenot in France! The idea is heresy!

However, with Mother's assurance that all would go brilliantly, arrangements were made for our royal procession to the kingdom of Navarre, so that the Prince and I may meet and she may be able to finalize the terms of the nuptials with his mother, Jeanne d'Albret. I have maintained outward calm, but inside I am simmering – *simmering* – with resentment.

They have tried to do this to me before. First, I was supposed to marry the Archduke Rudolf of Austria, a stiff and repulsive man; I'm very glad that never came to fruition. Then there was a plan for me to wed the son of King Felipe of Spain; I'm not sure what went wrong there but he ended up marrying my sister Elizabeth. After that, they tried to wed me to the King of Portugal, but he didn't like the way the Huguenots were being "suppressed", as he put it, and withdrew his agreement. It's embarrassing to be the subject of all these failed attempts, but of course, Mother and her cronies never consider my feelings in their schemes. I have half a mind to sabotage this next attempt myself.

(I see the bishop is not dead; a relief. He's been given a flagon of wine, and they are transporting him to our supply wagon for the rest of the journey. Will the other bishops swoon away in envious imitation? It remains to be seen.)

Henri came to me a few nights ago. A hidden stairway leads from the grounds of the castle to my apartments, and I had recently allowed him to visit me there, but only with my ladies present. This time he appeared after my ladies had retired which was most forward of him and, considering the circumstances, dangerous. He found me in my bedchamber, reading.

"Henri!" I leapt out of bed, flustered. He had never seen me in my dressing gown, and I was also terrified of the repercussions should someone discover him there. There are spies everywhere in the palace.

"Marguerite, *ma rose*, forgive me but I had to see you before your departure." He flung his cloak and hat aside and clasped me into his arms, overwhelming me with a cloud of his hair powder. "This match between you and Navarre is madness."

"I know, but I'm sure it will come to naught. I intend to make myself utterly repellent to the man. Giggle inanely for no reason, mutter loud prayers to the Virgin at every lull in the conversation."

"That will accomplish nothing. You are the most desirable woman in France; everyone knows that." This comment might look romantic on the page, but he said it most accusingly. I believe he realized that, because he softened his tone and took my hand.

"Mon ange, forgive me. It's just that I feel so deeply for you, and it seemed you and I were achieving a special intimacy."

"Of course, but don't despair. Remember how Mother said Jeanne d'Albret agreed to this match 'in principle.' I'm sure the Queen of Navarre will find a way to scuttle negotiations."

"It's true that the woman is a known fanatic. Oh, Marguerite, you look exquisite in this dressing gown – no, don't blush! The way your breasts peek above the top of your gown, those perfect orbs I worship so ardently. Perhaps, at long last, we can take these final moments *before you leave and* turn them into a memory neither of us will ever forget." He drew my body closer to his, breathing into my ear, murmuring my name - and I was suddenly overcome by the sensation I always experience when Henri attempts to seduce me.

Queasiness.

I want to experience love. I've been proclaimed by many to be the most beautiful woman in France, and though Mother's strenuous protections have kept me virginal, I'm sure most people assume I am very learned in the ways of love. The fact is, however, that I haven't been able to overcome a strange revulsion whenever events with Henri take a carnal turn. I'm happy to flirt, kiss, dance, and play the coquette, but when it comes to the idea of consummation, I feel nothing, no stirrings within my soul. Is it the pomades and perfumes that Henri applies to his beard and mustache? His embarrassingly poetic style of conversing? Is it the fact that we are of almost identical height, or perhaps the taste of his kisses? (Yes, that most certainly has something to do with it.) As much as I want to become a *femme du monde*, I just can't overcome my inner disgust. And so, that night, I found myself once again resisting his increasingly urgent advances.

"Henri...my love, it's so late. Henri, let us not be hasty... Henri, no – please –"

"Your Highness? Is there anything you require before I retire for the night?"

We turned. Rosalind was smiling in the doorway. Henri, who had been pressing his advantage rather unfairly, drew instantly away from me and examined his sleeve with interest.

"Thank you no, Rosalind. The Duke was just taking his leave."

"Yes, yes," muttered Henri. "Always a pleasure." As he left, I mouthed the word *merci* to Rosalind. Henri in theory is a much more persuasive concept than the man in person.

Cardinal de Lenoncourt has been aroused from his slumbers within his litter, and is selecting a new bishop to carry the saintly relic. Of which saint are they the remains, I wonder? I suspect it's the vial of blood from St. Januarius, the patron saint of Naples. Mother has a particular fondness for him, being Italian. Born in the third century, he was beheaded for his Christianity, poor fellow. One could remark that those were savage times, but when I hear of the violent doings of Huguenots, I doubt they were any more savage than our own.

Whilst Mother terrorizes her entourage, I find myself contemplating her litter. Suspended between two black stallions it is itself jet black, devoid of ornamentation, and projects an air of deep gloom and possible menace. Even the leather interior is black. Contrast that with my litter, which is a lovely pale blue with ornate gold molding and fleur-de-lys decorations, suspended between two darling palominos. I chose the color scheme myself to set off my flaxen hair, I feel it conveys a more positive image of royalty for the world to behold. Instead of black for the Queen Regent's litter, why not the *bleu de France*? Or a commanding purple, to delight the eye? Mother, however, enjoys being perceived as wicked; it renders her opponents more pliable. I'll never forget the time when, with an ominous flourish, she offered a goblet of wine to a prelate with whom she was having a dispute. The poor man fainted dead away in fear. I've never heard Mother laugh harder.

We are an eye-catching processional, with two or three hundred in our entourage, (numbers are not my strong suit) some playing musical instruments, many carrying colorful banners. When we pass through the towns, there is much fanfare to acknowledge us and the townspeople present their sometimes-delightful local cuisine, as well as an entertainment. In the countryside, children run alongside our litters and try to catch a glimpse of our faces, even though we are masked. Now that the sun is out, wildflowers have cropped up everywhere; hyacinths, ranunculus, snowdrops, and lilies of the valley. When we encounter flocks of sheep, one can see the baby lambs prancing about, joyful to be alive. My ladies Rosalind, Maria, and Agatha ride behind; I can hear their distant laughter. They're probably talking about me and this ill-considered mission, and I don't blame them. I'd much rather be riding with them on horseback, my face naked to the world, able to laugh and look about; but this dreary *cortège* is the price one must pay to make an impression, and as I am repeatedly told, the impression is all.

The trumpets have sounded; we're moving again. I'm sure Plutarch is right, but I have not achieved inner calm, and outward reality remains the same.

6 May, 1581 – Agen

We're passing the night in one of our castles. As the rain has begun again, I'm happy to have shelter from the inclement weather. "Happy slumbers, Mother," I said as she made her way to her rooms with her usual headache. She turned and looked at me reproachfully.

"Happiness is the one thing we queens may never have," she responded darkly and left the room.

Mother and her moods. I'm afraid they're rather contagious, for since then I have sunk into a melancholy. My ladies attempted to lighten my spirit with amusing chatter and silliness, as Madame de Tournon removed my wig and readied me for bed.

It occurs to me that, currently, there are three Henris in my life; Henri of Guise, Henri of Anjou my brother, and now Henri of Navarre, whom I am supposed to wed. To avoid confusion, I shall call the Duke of Guise Henri, since he holds the highest place in my esteem, my brother shall be Anjou, and this hapless heretic prince who thinks he's going to marry me shall be Navarre.

Speaking of whom, why is it we who are making the journey to Nérac? Shouldn't Navarre be coming to us in Paris? I was given to understand that he is thrilled and honored at the thought of becoming betrothed to me. How thrilled can he be if he chooses to stay home?

I'm sure his mother isn't thrilled. I remember Jeanne d'Albret from my childhood, a tight-lipped Huguenot with no sense of humor. It's very hard to believe she would give her blessing to this union, but when I queried Mother about it, she replied, "The Queen of Navarre was simply delighted, once she had the stakes explained to her." It's hard to imagine Jeanne d'Albret being delighted about anything.

I wonder how Navarre has changed. My memories of him are dim. I do remember playing croquet with him on the grounds of the palace at the age of six or seven. I recollect that he was pale, mosquito-bitten, and a rather poor loser. He was Catholic then, and got on well with the rest of us, sharing our restful sense of place in the order of the universe. Then Jeanne d'Albret met an ex-monk who excited her in ways we can only guess at and converted her to Protestantism. With feverish zeal she extracted Henri from court and sent him to Bearn for indoctrination and military education; we never saw him again. It must have been confusing for him. I wonder if he remembers his days in Paris fondly.

My younger brother, Alençon, suffers from terrible hero worship where Navarre is concerned. When we were children, he used to follow the Prince around like a puppy dog, which explains why Alençon is in Nérac right now playing war games with him instead of being useful to the Catholic cause. Alençon's sudden embrace of all things Huguenot dismays me. I'm sure he's no more truly inclined toward the Protestant religion than he was committed to astrology a few years back when Mother introduced him to Nostradamus - an unctuous, odiferous man whose prophecies always seemed to me little more than good guesses (witness our three days of rain.) Alençon spent about six months under that man's thrall, then grew bored and took up hammer throwing. He simply blows with the wind, which I say with regret because he has a very sweet nature and is (I will confess) my favorite brother, especially now that Charles has become so insufferable.

I hope they are not expecting me to convert to Protestantism. If they are, they do not know me. I remember well the summer of my twelfth year when my brother Anjou, who had recently caught the Protestant fever, tried to force me to renounce my faith.

"Repent!" he bellowed, holding my head underwater in one of the palace fountains.

"Never!" I screamed when he gave me a gasp of air.

He plunged my head back into the waters. I would surely have drowned if one of our nurses hadn't come across the scene and pulled him off of me.

When Mother found out about it, she had Anjou whipped; that was how important it was to her that our Catholic faith not be jeopardized. She certainly has changed course. I suppose it's because these constant internal wars are draining the national coffers. Strangely, I see the logic behind Mother's attempt to unite the two religions; a weakened France means a weak boy-king, whose life is always in danger.

I think Charles would be less agitated if Mother didn't insist on being his regent. Charles is seventeen, but he's immature and unstable, has a cruel streak, and is given to fits of rage - which I suppose doesn't set him apart that much from other kings. They're too alike, however, Mother and Charles. They feed one another's suspicions and hatreds, and Charles becomes most agitated in her presence.

The problem is that Mother thinks everyone at court is plotting to kill Charles. Probably a few of them are, but what can you do? She used every weapon in her arsenal to keep Francis alive and look what happened – the poor boy died of an ear infection at 15, an incident completely beyond her control. "Fate will find a way," as Virgil wrote. Perhaps fate will find a way for Mother to step into the shadows - but I seriously doubt it.

9 May, 1581 – Nérac

After a long, arduous journey replete with muddy roads, fainting bishops, mercurial weather and much discomfort within a bouncing litter, we finally passed the border into the kingdom of Navarre. Almost immediately the skies cleared and a cool breeze blew, which we took to be a good omen. We arrived at the gates of the chateau in Nérac with great fanfare; trumpeters trumpeting, drummers drumming, bells ringing, pennants waving, and ladies singing. Imagine our surprise when there was no one to receive us! No one but a clutch of bewildered citizens and a small retinue of soldiers, one of whom approached the caravan nervously.

"Your Majesty! The Prince of Navarre sends his greetings, and declares his delight at your esteemed presence here in Nérac!" he proclaimed. "He would be here himself to welcome you, but as it happens, he and his men have taken a vow of solitude from the company of women whilst they engage in military training. He is pleased, however, to be able to offer you accommodations on a suitable property outside the castle, where your every need will be attended to until such time as they have completed their training."

"For what are they training?" demanded Mother. "We are not at war with Huguenots; we come in peace. I have brought my daughter, the Princess of France for that very reason. Where is his mother the Queen of Navarre? I demand to speak to Jeanne d'Albret."

"The Queen is currently at her estate in Bearn, Your Majesty."

"At Bearn! With whom? Her monk?" I heard Cardinal de Lenoncourt snicker when Mother said this. There are, of course, many rumors about Jeanne d'Albret and the ex-monk she travels with. We don't know much for certain about that relationship but we do know that, because of his influence, the Queen finances her son's battles with the Catholics.

"This is an outrage!" Mother cried, then noticed the curious crowd that was growing in size around us. "But no matter! The Queen and I have already come to an agreement. Her presence here is not required!"

Interesting that the Prince of Navarre is as little inclined to meet with me as I am with him. I suppose I should be offended, but the truth is I'm rather relieved not to have to play out the charade of a betrothal. The property we were escorted to is lovely and, having dashed off a letter to Henri about the current state of affairs, I now have the leisure to read a bit of Plutarch and study my German.

Mother, however, is not to be deterred. "We shall divide and conquer, ladies!" She announced. Mother has in her entourage a collection of beautiful, educated, and charming young ladies of the court who have been rather famously labeled her "flying squadron." I wouldn't call them spies, but they are adept at ingratiating themselves with others, gaining information, and then reporting back to Mother. Perhaps they are spies. At any rate, she has set these lovelies the task of breaking down the will of the men inside the castle. Truth be told, I hope they don't. The weather is fine, the garden lovely, and I'm enjoying an excellent glass of claret.

2.

"The impediment to action advances action.
What stands in the way becomes the way."

Marcus Aurelius

10 May, 1581 - Nerac

Several of Mother's ladies have made attempts to enter the chateau, but with little success. Mme. de Tournon perched outside the gate playing her mandolin and singing the most enchanting melodies. She has a voice to melt the coldest heart, I felt sure she would be invited in to regale Navarre and his company. Alas, no response. Lady Maria then approached the guard with the urgent news that she carried a message for one of the nobles she knew to be within, the delicacy of which dictated it be delivered personally from Maria's lips to his ear. The guard suggested that rather than her lips, she should use her quill to inscribe the message. Rather rude, I thought. This is all a bit surprising given my ladies' enormous gifts to charm and suggests that Navarre must have issued extreme edicts carrying hefty punishments for violation.

Rosalind, however, has just come to us with an interesting piece of information, which she got from one of the tradesmen who deliver goods to the castle. "The Duke of Biron is within!" she exclaimed. Rosalind is fascinated with Biron because, although he is known for being a champion of manly pursuits like hunting and war, he tends to spurn the company of women.

"It is Biron who gave Navarre this silly notion of male isolation leading to enhanced warrior prowess," said Rosalind. "With Your Majesty's permission, I should like to have a try at him."

Mother gave her permission, and my other ladies and I had a lovely walk along the river Baïse in the Parc de la Garenne with its long paths of laurel and cypress trees. I must admit, Nérac is a principality of great beauty. We came across the ruins of an ancient Roman villa, with mosaics on what used to be the floor of the structure that were splendid in design. Touching the tiles, which depicted a tiger attacking a centaur, I was transported, imagining the people who had trod the same ground as myself so many years ago. Were they happy? Did they suffer from constant war? Did they fall in love? I felt that if I stood there long enough, someone from the past might whisper to me the answer. There is an otherworldly quality to Nérac, as if time is suspended for its residents. I can understand why Navarre chooses to make it his home.

11 May, 1581 - Nérac

Rosalind proves to be the cleverest of ladies, as well as one of the love-liest. An accomplished horsewoman, she devised to ride her horse back and forth on the grounds outside the castle in a most picturesque fashion, and when she espied the Duke of Biron watching her from a window, she caused her horse to rear and subsequently "fell" in a most convincing fashion. She demonstrated the scene dramatically, to our great amusement.

"There I lay, alarmingly inert, counting on Biron to lose the war within his soul and come to my aid - which he did!" she proclaimed.

As Biron lifted her small, delicate frame into his arms, Rosalind roused from her "faint" and gazed helplessly up at him with those sky-blue eyes of hers, pressing her bosom to his chest as if clinging to him for very life. I suspect the poor man was lost at that moment. Reviving her with water from a nearby well, Biron was then treated to Rosalind's sparkling conversational prowess.

"I touched on every subject, Your Majesty, from philosophy, to love, to Cicero's views on war. I regretted the fact that we were not to meet again, but asserted my delight at having been able to enjoy his delightful company for even this brief moment. I will say, he's quite handsome."

The Duke of Biron stumbled back into the castle, a man transformed. I should not be at all surprised to hear there's been a change in the weather at Navarre.

12 May, 1581 - Nérac

Last night inside the chateau, a conversation took place amongst Navarre, Biron, and some other lords whose names we are eager to attain. We have it from a serving person, who passed it onto a lesser lord, who told it to Lady Agatha. It went something like this:

"Hateful is the power, and pitiable the life of those who wish to be feared rather than loved," declared the Prince of Navarre, quoting the Roman biographer Cornelius Nepos and thus launching the topic of conversation. The Duke of Biron, still glowing from his encounter with Rosalind, saw his opportunity and seized it.

"I'm not sure the Queen Regent subscribes to that philosophy," he averred, which drew some chuckles around the room. (Alençon was not amongst them, or he would most definitely have weighed in on the subject of his mother.)

"Surely the rumors surrounding Catherine de Medici are, for the most part, fabrications," replied Navarre. "I knew her when I was a child. She may look like a witch, but she didn't seem all that fearsome."

"Indeed?" said Biron. "What of those who opine that she poisoned Francis III to achieve the throne for her husband, and poisoned her elder son to put Charles on the throne? Do you dismiss those rumors?"

"I do. Bosh!"

"But the King was a completely healthy man. One doesn't simply fall ill playing tennis and die."

"Actually, one does, occasionally."

"Sebastiano de Montecuccoli, her kinsman, confessed to preparing a poison for the Queen," asserted another of his guests.

"Montecuccoli was tortured. He would have confessed to anything."

"I must say, you're quite sanguine about de Medici. Did she tell you bedtime stories as a child?" jested Biron, which drew laughter.

"I simply haven't heard enough to cause me concern. Why, Biron, what do you know?"

There are some rather shocking stories circulating regarding Mother; stories that one really shouldn't repeat unless you are, say, Rosalind and find it expedient to do so. Biron repeated the stories she told him, and the names of those who died of mysterious causes at moments advantageous to Mother. He spoke also of her reliance on Ruggeri, her trusted necromancer, who specializes in the dark arts. Once Biron completed his ghoulish death list, there was silence around the room. Navarre pulled at his beard thoughtfully for a moment.

"Perhaps we should make an exception for the lovely ladies who have come to us with such good intentions," declared Navarre. And so, we are invited to a ball.

I receive this information with mixed emotions, as I never wanted the encounter to occur in the first place. Now that it's happening, it's sure to be horribly awkward. However, there is something about being barred from a premises that makes one determined to enter, and I am happy we have managed to both win this skirmish and assuage Mother's wounded pride. She has been particularly unpleasant of late.

I played chess with the Cardinal de Lenoncourt this evening; I must say, for a man of the cloth he's a very poor loser. "Damn the queen!" he exclaimed, then clapped his hand over his mouth and begged forgiveness for the profanation. There has been a change in the rules of the game of chess recently which have increased the queen piece's powers; she can now move as far as she wants and in any direction. He keeps forgetting this, and it drives him mad. I, however, find it a very welcome change.

15 May, 1581- Nérac

And tonight - a visit from brother Alençon! Ever ingenious, the dear boy managed to slip the guards at the castle and make his way to our lodgings.

"Darling boy!" declared Mother. Alençon is her favorite child and deservedly so, he has such a light and playful way about him. He'll never be king, he has too many brothers ahead of him, and perhaps for that reason, he tends to take life more lightly than the rest of them.

"Mother dear!" he replied, bowing deeply and then falling into her embrace.

"What madness is going on within that chateau?" demanded Mother. "How dare they treat us in such a disrespectful manner?"

"They're very serious about enhancing our warrior prowess, Mother. We have to train every morning from the break of day 'til sunset, eat the most spartan of meals, and pray three times a day."

"Pray! To a Protestant God? Don't break my heart, son."

"Oh Mother, don't worry, I slip in the odd Hail Mary," he said with a wink. How on earth he manages to jolly my mother out of this most deadly serious of subjects I'll never know, but he always does. "And then we have to bathe! At the end of every week! There are rooms in the chateau for nothing but bathing!"

"Alencon!" I was dismayed. "You know that water opens the pores and allows plague into the body."

"There's a new science that holds otherwise. Navarre bathes regularly and has reportedly maintained excellent health."

"What is all the mystery, Monsieur? Who is within the chateau?" inquired Mother. Monsieur is our family name for him. I leaned forward, eager to hear the names of the people who had sat around the night before discussing Mother.

"Well, the Duke of Biron, as Lady Rosalind will attest. Biron is a friend of mine; you might even say a confidante. You have made quite an impression on him, Lady Rosalind." She blushed prettily. "Then there is the Prince of Condé."

"Condé." Mother leaned back in her chair, reflecting on this. "I have tried to negotiate with him numerous times on the Huguenot question, but he is impossible."

"And lastly, Admiral Gaspard de Coligny."

I have heard a great deal about Coligny; Henri detests him. It is Coligny who is responsible for Henri's father's death in the Siege of Orleans. I don't believe Coligny held the sword but he certainly ordered the death. Henri speaks of Coligny often and with deep loathing. Should he know of this? Should I write to him?

"Coligny and Condé are traveling incognito under the pseudonyms Dumain and Longaville," continued Alençon. "Of course, everyone knows who they are, but it's fun to play along. Then there's one more man of note, the Earl of Oxford."

"An Englishman?" Mother looked quite alarmed. "What is he doing there?"

"I don't know. He doesn't speak much French, and neither does his travel companion, a young poet who has become quite celebrated in London. Monsieur Chaquesper, or something like that. The boy lurks a bit, observing and taking notes. Is he truly a poet, I wonder? Or a spy for Queen Elizabeth?"

"This isn't humorous, Monsieur. You know full well that Elizabeth, as a Protestant, is becoming more and more involved in our troubles."

"I can't speak to that. But oh, Admiral Coligny! What a stiff creature he is!" Expertly diverting the conversation, Alençon performed a hilarious impression of Coligny, a rigid Huguenot who deems the Catholic church too soft and sinfully corrupt. Alençon strutted around making pronouncements, twirling his mustache in the manner of the Admiral, and had us all laughing heartily, even Mother. (She has an odd way of laughing, as if it's against her will.) It was wonderful to have this comedic interlude when these constant wars wear us down so dreadfully.

But Mother is alarmed, I can tell. Three prominent Huguenots in Nérac at the same time as an English emissary? What treachery are they planning? It was foolish of Alençon to reveal that to us, (though I'm glad he did.)

Mother begged Alençon to stay with us but he demurred, determined to be with "his men," which makes me laugh; he's such a boy.

To have a moment alone with him, I walked with my brother to his horse.

"Monsieur, in all seriousness – why are you playing this dangerous game? You are no more a Huguenot than I am a Moor. Navarre must know that."

"I'm sure he suspects, but he doesn't care. Some of us are allowed to play outside the rules, Margot, in the name of friendship. Anyway, I enjoy the training; the swordplay, the wrestling, the strategizing of troop movements on a game board, and especially the ordering around of the soldiers. The only thing I detest is the actual battlefield. The sight of blood causes me to lose consciousness."

"Well, that seems inconvenient."

"Yes. I wish there were a way that battle itself wasn't so...physical."

Alençon himself is not very physical, being little taller than Mother and having a slight deformity of the spine. I suggested he find a way to enjoy the former activities without actually placing himself into the latter, and relayed the story of Lord du Plooy, who regaled his friends with great tales of his heroic missions in the field of battle, without once ever having been there.

"Brilliant idea, Margot!" He exclaimed. "It will give me great relief of mind to do the same." I'm surprised the idea had not occurred to him before.

I don't think I'll write to Henri of Coligny's presence here. I don't particularly relish the idea of being party to a revenge murder in the middle of a ball. These men and their blood lust.

However, no matter. A grand ball tomorrow will be a lovely diversion, however little I wish to go through the motions of meeting Navarre again.

3.

"For her beauty, as we are told, was in itself not altogether incomparable, nor such as to strike those who saw her; but converse with her had an irresistible charm, and her presence, combined with the persuasiveness of her discourse and the character which was somehow diffused about her behavior towards others, had something stimulating about it."

— Plutarch on Cleopatra

20 May, 1581 - Nérac

The day began festively. My ladies had concocted the delicious idea of going masked to the castle and having the gentlemen guess at our identities. I was very taken with the idea of masquerading as a lesser mortal and entered into the fun, trying on my ladies' clothing with much giddiness. It was during this interval that I was given the news that my mother the Queen required a private audience with me. I was shocked. In all my years, I cannot recall ever spending a moment alone with my mother, and the very idea terrified me. What had I done wrong? I racked my brains trying to recall some offense that may have merited a private reprimand, but could find none.

My mother desired that we should walk in the Parc de la Garenne together. Mother is short in stature, as I have mentioned, with coarse black hair and a rather aquiline nose, and since I have grown to womanhood and been deemed a beauty, I have always sensed her discomfort in my presence. However, today she was willing to walk side by side with me despite the disparity in our heights. This time I was impervious to the Parc de la Garenne's mystical beauty, so worried was I to discover my offense. We walked at great length in silence, and finally, my mother spoke.

"I wish to say that I regret the... awkwardness between us lately," referring, I suppose, to the day she and Charles beat me black and blue. "Perhaps I was hasty in assuming you were in love with the Duke of Guise. I see by your recent obedience that such is not the case." I said nothing. My mother had just come as close as she had ever come to apologizing to me; I didn't want to ruin the moment.

"Your brother relayed to me the content of a recent conversation with you recently. He considers you very clever, and says he treats you no longer as a child, therefore neither shall I. For the future, you will freely speak your mind, and have no apprehensions of taking too great a liberty, for it is my desire we become better acquainted."

The greatest thrill ran through me hearing these words. Speak with Mother? Offer my thoughts unbidden? I felt a welling of satisfaction unlike anything I have ever felt, as well as a sudden shame at the childishly vain amusements of a few hours before.

"I'm sure it will come as no surprise to you that the Duke of Guise has recently asked for your hand in marriage," began my mother.

"Oh! That is a surprise." I was offended that Henri would take such an action without consulting me.

"You did not know?"

"I did not, Mother, I promise you."

"I'm sure he thought I'd be faint with joy at the notion of joining the House of Valois with the House of Guise; such is the arrogance of that family. Perhaps you were even hoping for the union yourself."

"I – I had not given thought –"

"If so, you are not fully aware of the vicious and predatory nature of the House of Guise. They are ever watchful for a moment where they might circumvent our will and undermine the house of Valois. They may smile, the Duke may flatter, but you must remember, Marguerite, their only intent is to wipe out the Valois line."

I received this information with mixed emotions, as I am fairly sure Henri's feelings for me stem primarily from my power to charm. However, I am also aware of the strength of the House of Guise. Henri's aunt is mother to Mary, Queen of Scots, and his brother Louis a Cardinal. There is great ambition in that bloodline.

"I trust," my mother continued, "that you have not been so foolish as to make the Duke any promises."

"Indeed no, Mother," I replied. "I find the Duke amusing, and his attentions flattering, but I believe his primary attraction for me has been his nearness to power. I've been reading the book by your father's friend,

M. Machiavelli, and it caused me to realize the importance of allying with a man whose family is historically significant."

My mother raised a quizzical eyebrow. "Signor Machiavelli was my father's friend for a brief while - until the need arose to execute him. However, you are correct; the man's writings contain much of interest." She regarded me thoughtfully. "It is too bad you cannot ever inherit the throne, Marguerite. You're surprisingly intelligent; better read than your brothers, speak how many? Five languages fluently. You're certainly as astute as Elizabeth of England who, I'm told, has grown quite ugly since the small-pox. Yet sadly, Salic law forbids your ever becoming queen – unless, of course, you give birth to a male heir and your husband the king dies."

At this point, my mother did the most astonishing thing; she winked! It was just the slightest wink; it could even have been confused for a slight tic. Yet no, I could tell by the look in her eye that she was sharing a brief moment of her strange humor with me, of collusion, even. Was I meant to laugh at the death of my father? Horrifying thought, yet the opportunity to share in this odd "jest" with her was irresistible. To my shame, I produced a small giggle in response. I so wanted to retain Mother's confidence.

"And so," she continued, "We must look for other uses for your gifts. Fortunately, your value at this moment is immense. You are much sought after, Marguerite, as I'm sure you are aware. With your cooperation, we can put an end to these wars which are weakening the crown and causing other countries to look at us as easy prey. Why, you may well go down in history as the woman who brought peace to the land!"

I was stunned. Until that moment, I had never considered my place in history. But as Mother spoke further, sharing her vision for the future of France, I was suddenly filled with the import of our mission here in Nérac. What did my personal feelings matter where issues of state were concerned? If we can prevent the deaths of hundreds of Catholics with a simple mar-riage vow, it seems entirely right and proper that we should do so.

I returned from my interview with Mother a changed person. I informed the ladies that they could proceed with their foolishness, but that I would represent myself to be who I am; Marguerite de Valois, Princess of France.

Yet I will admit to the small part of me that still had hopes for a match with a man to whom I was attracted, who appreciates my intrinsic value as a person. Perhaps that just is a foolish dream. As I prepared for the ball, I forced myself to relinquish naive thoughts and commit myself to the mission at hand; bringing peace to France.

Madame de Tournon attired me exquisitely in a gown of crimson Spanish velvet richly trimmed with gold, and a toque of the same material adorned with jewels and bright feathers. Large pearl stones adorned my hair. My ladies assured me I had never been more beautiful.

We were ushered inside the castle and the festivities began in the inner courtyard. My ladies played their masquerade game with much giggling and silliness, and the men were both dazzled and charmed. I watched from an upper window and was told later that Navarre watched similarly from the window opposite, dismayed by what he perceived to be the indignity of seeing his warriors so quickly conquered. He vowed not to be so ridiculously overpowered himself.

But when I was announced, that vow evaporated. Exercising all of my powers to captivate, and aware of the gift God has given me to please the eye, I presented myself to the Prince of Navarre in a manner most pleasing to him. What surprised me, however, was how pleasing he was to my eye. Gone was the pale anxious boy of our youth; in his place was a tall, elegant man with luminous brown eyes, thick wavy brown hair, and a quite muscular physique.

"Sweet Princess, welcome to the kingdom of Navarre. You honor us with your presence."

His face was framed by an exquisitely fluted lace collar. He emanated a scent I had not experienced before, which I learned later was a mixture of the oils of pomegranate and lavender. It was intoxicating: I remembered his affection for bathing and instantly rethought my convictions against it. His voice was sonorous and musical, his conversation pleasingly decorous. The moment I entered his sphere of influence something occurred within me, a feeling that I fear I will not find the right words to describe. The feeling took place within my breast, but also somewhere else. It was a sensation that seemed to emanate from within my very being, as if it had been there all my life waiting to be set in motion, and it pulled me toward him in the most palpable fashion. The same thing seemed to be happening to him, and when he kissed my hand, I could swear that a frisson of something like lightning charged from his body into mine.

What can I say about the next hours? We danced, we dined, we spoke quietly to one another in a language that felt as if it were all our own, a delightful mixture of badinage and serious interlocution. A level of intimacy was achieved which I never would have believed possible in so short a time.

"Ah yes, I remember well our days at the Louvre Palace," said the Prince, with a mischievous twinkle in his eye. "I remember you hit me once with a croquet mallet."

"What! I never did!" I exclaimed, but in fact, I did have a distant memory and was glad we could laugh about it now.

We danced all night. Our emissaries scuttled back and forth, negotiating the terms of our nuptials. By evening's end, a tentative date had been reached for the wedding. Meanwhile, my ladies discovered the reason for all the military training – there had been plans to lay siege to St. Jean d'Angely within a fortnight. There is a rumor that Queen Elizabeth is supplying funds for such endeavors, which would explain the presence of the Earl of Oxford. It was to have been a surprise attack, which undoubtedly would have led to many deaths on both sides. Those plans have now been suspended, as slaughtering hundreds would have been an unhappy follow-up to our becoming engaged. To think - I have saved lives, by falling in love!

Our side is very gratified, but a number of his party are disgruntled. To witness their prince, who had issued the strictest of orders regarding the society of women, falling captive to one so quickly must have been a shock. To me, the surprise isn't his feelings toward me, but mine toward him.

Mother, of course, could not be happier. Indeed, late in the evening, I found her boasting of her successes to the English poet M. Chaquespere, which surprised me greatly as Mother doesn't generally take to strangers. Perhaps she was trying to assess whether he really were a spy, or perhaps she was truly charmed by him; the young man does have very soulful eyes. At the time I came upon her, Mother was recounting the death of François of Guise, Henri's father killed by Coligny.

"Poor man. But that I hated him deadly, I would have lamented his miserable state," she chuckled.

"Ah, *oui*, excellent!" The poet's quill scribbled away as his translator interpreted her words.

What a magical evening! Henceforth, I have decided that Navarre shall be referred to as Henri in my writings, not Henri of Guise who must now be relegated to being called Guise, or the Duke. After all, we were just playing with one another, it wasn't as if either of us was actually in love. And Navarre's kisses are far, far sweeter.

14 June, 1581 - Paris

We have returned home to the Louvre, having spent three magnificent weeks in Nérac. During that time, Henri and I have grown to know one another intimately. We took long walks in the park, went boating on the Baîse, and enjoyed many fetes and balls. It is not just the two of us who have fallen under Nérac's spell; my lady Rosalind may well have conquered the Duke of Biron, but he seems to have had a similar effect on her.

"Nérac has caused me to quite lose my head, and Biron my heart," is how she put it. Lady Maria has transferred her affections from Condé, who is, in fact, quite married, to Admiral de Coligny, whose wife is dead. Coligny is old, I'm guessing fifty, and just as strait-laced as Alençon painted him but somehow endearing for all that, and courts Maria in a very sweet old-fashioned way. We still laughingly referred to him as "Longaville." The weather was consistently fine, and the moon in its heaven seemed to smile down upon us encouragingly during our evening activities. Henri daily grew more handsome in my eyes, if that were possible. It seemed that love was in the air everywhere, that kindness and compassion would rule our lives from that moment forward.

It was an illusion.

Soon after our triumphant return to Paris, Henri's mother, Jeanne d'Albret, paid me the honor of a visit. (Her monk was nowhere to be seen.) The Queen of Navarre is a severe, hatchet-faced woman who, despite her husband Antoine de Bourbon's objections, embraced Protestantism with surprising fervor at a late age. Even when Huguenots sacked and burned the town she was visiting, causing her to witness much death and mayhem, she stood firm. Even when her husband died in battle against Huguenots at the siege of Rouen, she stayed loyal to her new cult. I marvel at her inexplicable tenacity. She has garbed herself in black ever since her husband's death, and it was in black that she arrived before me. Alas, hers was not the face of unmitigated delight that my mother had painted to me.

"Are you prepared to convert to Protestantism?" She demanded bluntly.

"Indeed, no, your Majesty. It is a question that has never come up."

"The Queen your mother didn't tell you it was my primary demand?"

"I'm sorry, she did not. She spoke only of your delight at the match."

"Is that so?" If a woman could purse her lips further than they were already, Jeanne d'Albret accomplished the task.

"You are a lovely young lady, Mademoiselle. I have watched your growth from child to young adult with some surprise since the rest of your siblings are so blighted by physical or mental defects. You alone have escaped that curse, which I take to mean that you have God's approval. But there has been a misunderstanding. A marriage between my son and a Catholic is unthinkable. We have labored long enough under the corruptions and abuses of that abominable religion. "AFTER THE DARKNESS, THE LIGHT!"

The zeal in the Queen of Navarre's eye as she fairly shouted the well-known Huguenot call-to-arms was unsettling, to say the least; she seemed momentarily possessed. I was shaken by the interview and afterward requested an audience with my mother. But when I relayed all the Queen had said to me, Mother merely smiled.

"I see. She would like to re-open the terms of our negotiation." For a woman with a rather dark nature, Mother can be surprisingly optimistic.

"I don't think that's it, Mother. She seemed most forceful in her opposition."

"Yes, yes. I will delegate that responsibility to Guise. It is possible the Queen found my manner a bit abrasive, but Guise can be most persuasive when he wishes to."

"Are you sure he will wish to?"

"Don't overestimate your charms, daughter. The Duke is quite recovered from whatever romantic setback you may have dealt him, and he understands the necessities of the crown."

Indeed, when I encountered Guise later in the day, he was a different man from the ardent suitor who had fled from my chambers mere weeks ago. Guise is by nature a pointed man in appearance; pointed beard, pointed nose, and eyebrows that point upward in the center. That day, his mouth was so tight that his cheekbones seemed to be ready to pop out of his face. I marveled that I had ever kissed that mouth.

"Your Highness, the Queen your mother has informed me of the recent impediment regarding your forthcoming nuptials. I assure you I will do all in my power to restore the situation with the Queen of Navarre. We are all eager to see this alliance take place to further burnish the glory of the crown." Gone was the man in love, and in its place was a proper and punctilious chancellor, all business. He seemed unable, however, to look me in the eye.

"I am grateful for your efforts, Henri," I replied. "Though difficult for both of us, I have always held you in the highest regard, and cherish our friendship." Using his given name produced no effect, and he seemed to stiffen at the word "friendship." I continued to be "Your Highness" for the rest of the conversation.

Life at court can be extremely dull, however amusing it may appear to the outside observer. It's the same group of people over and over, therefore certain intrigues do develop. For a princess, it is important that those intrigues not lead to a situation that can sully her reputation, but avowals of love and eternal devotion do take place, and I'm afraid the Duke of Guise and I may have wandered down that verbally demonstrative path too far upon occasion. No one takes it seriously. Well, perhaps some do, but anyone with any sense realizes it all rather a game, something to pass the hours. I'm very much hoping that Guise, with his great acuity in political affairs, has a similar facility for this particular sport. It would be rather dreary if he doesn't.

22 June, 1581 - Paris

Yesterday Jeanne d'Albret presented herself before my mother to announce her intentions to leave Paris and return to her castle in Bearn.

"Indeed?" My mother stared at the Queen with a blank countenance.

"Unfortunately, yes, Your Majesty. I have a demanding business there which cannot be ignored. I regret that we have not come to terms on your proposal regarding my son. Perhaps we can address them at another time."

My mother smiled at her with what passed for warmth. "Of course. I wish you the safest of travels. We will miss you a great deal, Jeanne. You feel to me already like family. In fact..."

Mother rose and moved toward d'Albret, whose eyes widened in alarm. She was even more surprised (as was I) when Mother enveloped her in an embrace. Then Mother gave a signal, and her personal perfumier, Renato Bianco, placed a luxurious pair of Florentine gloves, scented by Bianco himself, into Mother's hand. With a flourish, she presented them to Jeanne d'Albret.

"For you, my dear," she said.

It was an awkward moment. D'Albret hesitated, then took the gloves with little acknowledgment and handed them over to her waiting lady. I could see my mother stiffen at the insult, but the message was clear: Jeanne d'Albret is not to be influenced by a pair of gloves, even scented by the most famous perfumier in the land.

D'Albret is now on her way back to her castle, with nothing concluded. I had hoped the two women could get past their personal difficulties, but today I heard that a rumor has reached Mother's ears; d'Albret has been referring to her as "the Florentine grocer's daughter." Mother is very sensitive on the subject of her Italian heritage, as well as her early life as a relatively impoverished orphan. This does not bode well for the future of negotiations.

30 June, 1581 - Paris

News has come of a terrible battle in Montcontour. Scores of Catholics and Huguenots have lost their lives, with nothing to show for it on either side. It's all so pointless! The thought that Henri might have been in that battle chills my heart, although I've been assured in a recent letter from him that he is still in Nérac.

What's worse, we've learned that Jeanne d'Albret financed the bloody siege with her crown jewels, and has vowed to continue to do so. What a waste of jewels! Guise has been dispatched, with much choler on Mother's side, to press our case with d'Albret in whatever manner possible. He has been ordered not to return until he has gained permission for our marriage to go forward. The enormous loss of life does seem to have jolted Guise out of his resentment of me; he made for Bearn with great haste.

How I long to see Henri again! The memory of his kiss lingers on my lips. He writes me the most beautiful words of love, sometimes I feel almost faint reading them. Here is an example:

Will I compare you to a summer day?

You are more beautiful and more temperate.

The strong winds shake the cherished buds of May,

And the summer lease has only too little time.

Sometimes too hot the eye of heaven shines,

And often her golden complexion is faded;

And from every fair, fair sometime declines,

By chance, or the changing course of nature, unhewn;

But your eternal summer will not fade,

Nor lose possession of the beauty that is thine,

Nor will death boast that you remain in its shadow,

When in the eternal lines of Time you grow.

As long as men can breathe, or eyes can see,

So live this, and it gives you life.

What a charming poem! It is marvelous to think that in addition to being a virile and commanding warrior, my intended also possesses the soul of a poet. Rosalind reads this to me aloud every night before I go to sleep, and today I have made bold to write a poem back to him. It pales in comparison with his, but it gave me pleasure to write it.

The moment I saw you, I loved you.

Among thousands, you alone penetrate the inner secrets of my mind and are received in my heart.

Conversation with you is like a prayer I want never to conclude. You are locked within my soul forever;

You alone suffice.

I would never have dared write such a thing to a man before, but since he made so bold as to share his soul, I feel free to share mine. O glorious freedom!

1 July, 1581 - Paris

Guise returned from his mission in Bearn and placed himself before me in my chambers today. If a bow can be said to be performed sarcastically, Guise accomplished the task.

"Your Highness, the Queen your mother wishes me to inform you that an agreement has been reached between herself and the Queen of Navarre. Imagine our universal delight at knowing that your nuptials may now take place." Guise made this announcement with all the enthusiasm of a soldier reciting a casualty list.

"Excellent news!" I responded warmly. "I'm quite sure the success of negotiations is due to your efforts, Henri. Was it difficult to achieve?"

"Concessions had to be made. Your mother is less than delighted with the terms, but she sent me to achieve her goals, which I assume are also your goals, and achieve them I did."

I felt a pang of sympathy for Guise. He had the stiff, brittle demeanor of someone who has allowed himself to be hurt and is furious about it. It was at that moment that I realized he had invested more in our relationship than I understood, and I felt a pang of regret for dropping him so precipitously. I spent a good deal of time praising his brilliance and prowess, but it didn't seem to dent the armor of indifference he had assumed. After I had exhausted myself with acclamation there was a pause. He seemed to be wrestling with himself, then he spoke.

"Why did you not tell me that Coligny was in Nérac?"

"Coligny?" I was seized with guilt. "I don't know, I barely saw the man."

"I heard you did. I heard you all socialized extensively. With my father's murderer."

"Henri, I was there at my mother's command. What could I do?"

Guise stared at me for a long moment. "Nothing, of course." Then he bowed, turned, and left the room. He did not beg my leave.

Ah well, I cannot dwell on past peccadillos. The wedding goes forward! That's the important thing. Jeanne d'Albret has agreed to return to Paris, where she will be received with fanfare befitting the mother-in-law of a Valois princess, and proceed to have her gown fitted for the wedding. Now that the last hurdle is removed, I am optimistic there will be no further obstacles to our lasting joy.

And so, my prayers to the Virgin have been answered. If this doesn't prove the power of the Queen of Heaven, I don't know what does.

23 July, 1581 - Paris

Jeanne d'Albret is dead. We are all deeply shocked. She arrived in Paris, was fitted for her gown, took sick, and died the next day in her bed. Enormously unfortunate! Already rumors are circulating that it was "the Queen's poisoned gloves" that were the cause of the illness. It amazes me how stupid people can be, and how susceptible to rumors. What motivation could my mother possibly have for eliminating the Queen, when they had just come to terms on our wedding? I'm quite sure Mother will adhere to those terms regardless of the Queen's death - but even if she doesn't, it's absurd to think she would kill the mother of her future son-in-law before the wedding, thus casting a shadow upon the entire event. Mother is a firm believer in omens; killing Jeanne d'Albret would have been a bad one. Her natural death is, of course, not propitious, but it was known she was in poor health, and these things happen.

Henri was informed and wrote to me immediately. He is, of course, very sad, but in times like this, it is perhaps good not to have known one's mother very well; the grief one feels is undoubtedly more manageable. At any rate, for the good of the country, the wedding will go forward as scheduled.

It has not escaped the attention of either of us that with the passing of Jeanne d'Albret, Henri is now the King of Navarre and, when we marry, I will be queen. I can't help but be a little bit excited about that, which I know is sinful. I intend to be very sad for at least today, and possibly tomorrow.

Henri sent me another poem. This one I liked less well, as it began, "*When forty winters besiege thy brow...*" It seemed to argue against his first poem, which stated that my beauty would never fade. On the positive side, it expressed the hope that one day we would have children. But I did find the poem in general depressing. I can't imagine ever being forty winters old.

18 August, 1581 - Paris

My wedding day dawned very warm, the sun scorching the streets from early morning on, but this did not dissuade the crowds from turning out at the bishop's palace in large numbers. Henri and his retinue arrived in Paris two days ago in mourning clothes, an atmosphere of grief and propriety surrounding them, as was most appropriate. As events propelled us toward the wedding, however, all grief was forgotten, and they arrived at the palace attired in the finest clothing, sparkling with jewels. Henri looked impossibly handsome in his silk tunic emblazoned with the symbols of Navarre, a fur surcoat, and a bejeweled crown. I wore a more delicate but equally dazzling crown and a coat of ermine ablaze with diamonds down the length of it. I can't tell you how heavy it was; it took three of my strongest princesses to support it. A long platform draped with a golden cloth had been erected, which led from the bishop's palace to the Church of Notre Dame. On the grounds below stood throngs of people eager to view the procession. If they looked miserably hot, you can imagine how challenging it was for me in that ermine coat. I nearly fainted numerous times.

The wedding was magnificent. Pope Gregory had been unhappy about the notion of Henri being in the church, but after much wrangling a solution was found: Henri agreed to be absent for the Nuptial Mass. Instead, he stood in front of the cathedral during the ceremony and the blessing, accompanied by his kinsmen. We were received at the church door by the Cardinal de Bourbon rather than Pope Gregory, and it was the Cardinal who pronounced the nuptial benediction and the saying of the vows. After that, we departed through separate entrances.

That may sound awkward, but it was beautiful, beautiful, beautiful. I believe I actually saw tears on Mother's cheeks, although it may have been the heat. Afterward, there was a nuptial lunch followed by a magnificent ball. Then, we were ushered with great ceremony to our matrimonial chambers.

The events immediately following seemed rather odd, but as I do not know to what to compare them, I shall merely make note of it here without comment. Since neither of our fathers is alive, it fell to our court physician, M. du Lauren, to observe the activities of our wedding bed, as is the custom. Before Henri was introduced into my chamber, M. du Lauren gave me a tutorial on what to expect. Producing his own manhood, he encouraged me to examine it closely and even to interact with it. As his manhood did not look in any way pleasant to me, I was hesitant to do so. Happily, Henri was brought to me at that moment, and so I was spared the activities in which M. du Lauren was encouraging me to partake.

Once Henri and I were disrobed, I was happy to see that his manhood was much smaller, pinker, and infinitely more attractive than M. du Lauren's. Perhaps that was the physician's purpose; to defray my anxieties. At any rate, we then proceeded to demonstrate certain activities, as directed by M. du Lauren, until we had achieved their performance to his satisfaction. I will attest that there was a surprising amount of pain involved, but I was determined to display as much bravery as I could summon. Henri appeared not to be having the painful experience I was, which made me happy for him. I was surprised, however, that M. du Lauren's role seemed not only to observe but to interact with himself during the observation. At length, however, the physician declared himself satisfied with our accomplishments, removed the sheet that had been placed beneath me to absorb the blood that had been invoked, and retired. At last, we were able to have our first moments of privacy.

Oh, that I could describe the happiness that was then ours! All others forgotten, we lost our shyness and proceeded to learn the landscape of one another's bodies at our glorious leisure. Henri taught me how to give him pleasure, introducing activities that I never would have guessed at but, once learned, seemed perfectly obvious and enormously fruitful. I know enough about the ultimate goal to report that Henri achieved that goal many times. I believe we are destined to produce many children.

The next morning was perfect. We dined alone in our chambers, taking delight in one another's every gesture, every sigh. He fed me breakfast as we lay in bed and there was much playfulness and laughter, as it turned into a very messy affair. Afterward, he sponged me down with water from a basin, and I relinquished all fears that it might lead to a bout of the plague. I believe that morning may have been the happiest of my life.

Later that day I had another private interview with Mother, and this time it did not cause me fright. She asked me about the events of our wedding night and, freed by her request that I be most candid, I told her every detail. When I reached the sequence regarding M. de Lauren, I saw an emotion flit across her face. Mother is most skilled at keeping her features completely neutral but this emotion, though brief, seemed intense.

"Repeat that, daughter," she commanded. "He did what?"

I repeated the information regarding M. de Lauren's participation in our connubial activities. There was a pause. Mother seemed to be struggling for a response. Finally, she nodded and prayed for me to resume. By the end of our encounter, she embraced me, and I could feel something like emotional warmth coming from her. It was extraordinary.

Henri has retired to his chambers with his gentlemen, many of whom have been participating in the celebrations taking place in the city. There will now be four days of balls, masques, concerts, ballets, and banquets at the diocese and the Hôtel d'Anjou. Every person of significance has been invited; Protestants included. It will be heartening to see them celebrate together, ushering in a new era of tolerance for France. To think that I am the cause of it is most gratifying.

This moment of solitude, however, gives me a moment to relish the experiences, the sensations, and the vast happiness that lies within my soul. I am loved, and I love. It is a sensation I never knew was available to me. Ah, that this happiness could last forever!

22 August, 1581 - Paris

Of course, the happiness did not last forever; how naïve I was to write that. In truth, I am filled with horror. I don't know how to comprehend the events that have taken place since my wedding night. Where is the girl who was filled with such hope and delight mere days ago? I cannot access her. I can barely breathe.

Where to begin? My joy, so palpable to me, was apparently not shared by the populace of Paris. I had observed an odd silence after our ceremony, a distinct lack of celebration, but gave it little note in my euphoric state. I now recognize that lack as resentment and hatred, and perhaps the most deeply aggrieved was one of the most powerful: The Duke of Guise. He has, of course, never countenanced this match, is plainly upset with me, and has been furious about the presence of all these Huguenots in Paris. To that end, he extracted permission from Mother, who was anxious about his rancor and wanted the wedding to go well, to eliminate a certain individual.

Yes, that is correct. Mother gave her permission, during my wedding, for one of my guests to be killed. It is with deep sadness that I relate the name of that someone: The Admiral Gaspard de Coligny, our strait-laced friend to whom Lady Maria took such a fancy, and who we were amused to refer to as "Longaville" in Nérac. Guise has been forever seething at the fact that the Admiral is responsible for his father's death.

As happy as I was at the nuptial lunch, even I could see the manner in which Guise was glaring at the Admiral. Every bite the man took seemed to enrage him further. Mother was anxious (she explained later) that he was going to cause an ugly public scene, so she ushered Guise aside and, after listening to his grievances, gave her consent that Coligny should be done away with at a later date, in the name of peace.

Unfortunately, the assassination did not go well.

The first problem was that Guise interpreted the expression "at a later date" to mean now; he dispatched his assassin for the next day. The second problem was even more egregious.

"What assassination?" Charles asked when told that it did not come off as planned. He was then informed that Guise's assassin had shot Coligny in front of a group of his fellow Huguenots, but that the bullet only maimed him.

"And I was not consulted? How dare you, Mother!"

We could hear Charles' voice even from my chambers, squawking with anger. Charles quite liked Coligny; chances that he would have agreed to him being killed were slim. Perhaps Mother knew this. At any rate, Charles, enraged, sent for Guise, all the princes, and the Catholic officers to meet with him and Mother at the Tuileries Palace. I'm told the meeting was heated, with a great deal of screaming on Charles' part followed by a lengthy discussion of what "at a later date" means. Guise gave a heated defense of his actions, but Charles insisted that he be punished. It was Mother, I am told, who convinced him that things had already gone too far to turn back, that they needed to take action or risk being killed themselves. Dread, and a sense of self-preservation, extinguished Charles' desire to argue. Now it seemed advisable to finish the job of killing the good Admiral. Later the next day Guise's men found Coligny in his lodgings and killed him, along with several of his men. Coligny's body was thrown from the window into the street and was subsequently mutilated, castrated, dragged through the mud, thrown in the river, suspended on a gallows, and finally burned by the Parisian crowd.

Burned by the crowd! The very people I had felt sure would be rejoicing at the new peace I had brought to them. My sense of betrayal when I learned this news can, I am sure, be imagined.

But while it was going on, I was alone in my chambers and completely ignorant of events. I sensed a disturbance within the palace; there were distant shouts and loud noises I could not identify. When I asked about it, no one would tell me what was going on. The Huguenots have a deep suspicion of me because I am a Catholic, and the Catholics because I am now married to a Huguenot.

That night, still oblivious to any evil doings, I went into Mother's bedchamber and sat next to my sister Lorraine, who seemed extremely nervous. Mother, too, was out of sorts and the minute she saw me, she bade me go to bed. This seemed rather abrupt, given our new understanding of one another, but I made to comply. As I was taking leave, my sister seized my hand and began to sob, "For the love of God, do not leave this chamber, Marguerite!"

This surprised me greatly. Lorraine and I have never been particularly close. In addition to being six years older, she suffers from a hunchback and a club foot. I have always perceived her to be envious that I did not inherit these deficiencies, therefore I was greatly alarmed at her sudden concern for my well-being. So, indeed, was my mother, who called Lorraine to her and spoke sharply. All I could make out was harsh whispers until I heard my sister say clear as day, "If you send Marguerite away now, she will die!"

You can imagine my astonishment. What on earth were they talking about? Mother then spoke for all to hear. "If it pleases God, Marguerite will not be hurt. However, it is necessary that she leave these chambers immediately. Suspicions will arise if she stays."

With tears in her eyes, Lorraine bade me a good night and, utterly confused, I rushed back to my bedchamber. As soon as I reached my closet, I threw myself upon my knees and prayed to the Virgin to take me into her protection and save me; but from whom or what, I had no idea. It was at that moment that my Lady Maria came to me in a fit of hysterics to relay the news of Coligny's terrible murder. She had fallen in love with the Admiral, so you can imagine the state she was in. We put her to bed with a strong dose of laudanum.

I was sorely tempted to take the laudanum myself, but at that moment I was given the news that my husband was sending for me. I went to his rooms and found Henri in bed surrounded by about thirty of his men, among them my brother Alençon and the Prince de Condé.

"We must have vengeance!" shouted Condé. "An eye for an eye!"

There was blood lust in every man's eye, even my brother Alençon's. What followed was a long night of angry denunciations and (to my mind) a rather rash plan for revenge. Concerned, I pulled Henri aside.

"Dearest," I said. "It seems to me that, as small a party as you are at the moment, seeking revenge at this point can only lead to your annihilation." Henri shook his head dismissively, then seemed to reconsider my words. At length, he went back to his men.

"We must seek another way," he told them. More talk occurred, and finally, they came to the resolution that Henri would go to the King and demand justice. If it was refused, they would take matters into their own hands. Whereupon, exhausted as I was and as loath to be in the middle of this treasonous situation, Henri required me to bear witness as each of them, including Alençon, signed a blood oath to avenge Coligny's death.

I stumbled back to my rooms expecting to fall fast asleep, but tossed and turned the entire night, so haunted was I by the events of the day and the sense that I might die at any moment. As soon as day broke, I arose, ready for the next calamity.

Henri sauntered into my chambers and announced he was off to play tennis.

"Tennis?" I echoed incredulously.

"It's well known that the King is a late riser. I see no reason not to get a bit of exercise before I confront him," Henri replied calmly.

Oddly, I found this attitude comforting. If one can play tennis in the midst of an uprising, certainly the danger is not so great. Soothed by this notion, I relaxed enough to get some sleep, but about an hour later I was awakened by a violent noise at the door, and a voice calling out, "Navarre! Navarre!" Mme. de Tournon, thinking it was the King at the door, rushed to open it, whereupon a stranger ran in and threw himself upon my bed. He was bleeding profusely, having received a wound in one arm from a sword, and another by a pike. Four soldiers then charged into my bedchamber, their weapons raised.

Mme. de Tournon promptly fainted. I jumped out of bed and placed myself between the poor terrified gentleman and the soldiers, both of us screaming at the top of our lungs in fright.

"Leave him alone, for heaven's sake!" I implored.

"Yaaaaah!" he screamed.

At that moment, the captain of the Guard rushed into the bedchamber.

"What's this? What's this?"

I summoned as much dignity as was available to me in my nightgown. "How dare you pursue this man into my chambers, terrifying my women? I could see you hanged for this!"

The captain, seeing Mme. de Tournon in a crumpled heap on the floor and perceiving himself to be in a very poor position, turned on his men.

"Idiots! Remove this man immediately!" They made to drag their victim away, but I stopped them. "What are you going to do with him?"

"Begging your Highness's pardon, but he's a Huguenot."

"So is my husband! I demand that you spare his life, and find him medical aid! Summon M. de Lauren this instant."

"I'm afraid that won't be possible, Your Highness."

"Whyever not?"

"The court physician has, in a move surprising to all, taken his own life."

That *was* surprising.

"Well then, see this man to the gates."

"Of course, Your Highness." They dragged the whimpering man out. I do not feel confident they saw him to the gates.

A few hours later, I was told that Henri was again in his bedchamber. I rushed to his rooms and flew into his arms.

"Henri, something terrible is taking place within the palace."

"I'm aware."

"Did you speak with the King?"

"Er, yes. It didn't go all that well, I'm afraid. Your brother is taking the position that Coligny's death was an unfortunate accident."

"That's absurd! Let's go back and talk to him together."

"That won't be possible, I'm afraid, my dear. I've been informed I'm being placed under 'protection' until this unfortunate accident has played itself out."

I turned and noticed for the first time the heavily armed guards flanking the door.

"I'm staying here with you," I said.

"No, my dear, it's too dangerous. My captain will return you to your chambers. I won't have you drawn into this, Marguerite."

I whispered fearfully into his ear. "You drew me into it, Henri, when you had me witness your men's pledge of vengeance. If Charles or Mother knew my proximity to a coup, we would all be put to death."

"Which is why you must go."

Despite my protestations, Henri had the captain lead me from his rooms. As we passed through the antechamber, another man dashed in pursued by soldiers. They ran his body through with a pike right in front of me, and the poor man fell dead at my feet.

"Apologies, your Highness," murmured the captain, as if we had just encountered unexpected cobwebs.

"I cannot bear this!" I sobbed. Breaking free, I ran alone to my sister Lorraine's bedchamber where I collapsed, more dead than alive from terror.

I had barely caught my breath when Condé ran in, followed by Theodore d'Aubigne, another of Henri's friends.

"I beg you, Your Highness!" gasped Condé. "Help us!"

There is a secret exit from the palace through a hidden door in Lorraine's anteroom; each of us has one. (Guise made use of it, as I mentioned before.) I showed the men the stairway, and d'Aubigne shouted with relief as he ran down, "Poor fools who don't know to ask a princess when their lives are in jeopardy!" The joke seemed in rather bad taste, considering his dead kinsmen lying in the hallways.

That was only the beginning.

Within a few hours, every Huguenot within the palace who had not managed to escape was dead, except for Henri and Alençon. In terror for their lives, I ran to my mother's chambers and threw myself at her feet, begging her to show mercy. Mother, who was being made ready for bed, feigned surprise.

"Daughter. How could you believe that I would even contemplate such a thing as the death of your husband? I will admit to having acquiesced to the decision regarding Coligny, but that is all. I had no idea the citizens of Paris would elevate the situation to one so far beyond our control."

I made an effort to control my emotions. "How then, if you please, do you explain the murders which I have seen take place right before my eyes here in the palace?"

Mother placed her hand on her heart. "I'm sorry you had to witness that, child. It was an armed response to murderous provocation from within."

I thought back to the poor wounded gentlemen in my bedchamber, shrieking along with me in terror, and found her explanation extremely hard to credit.

Mother has always had a fluid relationship with the truth. As a child I found it confusing; today's truth was often tomorrow's lie and I was never sure what to believe about anything, which may be why I took such comfort in the eternal truths of the Church. But as I've grown, read, and educated myself on the thoughts of the great minds of the past - Sophocles, Marcus Aurelius, Boethius - I see the importance of finding one's truth and living it truthfully. Boethius introduced to me the concept of the hypothetical syllogism, whose logic is as follows:

If it is light, it is day.

It is not light. Therefore:

It is not day.

Mother's account of recent events is a fabrication, I feel sure of it. In addition, she has deeply misread the mood of the country, and we are now paying the price.

It is not day.

And she has entirely ruined my wedding.

4.

"In the late autumn of 88 B.C. The cities of Asia Minor were glad to obey the orders of Mithridates for a general massacre of the resident Romans."

Plutarch

24 August, 1581 - Paris

Oh, the atrocities that are taking place in the city at this moment! Paris has erupted with the massacre of Huguenot men, women, and children. Yes, children - what insanity is this? Hundreds of innocent civilians have been yanked from their beds and executed, not by soldiers but by ordinary people, by their neighbors! Two of my ladies, rushing back to the palace in terror, say Catholics are hunting Protestants through the streets, murdering them horribly, then collecting the bodies of the dead in carts and dumping them into the Seine. It defies belief! And now, it seems this madness has spread to regions outside of Paris. Could my mother possibly have foreseen the depth of the animosity of the common folk towards Huguenots?

To make matters worse, Charles has become extremely erratic. This happens to him occasionally; he'll seem to be himself for a long period, and then something will trigger a diabolical change of humor. The events on the street excited him to such a striking degree that I am told he stepped out onto the balcony with his pistol and started taking potshots, killing a dozen or so citizens. At his order, alarm bells have sounded and chains have been drawn across the streets, trapping Huguenots within the city whilst the killing continues. Then, in a bizarre attempt to disguise the level of horror going on, Charles proclaimed a day of jubilee in celebration of St. Bartholomew. How the saint must be turning in his grave!

This afternoon my mother called me to her chambers for a private audience. I could tell she was shaken because she smiled at me in a fashion most unnerving.

"My dearest child, such a turbulent time. I pray your well-being has not suffered overmuch." She took my hand which, of course, put me further on guard. I said I was doing as well as could be expected, considering the carnage taking place. She looked deeply into my eyes.

"Marguerite, I have so enjoyed the trust that you and I have developed over the past months. Can you give me some insight into the state of mind of your husband at the moment? He and his men must have been terribly weakened. Will they accept defeat, do you think?"

My heart began to pound.

"I'm afraid I have scarcely left my chambers these past days, Mother, so I wouldn't know."

"But surely, you've got an idea of whether they are defeated, or plan to retaliate? The peace of the country is at stake."

I have never lied to my mother. Oh, perhaps a sin of omission from time to time, on subjects such as court flirtations, things that were beneath her notice anyway. But I had the night before witnessed my husband, my brother, and his fellow Huguenots sign a blood oath to avenge the death of Admiral Coligny at any cost. What to do?

I am my mother's daughter. Having watched her so often master her features so that there is no evidence of feeling to be read on them, I returned her gaze calmly.

"I'm afraid not. Being a mere woman, I'm not privy to those conversations. Henri probably feels I wouldn't understand."

Mother frowned, a more natural look for her. "I completely understand your fright. You are probably regretting the choice to marry Navarre, and I don't blame you. Tell me, is there perhaps some grounds for declaring him 'not like other men?' If so, it should be easy for us to obtain a divorce."

I have endeavored all my life to see my mother in a benevolent light, to defer to her in all things and honor her as the Bible calls for a child to do. But no, I will not divorce the man I have just married so that Mother may have him executed. Calmly, I informed her that Henri was my husband "in all ways," and that there was no way I could claim otherwise. She was disappointed, but I could see she was impressed by my firmness.

"Very well. I am quite fond of Navarre, of course, but know that others see him to be a grave danger to the state. I'm afraid I cannot vouch for his safety."

I knew she was alluding to Guise. Now that Coligny is gone, Henri's demise would be the natural next step for him.

Later on, Henri and I conferred in his chambers. I must say, for someone whose life seems to be in constant peril, his calm demeanor was rather unnerving.

"Did you see my brother the King?" I asked.

"Yes, yes. He seems rather overstimulated by all this," he replied casually. "Someone should probably take his pistol away from him."

"What did he say?"

"He wants me to convert to Catholicism, or he will have me killed."

"He said that?"

"He didn't have to."

"What are you going to do?"

"I'm going to convert, of course."

"Oh! You would do that?"

Henri shrugged. "To retain my head, yes."

We haven't known one another that long, but I could tell his casual attitude was bravado. For my part, I was delighted to have the religious obstacle removed from our marriage. Alençon had likewise agreed to renew his vows to the church, although I don't believe his life was ever in jeopardy; Mother will view his disloyalty as a youthful indiscretion.

Henri's baptismal ceremony took place the next day, in the presence of the full court. The Pope blessed Henri with all the gravity the ceremony demanded, but with an air of sang-froid that suggested this was not the most moving baptism he had ever performed. His was not the only skeptical face, as Guise seemed barely able to sit still in his pew.

I am delighted that Henri has gone through with the conversion, thus saving his soul from damnation, but from that day forward his demeanor changed. The baptism was a necessary indignity that he might live to see another day, but he is grieving for his lost compatriots. Its greatest leaders, beginning with Coligny, are now gone and Henri is anxious that he not be seen as a traitor to those who remain. We still have our moments of intimacy, but the laughter is gone, and gone too is the doting lover of our first few days. Now he is fretful, I can see his mind is elsewhere. I suspect he deeply misses Nérac, and so do I. How I would love to be back in those first moments in the castle when we gazed upon one another and felt the purity of unsullied love. Instead, Henri is trapped now within the Louvre palace with me; Charles and Mother felt it inadvisable that he should leave. It may come as no surprise that captivity is not conducive to the successful flowering of a marriage.

I am a devout Catholic and nothing would cause me to question its tenets, but the events of the last week have turned my stomach and tried my soul. I vow I will no longer be a part of my mother's treacherous plans. After much prayer and reflection, I have determined that despite my deep attachment to his every look and touch, Henri must be released from his captivity. I know the Louvre palace like the back of my hand, and with the assistance of my ladies, I have devised a plan for him to escape, before it is too late.

I will join him in Navarre once he is safe ~ but safe he must be!

30 August, 1581 - Paris

Yesterday, on one of my perambulations around the grounds outside the palace, Lady Rosalind and I took a detour to the stables. There we encountered our stable master, M. d'Aubiac, currying the king's favorite horse. He's a portly, grizzled gentleman, with a kindly air about him.

"Your Highness!" he said with surprise and pleasure. "To what do I owe the honor?" The old man likes me and I him as we've known one another since I was a child. It was he who picked out my first pony, Bonbon.

"M. d'Aubiac, I wonder if you might do me a great favor."

"Of course, Your Highness."

"Could you arrange to have a horse and carriage at the ready outside my chamber window tomorrow at midnight?"

"Outside your chamber window? Would it not be more convenient –"

"Yes, outside my chamber window, Monsieur. As quietly as you have ever done such a thing."

"Ah. I see."

"I do not mean to cause you inconvenience. It is just that I require a great deal of discretion."

"Yes, yes, I understand. I am at your service, Your Highness."

"And I wonder, Monsieur, if you might have such a thing as a length of rope about you? Say twenty meters."

"I believe I do."

"Would you be so good as to procure that rope for us at this time?"

"Yes, Your Highness. One moment." He disappeared, and Rosalind and I waited nervously until he returned with a length of rope.

"Thank you, Monsieur d'Aubiac. And now would you be so good as to assist me whilst I wrap this rope around Lady Rosalind's undergarments."

The old man's jaw dropped. "Beg pardon, miss?"

"We need to bring it within the palace and wish not to be detected. Therefore, we intend to wrap it within Lady Rosalind's skirts."

"That's why I am wearing last year's fashion," interjected Rosalind. "I'm sure you were wondering. Last year the dresses were much more voluminous than this year, which features slimness. A rope of this length would clearly not fit under it."

M. d'Aubiac turned red. "No, quite right, quite right." Averting his eyes, the stable master assisted as we wrapped the rope around Lady Rosalind's undergarments, letting her overdress flounce over it.

"I do hope we're not seen," fretted Rosalind. "It's a scandal to be *wearing this dress, I shall never live it down.*"

"Your sacrifice is greatly appreciated, Lady Rosalind," I said and gave M. d'Aubiac a little wink, which delighted him.

Next came the challenge of disguising Henri and Alençon. They wanted to leap out of my chamber windows dressed in their usual attire, but I convinced them such foolishness would get them instantly stopped at the gate. Our only option was to thoroughly disguise them - and what better disguise than to be a woman? Lady Maria and I costumed them both in the season's finest gowns and periwigs so that they could masquerade as ladies of the court. I had chosen a night when there was to be no moon, to evade detection. We waited until the changing of the guard at midnight, and at that moment I threw open the sash, hoisted the rope out the window, and tied the other end to a bedpost. Alençon gave me a quick embrace.

"*Merci, Margot!*" he exclaimed, and we watched as he scaled his way down to the awaiting carriage below. He touched the ground, arranged his dresses around him, and curtseyed up at us, which sent the ladies into a fit of giggles.

Next came Henri's turn. He looked improbably beautiful in Lady Tournon's gown; it was rather titillating. He took me into his arms. "*Mon brave,*" I whispered, awaiting my big romantic kiss of thanks. At that moment there was a knock at the door.

"Quickly!" I whispered, and in a blink, Henri was out the window, without having kissed his wife goodbye. As it turned out, it was only my maid *de chambre*. Curses! How I wanted to climb down that rope for a final moment with Henri! But vigilance dictated we be as careful as possible. The carriage set off. It could only take them to the edge of the city, as the country roads are not passable by carriage. From that point, I had arranged with M. d'Aubiac to have two additional horses waiting, whence the two of them could doff their finery and ride to safety.

It seemed expedient to be rid of the rope, so I bade my ladies throw it into the fire. I don't know what it was made of, but the combustion that resulted, and the thick smoke that emanated from the chimney caused the palace guard to arrive, pounding at the door and yelling, "FIRE!" I leapt into my bed and pulled up the covers. Maria hastily put out the fire, and Rosalind ran to the door, to reveal two guards with axes.

"Oh, how lovely that you are here, gentlemen, but all is well! Like a silly thing, I turned the flue the wrong way!" They wanted to come in, but she begged them not to disturb me in my slumbers. It took some convincing, but they finally retreated.

Should I have gone with Henri and Alençon? The thought occurred to me, but I was afraid to be a burden to them in their flight, and I just couldn't face the thought of Mother's rage. As it is, she will most likely blame me for being an accomplice, though I doubt she'll be able to prove it. I don't doubt, however, Mother's capacity for vengeance. I look back upon my life at court, all the lies and convenient mortalities that have taken place here, and see that I have been most naive, seeing only what I wanted to see, to find my life here bearable. My eyes are now open; I vow not to close them again.

30 November, 1581 - Paris

It is three months now since Henri and Alençon fled the palace under perilous circumstances. A messenger arrived ten days after their departure with the news that they had both safely arrived in Nérac, and I have never been so relieved. I had hoped that, after Mother's initial fury had subsided, she would reconcile herself to the fact of his departure and allow me to join him. I had been assured that would be the case, once they had "sorted out" a few things.

Yet I am still here.

It is clear what is happening. Immediately upon having returned to Navarre, Henri reversed course and declared himself a Huguenot again. I don't know what this means to his immortal soul, but I do know what it means to Charles and Mother ~ that my alliance with him makes me a threat, and as a result, I am to be held prisoner in the palace.

Perhaps "prisoner" is overstating it. It's not as if there are guards at the gate, and I may traverse Paris freely. But they will delegate no funds for a journey to Nérac, no retinue to escort me there, and I certainly can't walk there myself. It causes me, regrettably, to feel a certain amount of pique toward Henri. Didn't he realize the troubles his renunciation of the true faith would cause me?

I have had time, therefore, to reflect at length, not only upon my state but indeed the state of so many titled women whose fate I have observed over the years and read about in history. If my tone sounds somewhat bitter, I apologize; I am lonely and sad.

It seems to me, upon reflection, that a young princess is given two messages growing up. There are in truth many trivial messages imparted to one regarding comportment and daily life, but these are the two that resound most deeply within the young soul.

Message Number One: <u>You are of enormous importance</u>.

As the offspring of the King and Queen, you are placed in the highest regard at court, your every whim catered to. You live in magnificent surroundings that reflect the illustrious history of your ancestors, the blood of whom you are constantly reminded runs through your veins. You are educated to the highest degree possible, surrounded by a retinue of servers and waiting ladies, flattered and admired by suitors, attired in the highest fashion, and given pride of place at every public event. When you travel, it is with all pomp and ceremony, in the company of a retinue which frequently numbers in the hundreds. This, I'm sure you might imagine, serves to build within the average princess a certain self-regard, except for the fact that it collides with the following:

Message Number Two: <u>You are of no importance whatsoever.</u>

Interestingly, this message is conveyed to you concurrently with Message #1. Yes, you will be educated, but the knowledge you acquire will be of no interest to anyone, except insofar as it may aid in the acquisition of a husband. Your father the King may dandle you on his knee and make you laugh for a few brief moments, creating a cherished memory you will never forget. But then he will dismiss you and go off to fight a war, or commence a year-long tour of the country with his men, or fight in a joust and be impaled through the eye with a javelin, die, and leave you fatherless. As you grow, your mother will find you to be an annoyance and focus her attention entirely on your brothers. Your ladies may flatter, courtiers may write letters of love to you but this is because, in addition to being a princess, you have somehow managed not to acquire the crippling congenital defects of your siblings. Beautiful baubles delight those to whom beauty is all. No one, except possibly your governess, will see your mind as a valuable resource, and why should they? It's not as if you'll ever inherit the throne; the Salic laws of France forbid it. Then, when you are deemed ripe enough for picking, you will be discarded the first moment an acceptable offer is made for your hand. That alliance accomplished, no one will give you a second thought until the day you return for, say, a state funeral. In short, you are, from the moment you are born, a chess pawn for the more powerful to play as they deem expedient.

Yes, I am angry, but I don't expect pity. I understand that there are a great many people who would sacrifice all to be a princess of France. I am merely pointing out that life as a chess pawn has its demerits. Mother and Charles are using me as one right now. Henri wrote that he is doing all he can to have me released, but just when he thinks he has reached an agreement with the crown, their demands grow higher, or they break off communications entirely.

Having said that, Henri's letters are fewer and fewer. I was so hoping he would include one of his delightful poems in the last one, but his inspiration in that regard seems to have evaporated, and who can blame him when the country is so deeply split in half? As Catholics, we have seen loved ones lost to the heretic religion; people we have previously regarded as perfectly rational have embraced the tenets of Protestantism with a bewildering fervor. Admiral Coligny was a good example; Lady Maria has lost much of her esprit de corps following his death. As a devout Catholic, she knows he is not assured of a happy afterlife and it pains her deeply, but there is no one in his family she can reach out to for succor; they, too, have gone over to the heretical cult.

There have been many pamphlets disseminated in the past depicting the evils of the Huguenots; I feel it may have led to the fervor of the recent massacre. Now Rosalind tells me of pamphlets agitating against the crown. This business of putting every loathsome thought to paper and distributing it to the public is diabolical. The printing press is a marvelous thing, but spreading ugly rumors is not the use to which its inventor intended it, I feel sure.

Though most of the Huguenots in Paris have been wiped out, it's like the plague; it dies out in one region and pops up elsewhere with new fervor. There has been a recent successful Huguenot uprising in Northern

Normandy, for example. I don't know if Henri is connected to that, and I have no idea if it increases or lessens my chances of release.

Once again, as ever, I am powerless, and it infuriates me.

5.

"But how are we to face Zeus when he pours down rain? And how the North Wind?"

— **Plutarch**, on Sulla

1582

3 February, 1582 - Paris

The coldest, most brutal month. Nothing seems to keep me warm, no matter how often they replenish the wood in the fireplace. No letter from Henri in a month. I have taken ill with a cold, and Rosalind looks like she may be next. The physician has prescribed an infusion of cabbage juice to purge the head, black beetroot and honey administered through the nose, and clover decocted in water and drunk hourly. I'm afraid I am not in the mood for the lively chatter of Agatha, though she's a sweet girl and I appreciate her intentions to cheer me up. I can't do much of anything besides sleep. I'm told Charles has taken ill as well, but Charles has consumption; one always expects him to be rather sick. Besides, I don't care how my captor is faring at the moment. Mother, of course, remains as healthy as an ox.

My detention in Paris now has lasted over five months. Everyone pretends I'm not being held prisoner, that they'd love for me to be able to join Henri in Nérac but the weather is bad, or the roads are washed out, or travel is dangerous with all of these battles cropping up left and right. I am being robbed of my liberty. Give it whatever name you wish.

The one bright spot was an interesting package that arrived today, though I don't quite know what to make of it. It's from that poet who was snooping about at Nérac so long ago, Chaquesper, though he seems to employ an S and a K in his name rather than C and Q. It appears to be a manuscript of some kind, but the problem is it is in English. I am fluent in Italian, Spanish, Latin, and Greek but I've never seen the need to acquire English, as any English noble we've come across has always spoken French as well. After all, they spoke Norman French themselves until only a couple of centuries ago. I was tempted to toss the manuscript aside, but there was a letter on top of it written in broken French which provoked much hilarity with my ladies.

1 January, 1582

> *Gracious Queen,*
>
> *I hope you will take no offend at my effrontery. The weeks I spent at the chateau of the King of Navarre is sculpted upon my spirit. So too your jolly semblance, as well that of your ladies, in my imagination. I have grasped the liberty of composing this divertisement, which I have greatly hopes our excellent Queen Elizabeth will one day regard at court. It was written with the deepest heat and estime for all of you who were the inspiration.*
>
> *I have lately heard of your maladroit current situation, and pray for a rapid resolution to reunite you with your bonnie husband, to whom I shall be forever heavy for his gracious hospitality. I hope this "play," for such it is called in our country, will bring you some relief from your durance in Paris.*
>
> *Respectfully,*
>
> *William Shakspere*

How very curious. He sends me a "play," apparently with the intention of having it read, but doesn't take the trouble to translate it to French? The gentleman certainly has a high opinion of himself! However, it occurs to me that my old governess, Mme. de Brezé, is currently at court. She has a knowledge of English and is a most intelligent woman. I will prevail upon her to translate it for me. There is very little of interest taking place at court right now, it might help to fill the tedious hours. With no communication from Henri, I am in much need of distraction.

30 February, 1582 - Paris

Mme. de Brezé, apparently as bored as the rest of us and having just recovered from her own ague, willingly took on the task of translating M. Shakspere's manuscript and has presented me with her work on the first act. My ladies and I have perused it several times and we are completely bewildered. It doesn't appear to be a mystery play, nor a morality play, nor a farce. It's certainly not a sotie, which is generally two idiots telling each other terrible jokes. So, what is it? The characters, mainly gentlemen of the court thus far, speak to one another much the way we do in life, with some ornamentation but in many ways in a natural fashion, which is curious and rather exciting for a theatrical piece. They discuss their vow not to allow women into the palace, which of course provoked great mirth because we all remember that little episode of our lives. There is the character of the King of Navarre, which is interesting because Henri was only a prince at that time. I suppose the playwright felt it necessary to elevate his status for dramatic effect. But this fictional King's reasons for barring women from his company are that he wants to spend three years performing academic study. This is how we knew it was going to be a comedy; imagine any of our young men forswearing battle for study!

Then it became quite interesting: One of the characters informs the King that the Princess of France is coming to Navarre to negotiate a contract of some sort. I am to be a character in this play! We all became terribly excited and immediately begged Mme. de Brezé to hasten as quickly as possible to translate Act II.

Meanwhile, we have all taken turns reading the male characters aloud. There is a Spanish character named Don Armado who Mme. de Tournon read most amusingly. Mme. de Tournon is rather rotund, which seems perfect for this character who is both licentious and unaware of his limitations. I read the King, and Rosalind makes a most convincing Biron - yes, he's in the play, as well as Congé and the late Coligny, but by the pseudonyms Shakspere knew them, Dumain and Longaville. This, of course, gave us a moment of sad reflection upon the Admiral's demise. Such a happy, idyllic time in retrospect, even if Mother was a part of it. Despite not being able to identify the exact genre of the play, it really is most diverting. The anticipation of receiving the second act has revived our spirits, and I find that my cold has disappeared.

15 March, 1582 - Paris

Mme. de Brezé delivered to us the second act of the play with many apologies, for she feels the original English to be very beautiful, and fears she is not doing it justice. She struggled a bit with the title, which she has decided is "The Work of Love is Lost." This sounds terribly sad, considering how humorous we have found the play to be thus far, but we were so eager to read the act that we rushed into my chambers to read it aloud to one another.

How delightful it is! The ladies of the play banter with the gentlemen in a most teasing and provocative manner, which made us thrill at their daring. The King explains his reasons for barring them entrance to the palace, and the Princess very gently but with much wit mocks his intentions, causing him to take her point without losing his regard for her; in fact, he is all the more intrigued. The same is true for each pair of lovers. Perhaps I should banter more with Henri.

We are accustomed in French comedies (of which there seem to be few, and most of them taken from the ancient Greek,) for a lower style of language to be employed. How refreshing to experience this altogether new and sophisticated form of discourse between lovers! Very wisely, no mention is made of war or religion or any of the depressing realities of the world. I'll admit I was startled to see one of the queen's ladies in the play to be called Katherine. She certainly bore no resemblance to my mother. Indeed, so far, there is no mention of any oppressive matriarchal figure hovering over the proceedings. Perhaps M. Shakspere thought that would take the fun out of it, as indeed it would.

16 March, 1582 - Paris

I had been requesting an audience with my brother the King for two weeks with no success. I felt that if only I could speak to him personally about my situation, he would take pity on me and let me set off for Nérac. He was kinder to me than Anjou was when we were children, but then that didn't require much. Every day I have been told that Charles is indisposed, or off hunting, or some other excuse.

Guise, in particular, has found every opportunity to be rude to me. After Henri escaped, the Duke mistakenly thought I would welcome a reintroduction of his simmering passion for me. As a Catholic, he expected me to thrill to his tales of manly conquest and ghastly Huguenot slaughter. When my reaction was less than one of admiration, he became surly and suggested that my loyalties weren't what they ought to be. Since that moment, he has tried to make trouble for me at every turn. I think he has Charles and Mother convinced I'm spying for my husband.

My suspicions were reinforced when, today, I was finally granted an audience with the King. I met him in my mother's chambers, though she was not in sight. Trying to set a reasonable tone, I reminded him that I had not married by choice, but because it was foist upon me. I opined that since Henri was their choice for me, they ought not to hinder me from joining him. Charles rolled his eyes.

"Don't be stupid, Margot. From the moment Navarre reverted to Protestantism, he has been a threat to us all."

"How a threat, brother? He is my husband, not my enemy. Do I not have a wifely duty?"

"Your duty is to the crown. Huguenots are our mortal enemy."

"Then let me plead with Henri to reverse course. You know I can be quite convincing, given the chance."

"Alas for you, then, that you will not be given the chance. You know far too much of the inner workings of the crown, Margot, for us to send you to him."

"Charles –"

"Your Majesty!" my brother snapped.

I bit the inside of my cheek. "Your Majesty, I assure you, I have no intention of becoming a Huguenot spy, whatever you have been told. I am a Catholic; I will always be Catholic. But whether I am here or there, I am still his wife. Please let me rejoin him. I ask for the smallest entourage, or no entourage whatsoever, just enough for my protection. I am desperately unhappy here. If you will not provide for my journey, I may well find the means to go myself."

"Is that so?" My brother laughed scornfully. "Sister, know this: If you join Navarre, you will make the Queen your mother and me your bitterest enemies, and we shall use every means to make you feel the effects of our resentment. Moreover, you will make your husband's situation worse instead of better. If that is the future you envision, by all means, leave!"

I'll wager Mother was behind the curtains, listening to it all. I could just imagine Charles turning to her upon my departure and asking, "Did I do well, Mama?"

I retired to my chambers in a dark mood. To escape my thoughts, I had Mme. de Brezé assist me in writing a letter in English to my little playwright. I thanked him for the play and related our enjoyment in reading it aloud. I'm sure he'd be amused at the notion of ladies performing in a theatrical piece. Such a thing is not done, but I don't think there's any harm, within the privacy of my chambers. I informed him of the correct spelling of Rosalind's name (with a D at the end) and wondered at his turning my mother into my waiting lady, in truth a rather entertaining concept. I wished him well with his theatrical aspirations and expressed the hope that his Queen Elizabeth, who is currently very much involved in support of the Protestant cause, will find the time to take an interest in his works. I asked that he express my deepest respect for Her Majesty and all of her endeavors, and show her this letter in support of his work.

In addition, I declared myself a friend to England, and whatever religion it chose to embrace. It was a small act of rebellion, perhaps even reckless. But it was very satisfying.

15 April, 1582 - Paris

My brother Alençon, who can seemingly commit the most reckless of acts and never suffer personal repercussions, appeared at the palace today. All is forgiven with Mother and Charles, who have welcomed him back into the fold. I won't waste words expressing my bitterness at the difference in my treatment compared to Alençon's. I, who am trapped here and have done nothing but obey their commands, am being punished and ostracized whilst Alençon, who for all I know has killed hundreds of Catholics on the field of battle with his boon companions, is welcomed with open arms. It's hard for me to be angry with Alençon, though; he was my playmate in childhood and can always make me laugh. What's more, I feel that he's the only person in my family who bears love for me.

Alençon came to see me after his interview at court. This may not sound like bravery on his part, but currently, I am living without a visit from a single person. None of my intimate friends dares to come near me, frightened that such a step might prove injurious to their self-interest. It is ever thus at court; adversity is solitary, whilst prosperity dwells in a crowd. You can imagine, then, my happiness at a visit from Alençon. I'm afraid I dissolved into tears upon seeing him and spent a great deal of time expatiating on my tale of woe. He listened patiently.

"Perhaps this will cheer you up," he said and drew a letter from his inner vest. I saw it was from Henri and fairly grabbed it from him. My tears vanished as I eagerly read.

> *Dearest Loving Wife,*
>
> *Though I am very much occupied with matters related to our noble religious cause, my mind is constantly on you. The unfairness of your treatment rankles me to the bone, and I am determined to once again have your lovely presence by my side. I am currently in Gascony, where we are forming a coalition called the Union of Provinces to protect the rights of Huguenots. I beg you for patience, my sweet wife, as*

I balance the demands of this endeavor with the delicate negotiations required to secure your release.

Your Eternally Devoted Husband,

Henri

Though not the poetry of previous days, the letter buoyed my spirits immeasurably. Determined to have me by his side – I like the sound of that. "Eternally Devoted Husband" also sent a thrill through my soul, and I found myself suddenly capable of listening to Alençon's complaints, which boil down to this:

He's sick of war. It has lost all entertainment value for him, and since many of his closest friends have been killed there is distinctly less pleasurable camaraderie for him. To be allowed to return to Paris, Alençon had to express public remorse for his involvement with the Huguenots, and the King interpreted this declaration as a decision to join up against them. This was not what Alençon had in mind. Charles recently announced the formation of something he's calling the Catholic League. (Actually, he didn't form it; Guise did, but as soon as he did Charles decided he was the head of it.) He wants Alençon to sign a document saying he'll be part of the League. He even wants to give Alençon an army!

"It's so exasperating," declared Alençon. "I couldn't be less interested in his ridiculous League. There must be some way to escape these endless wars."

"What did you say to him?"

"I took the army, of course. It's always nice to have one. But my heart isn't in it, Margot."

"Has the court ever considered the idea of tolerating the Huguenots and living in peace and harmony with them?" I inquired.

Alençon laughed long and hard. "No, but seriously," he resumed, "I've been giving it some thought and do you know what I'd very much like? To be King of Flanders."

"Isn't Flanders in the hands of Spain?"

"Yes. But I have it on high authority that everyone in Flanders hates Don John. He's trampling over all their most cherished French laws. Several nobles have come to me about it asking that action be taken to return Flanders to French rule."

"Aren't you just talking about more war, Monsieur?"

"No, no, no, silly Margot! Peaceful negotiations, that's how civilized people do it. The Flemish are most eager to be under French rule again. The minute French troops ride through the streets, our path will be strewn with flowers."

I had my doubts about this but I held my tongue, except to wonder why, if these nobles were so eager, they hadn't gone to Charles about it.

"Well, they wanted to, but Charles is preoccupied with our internal wars. No, I'm sure it would be a great relief to Charles if I took this on. After all, I was promised Flanders at one time."

"By whom?"

"By Francis, when he was king. He said it one day while we were hunting."

"But Francis is dead."

"Yes, but he did say it, and I'm quite sure Charles was there. Even if it wasn't, others will attest to it."

I was growing weary of this conversation until Alençon said something that captured my attention completely.

"Listen, Margot, if you're so tired of being in Paris, why don't you accompany Princess de Roche-sur-Yon to Spa?"

"For what reason?"

"To take the waters there. She's planning on setting off very soon, to treat her gout."

"How do you know that?"

"She's a friend of mine. I know she's a bit of a battle-axe, but she has the most entertainingly *risqué* stories about her old love affairs. Did she ever tell you about her tryst with Phillip of Spain?"

"No."

"Oh, do have her tell you, it's scandalously good."

"I'm not sure I want to know."

"Suit yourself. I'm merely saying, it would be a good way to escape Paris, and it should be easy to broach the idea to Mother. Just tell her the physician recommended it for that arm pain you say you're experiencing from writing so much. I'd be happy to vouch for you."

I cannot tell you how appealing the idea was to me. Spa is a town in Flanders that has become quite well known for the medicinal qualities of its waters. It's so popular that other locations with mineral waters are now calling themselves "spas," I suppose to trade on the fame of the real Spa. If I couldn't make the journey to Nérac, why shouldn't I accompany the Princess de Roche-sur-Yon? Yes, she talks a great deal about the triumphs of her youth, but any society is appealing to me these days, and the idea of removing myself from under the constant surveillance of Mother and Charles is irresistible.

"And it's just occurred to me." Alençon continued, "Since the trip will take you through Flanders, why don't you meet with a few of these nobles I've spoken of? You can test how willing they are to align with France again, and perhaps persuade those who are reluctant."

"I don't know, Monsieur. Would the Prince of Orange be happy to see Flanders go back to France? It used to be part of his rule."

"He has all the rest of the Netherlands, I don't see that he'd care. Anyway, he hates Spain."

"Hmm."

"You could be my ambassador! With your wit and charm, I'm sure they will fall at your feet."

It was flattering that Alençon thought me capable of manipulating Flemish nobility, and why not? I am accomplished, eloquent, and familiar with the teachings of "The Prince." Additionally, M. Shakspere has written a play about my wit and powers to convince, and I have read... well, half of it. Why not be as forthright and brave in speech as the Princess of France in his play? Inwardly, I leapt at the idea. However, seeing how keen Alençon was to have me do it, I realized I possessed some leverage in the situation. I disguised my enthusiasm and instead frowned.

"Oh dear, that sounds like rather a lot of work. There's only one way such a task would appeal to me."

"What is that?"

"If I were suddenly to hear that a peace had been negotiated between my husband and Charles, and that you had been the one to broker that peace, I would be so delighted, dear brother, that I would undertake your mission with great zeal."

Alençon looked at me in surprise. "My, my, Margot, are you negotiating with me? You *are* growing up! All right, I agree to attempt a peace treaty. The minute it is begun, I will make sure you know of it." I retained my calm until I got to my chambers - then fairly danced with excitement!

The Princess de Roche-sur-Yon, a woman of advanced years who rumor has it used to be a great beauty, was in her rooms working on her embroidery when I was announced. She hastened to rise but, seeing her painfully wrapped foot, I urged her to remain seated. We spent the requisite amount of time on the gossip of the court; who was entertaining an intrigue with whom, whose heart had been lately broken, who had been recently banished or killed for being a secret Huguenot. (That list was rather long.) The Princess also needed to spend a length of time bemoaning the death of her first husband, who left her spectacularly well off and has therefore gained heroic status in her eyes.

"Renee ~ the Marshall de Montejan, as you know - adored me! Simply worshipped the ground I walked upon. The way he gazed upon me as I crossed a room ~ Well, my dear it reminds me of the way the Duke of Guise used to look at you." I became uneasy at this subject, but the Princess continued.

"That poor man! He was heartbroken at your marriage, Your Highness. Heartbroken! He's always been a meticulous dresser, and I saw him the other day appareled in a doublet that had a clear stain upon it! Quite a changed man."

Hastening to change the subject, I broached the topic of my joining her on her journey to Spa. She expressed immediate delight.

"Oh, Your Highness, what an honor! Your presence will significantly *increase the size and prestige of our entourage!*" I recalled that the Princess has always been fond of pomp and circumstance.

The next day, with the Princess in attendance for support, I gained an audience with Mother. Guise was also in chambers, and it gave me a moment's uneasiness to have him listening in, but I decided to press on. Seeing the Princess with me, Mother raised her eyebrows, at once suspicious of this unlikely alliance. The Princess wisely stayed silent (she's terrified of Mother) and I launched into my proposal.

"Your Majesty, please don't take this amiss; I desire to remove myself from court."

My mother sighed. "Marguerite, stop with your wearying demands. You are not going to join your husband in Nérac and that is final."

"Yes, I understand that, and humbly accept your decree."

"Do you? How good of you."

"I think, however that it is ill-advised for me to stay at court. I have overheard others talking, and sense that my presence here is causing discomfort. Possibly it sends the message that the court has Huguenot sympathies."

Mother laughed. "I should think the deaths of thousands of Huguenots throughout France would assure the country that the court and Catholicism are in perfect alignment."

"Yes, of course," I responded and saw the Princess moisten her lips nervously. "But they might wonder if my estrangement from my husband for so long means that I have found someone else. You know how rumors spread in this city."

My mother glanced at Guise, who was feigning the reading of a document but who I could tell was listening to our every word. She knew the danger of rumors that I had reconciled with him.

"What is your proposal?"

"The Princess and I have been chatting, and she revealed to me that she is planning a trip to the city of Spa for the infirmity within her leg." Here the Princess nodded and raised her hem slightly to reveal her bandaged foot. "M. de Lauren, before his untimely passing, told me that Spa would be the perfect place for the relief of my recurrent arm pain. As this is the season, I petition the court to be allowed to accompany the Princess on her journey."

I did not expect Mother's reaction to be so immediate. "An excellent idea! I have very fond memories of Spa myself. A journey north can only be beneficial, and the good Princess de Roche-sur-Yon would be a very suitable companion." The Princess fairly glowed at the praise, and Guise looked up from his document with a frown.

"I wonder if that is advisable, Your Majesty," he interjected. "We have lately been discussing other courses of action –"

"No, no, this one seems to me most fortuitous. Take all the time you need, daughter. Months, if need be. Your health is the most important thing."

Surprised, and suddenly a little suspicious, I stammered my thanks. The Princess curtsied and began to back out of the room, but I needed to say one more thing.

"I pray, Your Majesty, that through your prudence, a peace may be affected between my husband and his Majesty the King, and that he is restored to his previous level of trust, perhaps even by the time I return."

Mother mumbled something noncommittal in return and I took my leave. In the hallway, the Princess was ecstatic with relief at having survived the interview.

"I've always wondered if the Queen held it against me that I fainted at her husband the King's coronation. I was nine months with child at the time and my corset was terribly tight. But I'm delighted ~ she seems to have completely forgotten it!"

With the assistance of her ladies, the Princess hurried away to her chambers. I, however, lingered, remembering the expression of relief that had passed over my mother's features at my request. I experienced the sudden wild thought that there might have been talk of ridding themselves of me in some less felicitous fashion than going to a spa. But I tried not to think about it.

17 April, 1582 - Paris

As I made preparations for our journey, Alençon came to me with the news that Mother and Charles plan to go to Poitiers to watch my brother Anjou's army lay siege to the town of Brouage and purge it of its Protestants.

"I wonder that they tell you these things, Monsieur. "

"They didn't tell me. But they tend to forget I'm in the room, and they see me as harmless, which amuses me. If this siege is a success, they intend to march into La Rochelle, and thence to Gascony to attack Navarre's troops."

I felt the blood drain from my face. "Where did you hear that?"

"I was feigning sleep and heard Mother and Charles discussing it.

"We must alert Henri!"

"I have already sent a messenger. Our best hope is that the sieges of Brouage and La Rochelle are a failure. It would make it much easier for me to negotiate a peace for you, and then you can win over Flanders for me!"

It occurs to me that Alençon, though often playing the fool, is much cleverer than I have given him credit for, and is serving as a most effective spy for the Huguenots. Does my Catholic blood recoil at the thought of my brother undermining our cause? I tried not to think about it.

Upon readying for departure to Spa, I was saddened to learn that our stable master, M. d'Aubiac, who was so helpful in orchestrating Henri's escape, has died suddenly, leaving his son to lead the expedition. His name is Jean, and he looks very young and inexperienced compared to his father. I am of course disappointed but see no alternative, as I feel we must make haste to depart before Mother changes her mind.

I examined my new litter; it is most impressive, with an interior lining of crimson velvet embroidered with gold silk thread. The windows are of glass, painted with interesting symbols that reference the sun and other astronomical phenomena. It will be followed by two other litters; in the one will be the Princess de Roche-sur-Yon; in the second Madame de Tournon, my lady of the bedchamber. As the roads are more passable going north, six coaches and chariots will carry religious eminences such as the Cardinal de Lenoncourt, ten maids of honor with their governess, and the rest of the ladies including Rosalind, Maria, and Agatha. The Princess is delighted with the spectacle we will present.

Madame de Tournon prevailed upon me to let her daughter Matilde accompany us. The young lady encountered a distressing situation that threatens to compromise her reputation and her mother is seeking my protection which, without asking questions, I am most happy to give. Matilde has a very charming countenance and, whatever occurred, I am quite sure it was the gentleman's fault.

I am distressed that Mme. de Brezé is not able to accompany us, as she has been ill of late. Unless we find someone else knowledgeable in English, it seems we will have to wait before we learn the rest of M. Shakspere's lovely story.

19 April, 1582 – *En route* to Spa

I am so relieved to be out of the Louvre I can scarcely control my delight. Our procession is a glorious one featuring canopies, musical instruments, banners, reliquaries, crosses, and flowers. My litter is larger than the last one; I can lie down in it, which is a relief for such a long journey. Frequently the ladies sing beautiful melodies accompanied by lutes, drums, cymbals, ringing bells, and other sounds to ward off demons and elicit divine grace. After dark, when they light the torches and the clerics start to chant, it is most mesmerizing and peaceful. Traveling across the countryside I'm sure we make a memorable impression, which is the goal of every royal procession; to remind the populace of their loyalties, and to bring a little magic into their lives. My new stable master, Jean d'Aubiac, has done everything possible to make the journey comfortable, but even he cannot protect me from a sudden

29 April, 1582 - Picardy

After ten days' travel, we have arrived in Picardy, the last French principality before crossing the Flemish border. Our welcome to the city was magnificent; we passed under a classical-style *arc de triomphe* created just for the occasion with living actors posed upon it standing in for what would have been statuary. We had to stop five times along the way for the presentation of a mystery play, and though I love Bible stories as much as the next person, I'll confess that by the third or fourth one, I was most eager for refreshment.

Thankfully, once within the city we encountered a civic feast celebrating our arrival and were served potage, stuffed peacock, roasted wild boar, and pears in red wine. After that, there was another play - a masque, which involved a great deal of music, dancing, and acting. It was adequately presented, but I couldn't help thinking of the play my ladies and I secretly performed in my chambers. Even Rosalind whispered in my ear, "This is nowhere near as entertaining as "The Work of Love is Lost."

A letter was waiting for me in Picardy, from Mother. She is very adept at her secret letter-locking technique, slicing the paper and using that slice as a key to lock the letter closed, then sealing it on both sides with wax. It's a challenge just to open it.

> *Catherine, by the grace of God Consort of France, to her dearest daughter Marguerite, by the grace of God illustrious Queen of Navarre, greetings and affection.*
>
> *I am desirous to be informed of your arrival at Picardy, and learn of your safety and that of the good Princess de Roche-sur-Yon. It is fortuitous that you departed when you did, for there has been much turmoil here in your absence.*
>
> *It is with sadness that I impart to you the news that the siege of La Rochelle has been a failure. Though your brother Anjou waged a courageous battle, our troops have been forced back to Brouage. With*

heavy losses, and another Huguenot army moving toward Paris, our younger son Alençon has offered his services in enlisting a negotiated peace, which seems desirable under the circumstances...

Hurrah, the battle has been lost! It is very strange to be writing this, yet my relief is great that there will now be no attack on Henri, and Alençon must follow through on his promise to negotiate a peace! I hastened to the chapel to thank the Blessed Virgin for hearing my prayers. I scarcely read the rest of the letter; I knew the real reason for the writing of it was to confirm that I had arrived in Picardy and not run off to Nérac which, though a sore temptation, would have been impossible given the size of our procession. I confess to harboring the fantasy that Henri would appear on the road and abduct me to Nérac, but Henri was at the time with his troops preparing for possible battle. How grateful I will be to Alençon if he manages successfully to negotiate this peace!

A gentleman has just arrived with the message that the Bishop of Cambrai will meet me on the borders of his territory in Flanders tomorrow morning. I shall now keep my agreement with Alençon, and do everything I can to win over the Flemish nobility.

30 April, 1582 - Cambrai

This morning the Bishop of Cambrai, a large, florid man in flowing vestment and a heavily bejeweled miter, met me on the edge of the city attended by a number of his people, who displayed all the rusticity and unpolished manners of their country.

"Bienvenidas, Your Majesty! Welcome to the city of Cambrai!" proclaimed the bishop, and from the language of his welcome, I perceived a firm attachment to Spain. It is also delightful to note that, now that I'm away from court, I have ceased to be "Your Highness" and, as Queen of Navarre, have become "Your Majesty." At the court in Paris there is only one Majesty, and that is Mother.

He proceeded to show me around the city. Although Cambrai is not as well built as some of our towns in France, it does have wide streets, large squares, and grand and highly ornamented churches. But what I admired most was the Citadel, the most strongly fortified in Christendom. I understood, looking at it, why Alençon was so interested in Cambrai. One could feel safe in a Citadel like that.

The governor of the Citadel is a gentleman named M. de Pirot, an extravagantly bewigged little man who, although maintaining the carriage and behavior of one of our most attentive courtiers, still manages to be quite dull. He escorted me to a grand supper given by the bishop and featuring Spanish cuisine which took some getting used to. After supper was a ball, to which were invited all the fashionable ladies of the city. My ladies and I were very interested in their style of dress, apparently modeled after Anna, the Queen of Spain. The ladies' gowns are generally of more subdued color than our own, but their arms are only half covered by the outer robe's sleeves, which fall away at the elbow and then drape freely behind the forearm, exposing a decorative inner sleeve. We've decided we quite like it, and I may try to sew such a sleeve myself. Princess de Roche-sur-Yon and the Bishop remained deep in conversation throughout much of the ball. As a famous beauty of a previous age, the Princess has many stories to tell and the bishop was most eager to hear them.

"Your Grace, he adored me. Adored me! But I could not engage in moral turpitude, even for him," I overheard her say. This runs rather counter to the stories I've heard about her, but then again court gossip can be quite controversial.

As soon as the ball was opened, the bishop withdrew and I was left in the company of M. de Pirot. He is a tedious lecturer, but I decided to find him delightful. This sounds easier than it is. I am by nature a serious person and, until recently, have not mastered the art of social laughing. My Mother is not given to spontaneous laughter, and though I've been told my father would sometimes roar with laughter, I don't remember ever hearing it. I have therefore had to observe the laughter of others in order to develop a laugh of my own suitable for social situations. My lady Agatha has a merry, tinkling laugh that serves to induce similar laughter in others, which I observe has enormous benefits. Through observation and imitation, I have managed to produce a laugh that can pass as spontaneous, which I employed with M. de Pirot. Inspired by our new friend M. Shakspere, I shall present it as a scene in a play.

Marguerite: (Laughing delightedly) Ah, such a pleasurable evening! I can't remember when I've been so thoroughly amused.

Pirot: It is our pleasure, Your Majesty. Your beauty and reputation for wit and charm precede you but I aver, your presence outshines all that mere words could have conveyed.

Marguerite: How kind. On another subject, M. de Pirot, you must be well pleased with your position as governor of the Citadel. Prince Alençon, my brother, has often spoken of it as the key to Cambrai's security.

Pirot: It is a weighty responsibility and one from which I do not shirk.

Marguerite: (Laughing merrily for no reason) I dare say! Flanders, as you know, has ever been dear to the Prince. He nearly became its king during my brother Francis's reign, and strongly hopes you will support his interests now.

Pirot: Ah yes, yes.... His interests ...to...?

Marguerite: Why, to regain Flanders, of course.

Pirot: I see! I had heard some talk but I didn't know...

Marguerite: (Tinkling laugh) Oh surely you had some idea, M. de Pirot!

Pirot: Well, perhaps.

Marguerite: You are, I know, a loyal friend to France. My brother confided to me as much, as well as his deep respect for your intelligence. He neglected to praise, however, your amiable skills in the art of conversation! I was unaware until this evening of the connection between Quintillian and Pliny the Younger.

Pirot: Oh yes, Pliny was his student! You know, I have in my possession Quintillian's twelve-volume textbook on rhetoric. Perhaps I might ride beside you on your journey to Namur and read to you the more salient passages.

Marguerite: Wouldn't that be a rare privilege! But I'm sure reading on horseback for such a distance would be tiring for you, Monsieur.

Pirot: Not at all, I excel in it! I shall solicit the bishop to grant me leave to travel with you immediately.

Marguerite: (Horrified, yet still laughing) Delightful! Am I to understand, then, that you look favorably upon the idea of Flanders coming under the protection of France?

Pirot: Yes, 'though I am not sure how the Prince of Orange would react.

Marguerite: (Laughing yet again) From what I hear, he'd be most happy to rid himself of the Spanish neighbors to his south!

I should like to attest that constant laughter is extremely tiring. Tomorrow M. de Pirot is to join our procession and I shall brace myself for a lengthy reading on the subject of oratory.

But no matter. Alençon is negotiating a peace and my Henri is safe, or will be soon!

6.

"Evidence of *trust* begets *trust*, and love is
reciprocated by love."

— **Plutarch**

1 May, 1582 - Mons

On the road to Mons, one of the horses bearing my litter started to develop a faltering gait. Jean d'Aubiac stopped the procession and examined the animal, finding him to be suffering from a gash upon his leg, possibly from a thrown rock. I expected him to replace the horse immediately with a new one, but instead, he informed us all that we needed to make our encampment for the night.

Whilst the tents were being erected, I watched as d'Aubiac produced some bags of herbs, wormwood among them, and made a poultice for the horse. He gently applied the poultice to the leg of the heavily breathing animal, all the while speaking to it in a soothing voice, as one might speak to a frightened child. Something about the melodic warmth of his voice caused the horse's breathing to slow, and after a while, it leaned heavily into him as if seeking comfort from his body. It was an enormously moving sight.

We're brought up to think of horses as beasts of burden or vehicles for sport or war and not much more, but the communication I saw take place between the stable master and the afflicted horse made me rethink my assumptions about an animal's capacity for emotion. I later went over to it myself and stroked its muzzle, and even used some of the comforting words and sounds d'Aubiac used, and the animal seemed to respond, nudging me gently on the shoulder as if in acknowledgment of my efforts. It was a remarkable experience. Returning to my tent I felt lighter in spirit than I have in some time. I was arrested, however, by the sight of Jean d'Aubiac under a nearby tree, having his meal and watching his horses. I wondered if he'd seen me, and was suddenly embarrassed.

3 May, 1582 – Mons

We arrived in Mons yesterday after a lengthy journey made ever so much longer by the roadside reading of Quintillian's twelve-volume book on rhetoric. I never want to hear that ancient Roman's name again.

I am being lodged in the house of the Count de Lalaing and his beautiful wife, who encouraged me to call her Adrienne, and whom I like enormously. She's an older woman of perhaps 38 with flashing brown eyes and a probing intellect. When the supper hour came, we sat down to a sumptuous banquet, after which came a ball that had us all dancing for hours. The Flemish ladies costume themselves more brilliantly than the Spanish, in vibrant silks with much ornamentation. It was a joy to watch them whirl around the room and then to participate in the whirling ourselves.

I invited Adrienne to pay me a visit in my chambers afterward and, invigorated by her presence, we stayed up until very late talking. After a while, it felt as if I had known her all my life.

"We heard many reports of the grandeur of your wedding, Your Majesty. I wish you much happiness." The subject of my wedding was painful, carrying as it did the burden of what came after, but I smiled.

"Thank you. To some, it may have appeared to be a political alliance that was forced upon me –"

"Oh, not at all!"

"I would understand if some leapt to that conclusion. As it turns out, the King of Navarre and I are very well suited to one another."

"How fortunate! That makes it very much easier, does it not? The Count and I have been married for twenty years, and we too have found that we endure one another's failings quite well."

I concurred that Henri and I were fortunate but it felt a bit strange because, in truth, my memories of our time together have already dimmed, and I find it hard sometimes to recapture the excitement of those idyllic days in Nérac.

Adrienne smiled as if reading my thoughts. "I'm sure you will regain much of the joy when these wars subside and you are able to spend more time together."

I hoped the sigh that escaped me at the moment didn't reveal too much. "Why do men feel the need to wage war?" I ruminated. "Why are they compelled to take one another's lives? I have never once felt that it was my right to end the life of another person, and I marvel that they do."

"It is the base instinct for domination, I believe. It goes beyond rational thought."

"Is it inherent within them to kill, or is it learned?"

"A little of both, I should think. It's not just men; some women seem to have no compunction about ending the lives of others." For a moment I feared she was talking about my mother. "But I believe it is primarily a male compulsion. I am of your mind, of course. Life is sacred, and our Savior teaches us not to kill. One must acknowledge, however, the realities of life. One must survive."

I was considering opening the topic of Alençon's intentions toward Flanders, but it was as though she read my mind.

"For instance, we feel that we suffer greatly under the yoke of Spanish tyranny. I feel a strong attachment to France, so you can imagine my sentiments about our current oppressive situation. We don't want war, but if war must come, we realize that necessity. The problem is that France right now is divided between two different religions, and I hope you agree it weakens the country."

"I do agree," I replied. "I pray every day for a resolution. The King of France is focused entirely on his antipathy towards the Huguenots, which perhaps limits his abilities elsewhere. My other brother Alençon, however, has a more nuanced view of matters. He also has sufficient means to offer protection, and feels it would be an honor to serve as Protectorate of Flanders. He is one of the bravest generals of our times, certainly the equal of any of his ancestors."

I formed a cross with my fingers to ward off ill fate when I said this. It may not be, strictly speaking, true about Alençon's military skill, but I wanted to engender trust in him within the Countess's heart. After all, Alençon is an excellent swordsman.

"The King has given him an army against the Huguenots," I continued.

The Countess looked surprised. "Has he? I'd been given to understand that your brother was fighting on the side of Huguenots."

I instantly cursed myself for having led the conversation in this direction and attempted to cover my indiscretion.

"That was true, but it was for only a brief period and my brother has since recanted and recommitted himself to Catholicism and the crown." Seeing the Countess's slightly puzzled expression I continued. "Young men may sometimes err on the side of fighting for its own sake, a subject we just touched upon. But when they mature, as my brother has, they come to a wisdom that causes them to reject their past follies." The Countess nodded thoughtfully. I pressed on.

"You could not ask for a prince who has it so in his power to defend his domain. Under the protection of France, Flanders need never feel vulnerable again. Of course, the Count may be assured of my brother's gratitude for his support, at whatever price he may wish to set." The Countess waved this away with her hand, as though money were of no importance, but I could tell she was keenly listening. "As for the wars, I am very hopeful that a peace will soon be reestablished with the Huguenots, and indeed expect to hear news to that effect before my return to France."

"Is that true?" The Countess brightened. "That would alter the scenario in my husband's mind." I said an immediate prayer that it might be true. We returned to other topics, and when the Countess arose to take my leave, she said,

"I wonder, Your Majesty, if I might be allowed to confer with my husband this evening, and perhaps the three of us can speak on the subject tomorrow? It would give me great pleasure to have my husband and your brother form an alliance, not the least reason being that I feel I have met a new friend."

I was elated to hear her say this. I was enjoying her company so much I had almost forgotten I was on a mission of state. The next morning, she came to me again, this time with the Count, an outwardly jolly man who has, however, a great many grievances against Spain which he was happy to enumerate. He went into a detailed account of petty offenses that I strove mightily to find interesting, advising me on where Alençon should make his first advance (Hainalt) and suggesting it would be helpful if I spoke to M. de Pirot for his expertise on this matter. Having spent more than enough time with that gentleman, I prevailed upon the count to perform that task himself. We then spoke in rather coded terms about the nature of reward that the Count could expect for his service to my brother. Not having the slightest notion what Alençon has in mind in this regard, I vaguely assured him that he would receive as large a share of power and authority as a person of his rank deserved. This seemed to satisfy the Count for now.

What an exhilarating day! Mere weeks ago, I was a prisoner in the palace, pacing the floor of my chambers, praying fervently to God and the Virgin to release me from my bondage. Now my prayers have been heard. I am free and out in the world, performing state business, being treated with utmost seriousness by figures of import to the crown. No ridiculous empty words of flattery about my beauty, as if that is all I have to offer the world. (Well, perhaps from the Count, but it was very pro forma.) I am of use. I am performing a useful service on behalf of the crown. It is enormously gratifying.

I will admit that there was a small part of me that was thinking, "Are these efforts worthy of Alençon? I remember the time when, thinking he could fly, he jumped off a parapet and landed in the cistern, or that time at the stables when he got his head stuck in a tie ring? True, he was only a boy, but I wonder sometimes if he has the seriousness of mind now to take on the challenges that lie ahead. Can I imagine him riding into Flanders on a white horse with a glorious army, received by a grateful populace strewing flowers at his feet?

Well, why not? Less likely victories have occurred in history; David and Goliath come to mind. It seems to me that what is required is a combination of good fortune and commitment. Fortune always seems to smile on Alençon and, when he's in the mood, no one is a more committed warrior. I choose to believe my efforts are of value.

Tomorrow I will be received by Don John of Austria, a perhaps confusing title as he was born in and represents the interests of Spain. I remember my older sister Elizabeth, God rest her soul, telling stories about him when I was young. Both Elizabeth and my cousin Mary, now Queen of Scots, spent their childhood in the royal nursery together, and they were much smitten with him. He was born to one of Charles V's mistresses, a commoner, then taken from her and brought up away from court. He did not know about his illustrious parentage until he was 14 years of age. Since then, it sounds as if he's been making up for lost time; fighting wars against the Turks in the Mediterranean and creating quite a reputation for dash and daring, which is, I suppose, what led him to be appointed Governor of Flanders. He's reportedly extremely attractive both in person and personality, at least Elizabeth found him to be so, but Mother arranged for Elizabeth to marry Phillip II of Spain and she died in childbirth at age 23. One could become quite sad about that, if one allowed oneself...

But to return to Don John. The Countess related to me the rumor that Don John recently had a daring plan to rescue my cousin Mary from her current imprisonment at Tutbury Castle, marry her, and make himself King of England. Ambitious plan, and of course it didn't come to pass, but it speaks to his bold character. So, too, does the fact that, though unmarried, he has many mistresses, several of whom have borne him children.

Clearly, there is no way he could know that I am here on a mission counter to his interests, but I find I am nervous all the same. I shall endeavor to defray any suspicions he might have about my presence here and make him a friend.

9 May, 1582 – Namur

We took our leave of the Count and Countess this morning, to my great regret and that of my ladies, who were enjoying the loveliest balls and banquets every night. The Countess and I had an emotional parting, and she made me promise to return by way of that city. I presented her with a diamond bracelet, and to the Count I gave an exquisite diamond star, to help him trust the sincerity of my brother's intent.

The Count de Lalaing and his nobles conducted me only seven miles or so until he saw Don John's men advancing to meet me, then he took his leave so as not to have to speak to him. (As I said, the Count has many grievances against him.) Don John approached, followed by a great number of running footmen, and escorted by about thirty fine-looking horsemen. He alighted from his horse to approach me in my litter and I got a closer look at him, immediately comprehending his allure to Elizabeth and Mary.

"Your Majesty!" He bowed deeply. "How honored I am to finally meet the beautiful Marguerite de Valois. Do you know I canceled a trip to Poland, just for the honor of basking in your renowned beauty? I see now that it was well worth the sacrifice."

He is a solidly built, darkly handsome man with an expansive personality, bright blue eyes and a brilliant smile. There's a dynamism to his character that many men lack, and his direct gaze is both flattering and disconcerting. I returned his salute after the French fashion and after a further exchange of compliments he remounted his horse.

Riding alongside my litter, he spoke amusingly on light topics until we reached the city. It was growing dark, but Namur glowed brightly before us with well-lit streets and a candle in every window, undoubtedly by directive to welcome us.

"As Your Majesty is no doubt fatigued by your long journey, I have arranged to have supper served in your apartments. I think you will not be displeased with your accommodations." Don John offered.

Indeed, the lodgings that he led me to are most impressive; a magnificent large salon and a private apartment consisting of lodging rooms and closets, each furnished in a most costly manner. The many pieces of massive furniture are exquisitely wrought, the walls hung with the richest tapestry of velvet and satin.

"I hope this meets with your approval," said Don John.

"Indeed. The furnishings are splendid."

"They came to me as a present from the Grand Vizier of the Ottoman Empire. I captured two of his sons and, after a productive conversation with the father, spared their lives and released them without ransom; he was very grateful. And now, with Your Majesty's permission, I will take my leave. In the morning I will conduct you to a chapel, where we may take Mass together. I wish you a good evening."

It is interesting to me that, even when he is speaking about such serious topics as capturing prisoners and taking Mass, Don John has a twinkle in his eye as if he is really saying something else. I don't know quite what to make of his manner, and keenly feel the importance of keeping my wits about me.

A messenger arrived with a letter from Alençon and I opened it with eagerness. I place the letter between these pages.

Francis, by the grace of God Duke of Alençon, to his dearest sister Marguerite, by the grace of God illustrious Queen of Navarre, greetings and affection of sincere love.

I trust that you have arrived at Namur without incident and that you are enjoying some success in the endeavor of which you and I have spoken. As I do not have our mother's gift for locking letters, I choose to write no more of this. I will inform you that thanks to my efforts, a treaty has been signed forming a reconciliation between the Crown and the Huguenots. It's going to be named after me; they're calling it "The Treaty of Monsieur." An honor, but already there are those amongst the Catholics who feel that it is too lenient toward the Huguenots, as it awards them the right to public worship and bestows reparations to the victims of the unfortunate events on St. Bartholomew's Day. But I'm sure they'll work it out. I have done my part; documents have been signed and with God's blessing, peace will now reign.

With this victory, I have decided to follow through on Mother's plan that I go to London and court the Queen Elizabeth. I'm sure you're surprised, and I'll admit I was, too, that Mother would send yet another child off to wed a Huguenot, but Mother feels an alignment between our families might temper Elizabeth's financial support of the Huguenots, and I'll admit the idea has its appeal. Wouldn't that be a feather in your little brother's cap, to become England's King! It would certainly bring Charles down a notch; he's become insufferably full of himself lately. Since my business here is done, I think such an endeavor is worth the effort, and your recent letter to me causes me to believe there will be successful news regarding Flanders upon my return. Well done, Margot!

You can imagine my delight as I read this letter. It reinforces my confidence in my brother, which had been perhaps flagging ever so slightly. I am astonished, however, at Mother's decision to send Alençon to England. He is not yet twenty-three years of age, and the Queen is forty-six. In addition, though charming in nature, my brother is quite small, his skin is pitted from the smallpox he had as a child, and his spine is visibly deviated, as tends to run in our family. Does Mother think Queen Elizabeth, after all the handsome suitors that have come her way and been rejected, will finally find in Alençon the man she is looking for?

Ah well, Mother has never been one to shy away from a challenge when it comes to unlikely matrimonial couplings, as I can attest. I'm just glad Alençon will be kept out of trouble on the battlefield.

7.

"Suspicions amongst thoughts are like bats amongst birds – they ever fly by twilight."

– Francis Bacon

10 May, 1582 ~ Namur

The morning dawned cool and beautiful, and we heard Mass cele-brated after the Spanish manner, with a great deal of music that was very pleasant to listen to. Afterward, there was a banquet. Don John and I were seated at a separate and elevated table from the others, and dishes were brought to us with, I felt, an undue amount of bowing and scraping on the part of the presenters, but I try not to question foreign ways. After a few moments of vigorous enjoyment of his meal, Don Juan looked up.

"Your Majesty, I am told you are making this very long trip through Flanders exclusively to receive the waters at Spa. How surprising that a young, beautiful woman such as yourself feels the need for medicinal atten-tion. I also wonder at the considerable number of stops you have made along the way." Realizing that Don John was indeed suspicious of my jour-ney, I responded in a tone that I hoped conveyed ease and sincerity.

"The Princess de Roche-sur-Yon is in delicate health, and I am accom-panying her as a dear friend. As for the many stops along the way, we are attempting to make the journey as easy as possible for her, poor soul." I glanced over at the Princess, who was relishing her meal with a gusto equal to Don John's, and made a mental note to encourage her to appear less healthy. Don John apparently observed the same thing, because he burst into laughter.

"Of course! That explains it all. I suppose you've been told this; you greatly resemble your sister Elizabeth. In fact, I avow you are even lovelier than she at your age, God rest her soul."

"You are too kind. Elizabeth told me once that she and our cousin Mary were acquainted with you."

Don John's demeanor changed, and his features grew dark. "Mary's misfortune burns me to the soul. It is a travesty that she is locked up in that castle when she should be ruling England. But the heretic religion seems to have taken a devilish foothold in that country."

"And the English Queen Elizabeth would appear to be a strong-willed woman," I added.

"She is doing what any monarch would in her position. Still, it pains me deeply to think of beautiful, delicate Mary in this distress. I came close to saving her.... but I was betrayed by the perfidy of others."

Suddenly his face grew dark and he pounded the table loudly with his fist. The room, which had been filled with gay laughter, grew silent. A few turned to look at us, but others stayed frozen in their seats as if waiting for a signal to flee the room. There was a nervous silence.

"It seems I am doomed to always be betrayed," growled Don John. "Trust no one! A lesson I must learn over and over again." He glared around the hall as if trying to determine who the next malefactor would be, and I watched his guests shrink in their seats. Aware that this was a moment in need of salvaging, I adopted a playful tone.

"Don John, forgive me for asking. My cousin Mary always spoke of you with such admiration. Were you two just a little bit in love?"

Don John looked up and saw me smiling at him teasingly. The moment could have gone quite wrong, but to my relief, his demeanor changed entirely yet again, and he laughed.

"Why don't you ask if I was in love with your sister Elizabeth?"

"Goodness! Were you?"

"Let's just say I have a weakness for flaxen-haired beauties from the house of Valois."

I laughed merrily at this, and the room relaxed and resumed its chatter. I also felt a thrill running through me at this turn in the conversation. I will admit that I was fully feeling the seductive power of the notorious Don John.

The tables having been removed, the ball was opened, and the dancing began. Don John is an excellent dancer and as I, too, enjoy it, we spent much time performing the Carole, the Basse Dance, the Estampie, and the

Almain. When we finally left the dance floor and drifted apart, I found myself in conversation with the Duke of Arscot, a gallant old courtier who had waited on my father when he was king.

"How happy it makes me to see you grown to health and beauty, Your Majesty," exclaimed the Duke. "Your father said to me once that of all his children, you were the cleverest."

"Is that true?" As I knew him so little, I was delighted to hear any stories of my father, particularly stories that featured me. I was eager to hear more, but at that moment Don John intervened.

"Your Majesty, other nobles are awaiting the pleasure of your company," he said briskly and drew me away without a word to the Duke of Arscot. I wondered at the abruptness of this action, and Don John provided no explanation until we were well out of his hearing.

"I advise you to have no further conversation with the Duke of Arscot, Your Majesty."

"Whyever not?"

"The man is a traitor, a secret Huguenot."

"Surely not! He was in service to my father the King for many years."

"That was then, Your Majesty. I know for a fact he is in league with the Prince of Orange, who hates the Spanish presence in the Netherlands."

The Prince of Orange is not popular these days with Catholics. When he converted to Protestantism, the King of Spain called him "a pest on the whole of Christianity and the enemy of the human race." It seemed to me unlikely that the Duke of Arscot would, at his late stage in life, abandon his religion and join with the man but, not wanting to offend my host, I followed Don John's counsel and reluctantly gave Arscot wide berth.

That evening we removed ourselves from general entertainment and indulged in the kind of playful conversation that takes place so often at court. I won't attempt to recreate it here, but suffice it to say Don John is a man of great wit and verbal dexterity. I felt proud that I was able to play that game with ease, at the same time acquiring a sense of how matters lay in Flanders.

Then came a moment that changed everything. Don John, completely unexpectedly, took a liberty that was both coarse and shocking. As I was gazing at the view from a balcony, he came up behind me and grabbed me in a very private place, at the same time burying his head in my neck and biting it. Yes, biting it! I was shocked beyond words and hastily drew away.

"Sir!" I expostulated. "How dare you?"

"How dare I?" He responded with a grin. "Don't pretend you haven't been leading me to this very moment, temptress!"

I was astonished. Prior to his indiscretion, it's true I was enjoying the company of this man. Perhaps I even, without realizing it, led him to think I was encouraging an intimacy. I am young, I enjoy being appreciated, blood runs through my veins. But I am the Queen of Navarre. Certainly, he didn't expect me to respond favorably to this type of coarse behavior.

"Monsieur, if I gave you the wrong impression the fault was mine. Let us forget this moment. It has been a lovely evening, thank you."

As gracefully as I could I disengaged and retreated from the room. I heard the anger in his voice as he called down the hall after me.

"You misled me, Madam! You are duplicitous and sly, and I know what you're up to! Flanders belongs to Spain!"

I found my way to my apartments, shaken. Had I unknowingly sent a signal that I would be open to such a crude advance? Would I have done so, if Alençon hadn't set me on this mission to secure Flanders for France? Why did I agree to essentially perform the duties of a spy, when a nice trip solely for the purposes of visiting Spa would have been so much more relaxing? I berated myself for having put my person into such a position.

Later, as Madame de Tournon was taking down my hair, she sensed my preoccupied air.

"Is all well, Your Majesty?"

"Yes, yes. A lovely evening."

"Don John certainly lives up to his reputation for providing excellent entertainment," commented Madame de Tournon. "He stayed far longer at the ball than I've been given to understand is usual for him. But then, that's easily explained."

I looked up at Madame de Tournon questioningly and she smiled. "He's finally met someone more captivating than himself."

Her compliment filled me with conflicting emotions.

11 May, 1582 ~ Namur

It has been an awkward day. We intended to set off upon the Meuse River for Liege this morning, but the boats that were meant to convey us are not ready, and so we are forced to stay in Namur a day longer. Don John and I did not intersect, but I observed him from a distance. His mood seemed dark and suspicious, and he abused his servants in a manner I found most disturbing. I don't understand why it should be this way. We had a bit of a misunderstanding, I set him straight, and that should be that. But that is manifestly not that, and so this very long day must pass.

Later, Jean d'Aubiac informed me that Don John had gone hunting. "Begging Your Majesty's pardon, but I don't like the way that man treats his horses," he muttered. I could imagine the manner in which a man like Don John, defrayed from his intent, might take out his anger on a dumb animal, and I was sorry for it.

Aware that we had a great deal of time to fill until we could sail, I asked d'Aubiac to lead my ladies and me on an excursion to view the citadel, the site where Julius Caesar defeated the Belgic Gauls so long ago. Built on the side of a mountain, it is an impressive site. As we approached, I thought to enter and seek out the Duke of Archot, whom I knew to reside within and who I felt bad about snubbing the night before. As he was an old friend of my father's, I was eager to hear more stories, and I thought he might respond with enthusiasm to the idea of rejoining Flanders to France. Then I recalled Don John's combustible temper, and chose not to.

No one was in particularly good spirits. I observed Jean d'Aubiac in somber conversation with one of our gentlemen, M. La Boessiere, who seemed distressed on some matter. And Madame de Tournon is very worried about her lovely daughter Matilde, who has recently experienced an alteration of her disposition much for the worse.

I know more about this story now; Matilde was visiting her sister in Spain when one of the houseguests, the Marquis of Varenbon, developed a violent passion for her. His feelings were apparently reciprocated and, once discovered, Matilde was removed from the house before any further damage could be done. She is traveling with us now to repair her reputation and set her on a more fruitful course. By unhappy coincidence, however, the Marquis of Varenbon is a guest at Namur this week. Matilde has been (according to her mother) desperately hoping that the marriage proposal he made in Spain would be repeated in Namur. But to the young lady's shock, the Marquis chose not to acknowledge her existence at all. The girl is devastated. At her mother's behest, Matilde accompanied us today on the trip to the citadel, but she looked as if she were sleepwalking. I noticed too that La Boessiere seemed not to be able to take his eyes from Matilde, and I'm afraid curiosity got the better of me. I went to Jean d'Aubiac for enlightenment.

"M. d'Aubiac, I observed you in conversation with one of our gentlemen, and I wonder if you can illuminate me as to what was said." He looked at me in great surprise.

"If it please Your Majesty, I am not sure of whom you speak."

"Young La Boessiere."

"Ah. Well, it was a matter of some delicacy."

"Surely there should be no secrets kept from me."

"No, no, of course not. Well, in point of fact... Monsieur La Bossiere is in love with a young lady who is above him by birth, and it is causing him much misery."

"Indeed."

"He feels that, in his heart, he must express his love for her, but he knows he is sure to be rejected."

"I see."

"And therefore, he unburdens his heart to me, as a friend."

"Have you given the man any advice?"

"No, Your Majesty. I merely listen."

"If you were to advise him, what would you say?"

Jean d'Aubiac stood across from me at the grave site, and for a moment our gazes connected. I saw within him the same pain and confusion I was feeling. And of course, we will never speak of it again.

26 May, 1582 ~ Liege

A letter has arrived from Alençon, who is now in London paying court to Queen Elizabeth, and his words raised my spirits somewhat. I was particularly struck by this paragraph.

> As for the Queen, though she is quite old I like her. She calls me her "little frog," which some have said is a derogatory expression, but I am sure it is because of the little jade frog brooch I gave her as a gift when I arrived. We have spoken words of love to one another, and she has avowed that she is much inclined to marry me. This would suit me very well, as I am loath to return to our mother and her machinations. I mentioned that you were much amused by the play written by your friend M. Shakspere, and she has said she will ask after him, and perhaps have it for an entertainment.

Her little frog! It is true that Alençon's eyes are somewhat bulbous. The idea of my little brother courting that intimidating woman is too delicious to contemplate and has almost restored my sense of humor. Does he sit on her lap, snapping flies out of the air for her? Croak love songs? How on earth has he managed to coax words of love from her? Monsieur never fails to amaze.

Additionally, it is nice to think I may have helped the soulful-eyed young poet, M. Shakspere, with whom I associate the joy and serendipity of being in Nérac. That magical time seems extremely far away at the moment.

28 May 1582 ~ Spa

The Princess desires to have the waters transported to her in Liege, but my ladies and I have chosen to make the trip to Spa ourselves, and we are glad to have done so. In addition to several suitable members of society being present, the waters themselves are delightful. I did not realize how much my body needed relaxation, but once I sank into those delightful warm waters infused with whatever mysterious medicinal elements they possess, not only my body but my mind felt infinitely more at ease.

The Duke of Biron is here. He was, unfortunately, wounded in a recent battle, and has come here to heal. Rosalind, who has always been attracted to damaged men, immediately ran to his side, and they have spent every minute together since.

"He is a shattered man, Your Majesty. Shattered in body, yet his delightful essence remains. I find I am more in love with him than ever!" I envied the sparkle of her eyes as the two of them bent toward one another in intimate conversation. Rosalind even performed some of "The Work of Love is Lost" for him, since she herself played the character of Biron in our readings. He was delighted at her portrayal of him, and I was amazed that she remembered so much of it.

Maria, who has been a shadow of herself since the terrible murder of Coligny, seems to have met a young woman who is helping her to forget. A tall, angular but compelling-looking woman named, I believe, Françoise. They, too, are spending many moments together, and Maria has regained her infectious laugh. I am so glad.

Normally, I would have found someone to amuse me, as well, but my recent encounter with Don John has caused me to feel less than flirtatious. I spent my time in conversation with a woman who claimed to be an old acquaintance of my mother's, Madame Chauderon. She's an eccentric-looking lady, with downy white-gray hair that appears to be flying in all directions; large, deep-set eyes and an extremely long neck. She reminds me of the ostrich that my father had imported into our short-lived menagerie.

"Your mother and I were very close at one time," she said. "We were novitiates at the Murate Convent in Florence together. Oh, but those were happy years!"

"Happy? Isn't life in a convent terribly austere?"

"On the contrary, it was beautifully simple and safe. One enjoys the company of others, but there is also time for reflection and prayer, and the rules are set by women. I could read as much as I desired and began the study of medicine. It was, I believe, the happiest time of my life."

"What was she like back then, my mother?"

"Oh, lovely! So very gay, and clever, and amusing!"

I was stunned. "You must be mistaken. My mother is Catherine de Medici."

"Yes, that's right. Quite the songbird, your mother. We were all enchanted by her."

I decided that the woman was suffering from delusions and made to move away, but then she said the most amazing thing.

"I don't suppose you know this, but your mother was barren for many years in her marriage from the age of 14 to 22. She wrote me of it in her letters; the poor girl was quite distraught."

I arrested my movement. "You have letters from my mother?"

"Of course! We told each other everything at the time! She was feeling quite desperate on the matter. The King's mistress had just given birth to a daughter, and she was afraid her days as a queen were numbered, but she summoned me to court and I happily assisted in her desire to become with child."

I was astonished to hear the woman speak so bluntly of my mother's intimate personal affairs, but also deeply intrigued. "How on earth did you do that?"

"It's a matter of positioning, my dear. Your mother has a uterus that tips ever so slightly forward, and your father's manhood pointed in the opposite direction, so I'm sure you can see that is not an ideal recipe for conception." I was gaping at her now. "All I did was advise her on how to hold her body during the conjugal act. It may have felt awkward at first, but from then on, she could do nothing *but* conceive!"

I was amazed. "How is it, Madame Chauderon, that she knew to come to you on this subject?"

"Well, she knew I was interested in the anatomy of the body, and that I was studying medicine. I am very well-known now in certain circles, my dear. If it weren't for your mother I would have been burnt as a witch many times."

"A witch! Why?"

"Because I know many other things as well, including ways for a woman to arrange it so she does *not* conceive. Men do not like for women to understand the workings of their bodies. They consider it a threat to their dominance."

I am a Catholic, and as such understand that any undertaking by a woman to subvert God's will that she become pregnant is a mortal sin. However, I am also well familiar with the despotic nature of men, and could not keep myself from asking the following question.

"Out of curiosity, how does a woman do this, Madame? Prevent it, I mean."

"There are several ways, Your Majesty, but perhaps the best way is to ﹍."

She leaned forward and whispered a formula for an herbal compound into my ear. May God forgive me, I have tried desperately to forget this recipe, but I fear it will stay with me to the end of my days.

20 June, 1582 - Liege

We have been in Liege for six weeks. It seemed as if life were finally assuming a normal pace when Mme. de Clerc, wife of the monotonous M. de Clerc and a tedious person in her own right, appeared before us in a state of abject hysteria. It seems that on the very day we left Namur, Don John mounted his horse with a great number of men and rode to the citadel. News that we had lingered outside the gates the previous day had reached his ears and was enough to arouse his easily inflamed suspicions. He demanded entrance to the citadel and, upon entering with his men, took possession of it by force. He arrested the Duke of Arscot and M. de Clerc as well as Mme. de Clerc herself, and made them prisoners of the castle.

"He was quite irrational!" exclaimed Mme. de Clerc. "Accusing the poor old duke of conspiring with you, Your Majesty, to overthrow his command in Flanders. The Duke kept protesting, 'But I only danced with her once!' Don John would hear none of it. He slapped the poor man until he fell, senseless, to the ground. *C'etait terrifiant!*"

After some negotiation, Don John extracted assurances of loyalty from the men, as well as promises of a considerable sum of money. He then held Mme. de Clerc hostage until the two men could return with the monies.

"I was alone with him for hours, Your Majesty. He kept pacing back and forth, ranting and raving as I sat there helpless, tied to the Toscano arm-chair," sobbed Madame de Clerc. "He could so easily have taken advantage of me!" she gasped, in a voice that betrayed possible regret he didn't try. "He is sure people are lying in wait to kill him - disbanded soldiers, desperados on the road, persons of high rank plotting his assassination. God knows he's made enough enemies it might be true, but the man was raving!"

The country is up in arms about the event, and negotiations are being led by the Prince of Orange to get Don John to relinquish the castle, but he will not be swayed. Mme. de Clerc, who upon release immediately fled to Spa to resurrect her shattered nerves, issued a parting shot at me before she left.

"Something changed the night of his ball for you, Your Majesty. He said the most terrible things about you in the castle last night, things I dare not repeat." Then she changed her mind and chose to repeat them. "He called you a hussy and a temptress! He thinks you have plans to overthrow Flanders, and he has issued orders to have you arrested and imprisoned!" I stared at her, astonished. "Of course, I vehemently defended you," Mme. de Clerc added as an afterthought.

Immediately following, a letter arrived for me from Alençon. It was delivered by a physically exhausted gentleman who had traveled day and night for five days from England. It was scrawled hastily without formal introduction.

Dear Sister,

Burn this upon reading. I am being summoned back to Paris. The King has discovered the nature of our mission in Flanders and is much angered. If I gave the impression that he had officially approved our mission, I regret the fact. My plan was to wait until we had some success to report and then delight him with the news. As it turns out he is not delighted, but feels that we have gone behind his back. He is sending troops to intercept and bring you back to court, whether you will or no.

From all reports, the King has become quite unstable. Not only is he dismembering small animals again, but he has fallen under the influence of Henri of Guise. It is Guise who has raised Charles' suspicions about you, and Guise who is responsible for my being ordered back to court. I have attempted to correspond with the Queen on this issue but received no response. I fear our mother's influence is waning at court.

Hasten back immediately, dear sister. Take all necessary precautions.

Your loving brother.

Curse my foolish brother! How could he not have told Charles? Was he indeed attempting a grasp for power? If so, I want no part of it. I need to return as quickly and safely as possible, so that I may clear my name with the throne.

"*Our mother's influence is waning at court.*" How can this be? Mother's influence has been the primary force not only in our lives but in the lives of all Frenchmen, ever since I can remember. Then again, the Guises have ever been nipping at the heels of the throne, and the Duke is particularly good at manipulation. Does he hate me so much now, that he would put my life in peril? He has always been a deeply proud man. I understand now that I toyed with his affections foolishly.

I shared the news of our current situation with the Princess and Madame de Tournon, who promptly became hysterical, weeping with fear and begging me to promise them that the journey back would be a safe one. I would have laughed if I weren't so paralyzed with fear myself.

I must consult with the Bishop of Liege.

28 June, 1582 - Liege

The Bishop of Liege, a doleful-looking man with a face rather like a Basset hound, was sipping a brandy when I rushed to his rooms. He heard my plight with muted alarm, and after some contemplation (and another tazza of brandy) offered the services of his grandmaster, M. de Molay, to accompany us through his territories. Molay is a bland, mousy little man of unimpressive appearance, but the bishop assures me he has the exalted connections required to offer ease of passage. This provided a moment of relief until the Bishop said that before I attempt to depart Liege, I must obtain a passport from the Prince of Orange.

"A passport? Whatever for? I made it this far without one."

"Things have changed, Your Majesty. The Prince of Orange's suspicions about you have been aroused. He may not like Spain, but he likes even less France purloining land he sees as rightfully his. He is a Huguenot, as you know."

"Doesn't that make it unlikely he will grant me a passport?"

"Perhaps. But it is necessary."

I have sent my man Mondoucet to obtain one.

I'm frightened. I have incurred the anger of not only my unbalanced brother but also the very mercurial Don John, and now the Prince of Orange. It is unlikely that I can employ my charms to extricate myself from this predicament. Charles will think my lingering in Flanders is evidence of guilt, not realizing I am here against my will. Don John thinks I'm a spy and wants me captured. The Prince of Orange – well, having never met the man I don't know, but what to do? History is replete with stories of dead princesses caught in the crossfire of politics at the whims of their powerful male relatives. In Greek history, there is Phaedre, Antigone, Iphigenia, and for a recent example there is my mother's cousin Isabella, who died mysteriously only recently when she became an inconvenience to her husband. He claimed she dropped dead while washing her hair, but wasn't it fortunate he had a mistress on hand to step in and dry his tears?

Why are men necessary? They only seem to wage war and destroy that which is beautiful. It seems irrational for God to create such deeply flawed creatures when women are so much more guided by reason. I keep returning to the rules of being a princess, as I have understood them. Rule #1: You are of vital importance. Rule #2: You are of no importance whatsoever.

My great fear is that I am drifting inexorably toward Rule #2, and no one will be able to save me.

4 July, 1582 – Liege

It has been six days, and Mondoucet has not returned. In addition, something worse has happened. Rosalind, who has been in Spa with the Duke of Biron, requested audience with me, and the minute I saw her pale countenance, I knew something was wrong.

"Your Majesty, I would not alarm you if I didn't think this were a grave issue."

"What is it, Rosalind?"

"You know that I have been nursing the Duke of Biron back to health. In that time, I have been privy to certain conversations between the Duke and various members of the nobility, some newly arrived. At times, I thought it best to be present but not visible, given my obvious alliance with the crown."

"Of course. I can see by your expression you have learned something."

"Yes, Your Majesty. There is a faction of the Huguenot party that thinks you are here on a mission to claim Flanders for France. They have come to the Duke with their concerns." My heart skipped a beat.

"Is that so?"

"The Duke was kind enough to offer his opinion that this was a baseless rumor, that you are here only for your health, but the Huguenots scoffed at that. They feel the King of Navarre has betrayed them and is secretly in league with King Charles, and they intend to punish him."

"I see ...how?"

"I don't know how to say this."

"Say it, Rosalind."

"Your Majesty, by killing you."

The blood drained from my head. Rosalind reached out to steady me.

"Are you all right, Your Majesty?"

"Yes. Thank you for telling me this, Rosalind. That is, indeed, a baseless rumor and I'm glad that Biron said so. I hope he believes it."

"That is hard to say. He believes my presence here has made his life worth living, so that may have colored his judgment. Shall I... do something?"

"Stay close to Biron, and report to me if you learn anything more." She curtsied and started for the door. "And Rosalind." She turned. "Please don't take any foolish risks. There is no need for you to be in danger." Rosalind smiled at me with tears in her eyes, curtsied again, and departed.

I'm trying to stay calm, but it feels as if I'm being closed in on from three sides. Charles has sent troops, Don John has vowed his vengeance, and now the Huguenots want me dead. I also suspect that the Prince of Orange intends to use my presence here as leverage by detaining me here. We must leave! But everyone, from the Bishop to Cardinal Lenoncourt, believes that we cannot move until we have those passports in hand.

I don't know what to do, or who to turn to. Dearest Virgin, please provide me with some guidance as to how to proceed.

5 July, 1582 - Liege

Beside myself with worry, I decided to go for a ride to clear my head. Jean d'Aubiac insisted on accompanying me for my safety and though I meant to ponder in silence, before long I found myself sharing our precarious situation with him. He listened to my account of events, the advice of the Bishop, the opinion of the Cardinal, and the declaration of my treasurer who seems to think we are running out of money. I told him there had even been a recommendation that our horses be taken from us, to guarantee payment of our growing debt. Jean d'Aubiac's eyes flashed at this.

"Your Majesty, I am not one to give advice."

"As you have said. Advise me now."

"We must remove ourselves from this place immediately."

"But the passport ~"

"~ is a ruse to keep you here. Something troubling is afoot. We must depart."

"Do you think so?"

"I know so. The animals are restive; something is not right."

In my heart, though he is of no eminence whatsoever, I know Jean d'Aubiac is more right about this than any of my advisors. Therefore, go we shall. I shall give the Bishop one of my larger diamonds, worth more than three thousand crowns, and shower his domestics with jewelry, then we shall proceed to the bishopric of Huy with no passport other than, hopefully, God's good grace.

10 July, 1582 - Dinant

Our entourage set off for Huy at night in hopes of traveling unde-
tected. We were accompanied by the grand master of the Bishop's household, M. de Molay, with the idea that his illustrious presence would
guarantee us safe entry into the towns within the Bishop's purview. Molay
is a dull, bureaucratic fellow with an alarmingly bulbous nose rather like a
purple cauliflower, but he carries an air of certitude that caused me initially
to have faith in his powers to protect.

"I'm well thought of throughout the land," Molay repeatedly said.
"You can be assured of that, Your Majesty. Very well thought of!" When we
arrived at Huy, however, there was no royal welcome, no official to mark our
presence there. Instead, the scene was one of chaos and fear, provoked by
Don John's assault upon Namur and his (now public) edict against me. The
townsmen felt sure that if I was there, Don John must right behind, waiting
to lay siege to their city, and for all I knew they were right. But they couldn't
just leave us outside the gates, so they rushed us in. It felt as if we were pigs
being pushed into a sty.

"Come on, move quickly! With haste!" they kept saying.

"Well, this is a surprise, I must say," was Molay's befuddled response,
rubbing his bulbous appendage.

They rushed me up into wholly inadequate quarters, rang the alarm
bell, barricaded the streets, drew up their artillery, and kept my divided
party isolated in different locations throughout the city. We were provided
a meager sustenance, which was essentially tossed through the doorway by
a terrified citizen who scuttled away as quickly as possible. At the break of
dawn an official of some obscure nature came rushing in.

"Time to go! Time to go!" he cried, upon which pronouncement we
were rushed from our quarters and out of the city, the streets of which were
lined with armed military.

Quite a far cry from our glorious entry into Flanders. The Princess is weepy and disconsolate. She is much regretting my presence now, I am sure, on what was to be her glorious wellness tour.

We are a smaller group now. I made the decision to leave behind the young girls and their governess, who I feared would not sustain the pace we mean to undertake. Rosalind is staying with the Duke of Biron in Spa, to relay any further intelligence. I have also given leave for Madame de Tournon, who is grief-stricken over Matilde's death, to stay in Liege for a time to honor her daughter's grave site. The Cardinal de Lenoncourt, despite his initial reluctance to depart Liege, is still with us, probably because he misses the excellent brandy of home. We have, however, added one member to our entourage; Lady Maria prevailed upon me to welcome her new companion, Françoise de Longwy, Duchess of Bouillon, as one of my ladies and I am happy to do so. The veil of grief has lifted from my lady Maria's face since she met Françoise, a happenstance for which I am most grateful. I wish that I were able to fall in love with a woman; it seems to me life would be so much simpler. I marvel, however, that the Duchess is so eager to join our procession, fraught as it is with so much peril.

Having been virtually thrown out of Huy, we made our way to the citadel in Dinant, unimpeded but with the sense that we were being carefully watched. My fear was that we would encounter more fear and chaos in Dinant, but *au contraire*. We arrived at the gates of the citadel to discover that the townspeople were oblivious to the current state of the country because they had that very day chosen their new burgher master, and it seemed that the entire town was intoxicated. We could see through the gates that the central plaza was filled with riot and debauchery, with no magistrate to acknowledge us. When M. de Molay finally succeeded in making our presence known, the townspeople sobered up immediately and became hostile.

"*La vache!* There's that reprobate Molay!"

It turns out that M. de Molay, our well-thought-of ticket to ease of entry, is someone they detest. He did them some disservice in the past that they have not recovered from, and consider him the direst enemy. The citizens took up arms and barricaded the gates, and some of them even started throwing stones at us. Amazed, I sent my first esquire with my harbinger and quartermasters, to beg the magistrates to admit me to stay just one night in the town. We waited a considerable length of time, during which M. de Molay apologized profusely and at great length.

"I'm sure this is a misunderstanding, Your Majesty. They have me confused with someone else."

"Yes, I'm sure."

"Once your harbinger explains the situation, I feel sure that all will be well."

"Kindly stop talking, M. de Molay. I'm trying to think."

Suddenly we heard yelling from within, "*Au secour!* We're being taken prisoner!"

What to do? Jean d'Aubiac, who I could see in conference with some of the citizens, now broke away from them and rushed over to me.

"Your Majesty, ask to speak to Dupree."

"Who?"

"The town's new burgher master, Dupree. He's quite popular."

This seemed sensible advice, given all the celebration we had witnessed, so a message was sent inviting this man Dupree to an audience with me. After a lengthy period (during which we heard much loud debate within) the gates opened, and the burgher master Dupree came reeling out drunkenly in a filthy wine-stained jerkin, to the applause of the citizens. He staggered over to my litter and breathed a few words that almost caused me to faint from the fumes. I congratulated him on his new position. In response he bowed deeply, then turned to M. de Molay and *punched him in the face*, knocking him to the ground. The citizens cheered, confirmed in their conviction that they had chosen the right man.

I was now at my wits' end, but Jean d'Aubiac did not seem ruffled at all. He smiled and whispered to me, "Now speak to them."

"Whom?"

"The citizens."

"Why?"

"You just allowed their burgher master to punch Molay in the face. You have gained an advantage."

"I don't see how that follows."

"Just do it. And mention the Baron Von Duffel."

"Von Duffel? Who, pray tell, is he?"

"Doesn't matter. Just say you know him."

It seemed like nonsensical advice, but at the moment I saw no other recourse. All my titled counselors were arrested and M. de Molay lay on the ground with a bloodied nose. I rose from my litter and turned to the crowd.

"Citizens of Dinant, I am the Queen of Navarre!"

"A Huguenot!" someone shouted.

"No! I retorted, "I am a Catholic like yourselves and a sister to the King of France traveling for personal reasons having to do with my health. It is far from my intention to do any of you harm. I only beg that our party be admitted for a night or two, perhaps only the women, or whoever else you think proper, and then we will be on our way. I did not know that the grandmaster of the Bishop of Liege is a person who has not met with your pleasure, and apologize for bringing him here." De Molay looked crushed. "However, I'd like you to consider the consequences of giving offense to a person like myself, who is a friend to the principal lords of the States."

The crowd gaped at me dully, unmoved. I glanced at Jean d'Aubiac, who raised an eyebrow.

"I am also a friend of the Baron Von Duffel."

A gasp from the crowd. Someone called out.

"You know the Baron?"

"I do." D'Aubiac nodded encouragingly. "He's a close friend. In fact, I believe we are blood-related."

The alchemical transformation that took place within the crowd was instantaneous. They exclaimed amongst themselves, the gates opened, and the citizens poured out to receive me. I exchanged a grateful look with Jean d'Aubiac as they escorted me and my ladies within the citadel, whence I am now writing these wondrous recollections. Every time I mention the name of this mysterious Baron Von Duffel some new service is done for me or my ladies. Jean d'Aubiac tells me he learned of the man's influence in conversation with the citizens.

It is a lesson to me: If you want to know what's going on in a country, ask the common man. Or perhaps I should say, ask a man who feels comfortable speaking to the common man. Jean d'Aubiac saved the day.

13 July 1582 – Florennes

This morning I woke up safely inside the citadel of Dinant. After all the chaos and pandemonium of the day before, it was a relief to hear the everyday sounds of a French town as it woke up; bells ringing, hooves clopping on cobblestones, a smithy plying his trade, the muffled sounds of the townspeople pursuing their business. I stretched contentedly and arose with the intent of going to Mass when Maria entered, looking flustered.

"Your Majesty, there is a man downstairs named du Bois. He says he is the King of France's special emissary on behalf of Don John."

"That makes no sense. Why would Charles send an emissary for Don John?"

"I don't know, Your Majesty, but he's quite sure that's who he is, and he has requested an audience with you."

After bathing and dressing, I ordered the man sent up. He was a tall, gangly individual whose arms were noticeably too long for his uniform.

"Your Majesty, I am the King of France's special emissary on behalf of ~"

"Don John, yes, so I've been told."

"I am here to tell you of the imminent arrival of Monsieur Barlemont, who will soon be outside the gates with his cavalry."

"I see. What does this M. Barlemont want with me?"

"He has been ordered by the King to escort you to the safety of Namur."

"To Namur. Why not Paris, whence I've been informed the King wants me to return?" Du Bois squirmed in his uniform, which I began to question was his own.

"I don't have the answer to that, Your Majesty. I'm sure all will be revealed, but at the moment what is required is that you tell the citizens to admit Barlemont and his troops through the gates."

In the great wisdom of a later era, one may look upon me as naive in many ways, but I should like to receive credit for immediately recognizing the absurdity of this demand, which I perceived to spring from the feverish mind of Don John himself. He was clearly hoping this gambit would enable him to take possession of both me and the citadel. Gathering my wits, I feigned acquiescence and expressed the desire to share the good news with the Cardinal de Lenoncourt. I left the room calmly, then dashed down the hall to the Cardinal's rooms to relay the man's proposal. The Cardinal agreed with my assessment.

"It does indeed sound like a ploy. Speaking for myself, I have no interest in falling into the hands of the Spaniards at this point in life," he said.

"Nor I. What shall we do about this man?"

After some discussion, it was decided that I (the intimate friend of the illustrious Baron Von Duffel) should alert the townspeople to the situation, whilst the Cardinal stalled du Bois. I summoned Jean d'Aubiac, apprised him of the situation, and he gathered as many citizens as he could to meet with me. Once assembled, I informed them that if they admitted Barlemont's troops within the citadel, he would most certainly take possession of it. Although many of them seemed to be nursing intense headaches from the day before, this news was enough to snap them out of their lethargy.

"'Zounds! What are we to do?" one of them asked.

I never learned who any of these people were, or their titles, and the burgher master was notably absent, so at all times I spoke to them as a collective.

"Our best recourse is to allow Barlemont, and only Barlemont, within. Put on a show of all your weaponry as you do so, and behave in an intimidating fashion. At the same time, M. d'Aubiac will escort the Princess de Roche-sur-Yon and the rest of my retinue outside the gates. I advise everyone to speak in loud terms of the fact that we are preparing for our journey back to Namur."

They agreed to follow my counsel and swore to protect me at all costs. (I found I was growing ever fonder of this motley bunch.) I then went to my ladies and informed them of the situation. The Princess, I regret to say, was taken with a fit of hysterics.

"All I desired was a quiet trip to take the waters, and now I'm going to die here in this backwater Armageddon!" She wailed. Maria and Françoise gave her a dose of laudanum and stayed by her side as I explained our plan of action.

Meanwhile, the Cardinal had received M. du Bois, expressing great interest in his welcome news. He asked that I be given time to prepare myself for departure to which du Bois, pleased with how well his mission was going, readily agreed.

The citizens now went to the gates and made a great loud show of mass ferocity, managing to let only Barlemont within. At the same time, the Princess and the entire retinue descended in preparation for departure.

"We are going to *Namur*! Indeed, that is our destination! I am so looking forward to being in *Namur*!" The Princess kept exclaiming, with an edge of hysteria to her voice.

The aforementioned Barlemont was a coarse shifty-looking creature in similarly ill-fitting military attire, who immediately started to swear ugly oaths and argue that his troops be allowed within. At this, the citizens flew into a violent rage.

"Varlet! Infidel!" they shouted. They dragged Barlemont from his horse, handcuffed him, and started to drag him toward the scaffold. "String him up!" they yelled.

Barlemont suddenly lost his swaggering demeanor. "Have mercy! Tell me your demands and I will meet them!"

"Order your men out of sight!" they shouted. "If you don't, we will fire on them now with our great guns!" I was very impressed by their showmanship since they, in fact, do not possess great guns.

Feeling the tightening rope at his throat, Barlemont yelled to the troops without. "Withdraw to the woods and await further orders!" They did so. At that moment, Jean d'Aubiac came out of the building and approached Barlemont, smiling genially.

"Monsieur Barlemont, is it? Pleasure to meet you, I am D'Aubiac, the Queen's stable master. Sorry for the rather rough reception you just received. The town of Dinant is small but powerful, and they know they are living in fearful times." The townspeople growled and shook their fists. Barlemont, the rope still around his neck, nodded nervously. Jean d'Aubiac turned to du Bois.

"The Queen is most grateful for your offer of a safe escort, sir. She has gone directly to the chapel to take Mass, so that she can thank the Lord her prayers have been answered. Meanwhile, I've been instructed to lead her retinue outside and prepare the horses for the journey. Your servant, sir." Jean d'Aubiac bowed, then turned and led the benumbed Princess and the rest of my retinue outside the gates.

Regardless of the noose still around Barlemont's neck, Jean d'Aubiac's pleasantries seemed to convince du Bois that things were going his way. He took a seat, and the Cardinal engaged him in a diverting conversation about the book of Exodus. Meanwhile, outside the gate, my retinue hurried down the hill and toward an awaiting boat on the river Meuse below. Many trips were made until they were all ferried to safety on the other side. I watched from a tower window until the last of them was safely across. Then I started down the stairs flanked by my new closest friends, the citizens of Dinant, and approached du Bois.

"*Bonjour*, monsieur! I trust you have enjoyed your conversation with the Cardinal de Lenoncourt. Isn't he a stimulating man? And what lovely weather! I'm so looking forward to this excursion." I swept past du Bois, further extolling the virtues of the current weather as I made my way out the gate and down toward the river.

"Your Majesty," interjected du Bois. "You are, I think, going the wrong way."

I laughed merrily. "As my old friend Baron Von Duffel has so often told me, there *is* no wrong way when the time has come to take one's leave." I continued down the hill, flanked by my new security detail.

"Your Majesty, please, this was not the plan. I was given strict instructions!" pleaded du Bois. I strode forward, anxious someone might try to physically detain me until I saw Jean d'Aubiac at the helm of the awaiting boat, smiling encouragement. On the other side of the river were my company, safe and sound. D'Aubiac extended his hand. I took it and turned to face du Bois.

"Au revoir, Monsieur du Bois," I breezily replied and climbed into the boat.

"You do wrong, Your Majesty," pleaded du Bois. "You are acting in disregard of your brother the King's intention."

"Oh dear! When I get home, the two of us must have a nice chat about that."

Barlemont, who apparently had broken free of his restraints, came running out of the castle toward us, cursing and throwing ugly epithets our way as we crossed the river, but he was no match for the townspeople, who tossed him into the waters, laughing and poking at him with glee. One day I shall erect a plaque to the citizens of Dinant. I turned in relief to Jean d'Aubiac.

"Well done, Your Majesty," he said with a wink. My reflexive response was to be affronted; it is not a commoner's place to pass judgment on the actions of his sovereign. But the larger part of me was absurdly happy at his words.

"Thank you, Monsieur d'Aubiac. I couldn't have done it without you."

14 June, 1582 – Florennes

I must continue yesterday's story because it is just too good, and I have a moment's leisure to do so.

Having just escaped Dinant, and aware that Don John's men were behind us, we hastily made the best time we could to a strong castle in Florennes which our ever-helpful envoy, M. de Molay, assured us would offer a warm welcome. Remarkably, that gentleman was again incorrect! When we arrived, the master of the castle was nowhere to be seen. As we entered the courtyard, the lady of the castle saw us from her window and screamed, "Invaders!" She then ordered that the bridge be drawn up and ran to hide in the tower. I don't know what kind of invader she thought would arrive in a litter and with an entourage, but clearly, she was convinced we were up to no good. My men shouted our business to anyone else who might be within, but to no avail.

"I say, this was not expected," was de Molay's glum commentary.

The Princess was again becoming querulous. "Oh, to be back in the warm waters of Spa!" She kept moaning from her litter, but talk of warm waters triggered her own call of nature. Her lady escorted her to a suitable spot to relieve herself, and was just bringing her back to her litter when Jean d'Aubiac said in a low urgent voice, "Your Majesty, turn and look behind you."

I turned. Not a thousand yards away, at least three hundred of Don John's soldiers were pulling their horses up onto the rim of the hill. It was only dumb luck that the setting sun was in their eyes, or they would have spotted us immediately.

"Princess, quickly!" I commanded. "Back into your litter. Ladies, Cardinal! Stay within your coaches and be absolutely still! The rest of you maintain attendance. They must believe we have already gone inside the castle, or we will surely be apprehended." I retreated into my litter, pulling

Jean d'Aubiac into it with me. My hope was that those still visible would appear to be our attendees, waiting for our return.

A reasonable plan. But why, one might ask, did I pull Jean d'Aubiac into the litter with me? Surely, as stable master, he should have remained with his horses. I'm aware that would have made more sense, and my answer is... that I have no answer. It was an impulse. I panicked. I was aware that we were in a courtyard surrounded by a less-than-impressive wall, shut up by an equally weak gate, and that there were hundreds of armed men on the hill itching for the opportunity to commit violence. I knew, too, that it was very possible we would be forced to stay within our carriages until morning, as they watched from that hill. All I can say is it seemed... expedient. We lay in the litter side by side, hardly daring to move. At one point, Jean d'Aubiac whispered, "Your Majesty, perhaps I should ~"

"No!" I commanded. "Do not leave me."

Night fell, and sound seemed to travel further. We could hear the soldiers' horses snorting in the distance, and the howl of distant wolves. I could feel them watching, watching. The moon was sickle-shaped, thank the Virgin, so we were not brightly illuminated. Beside me in the litter, I could hear Jean d'Aubiac's even breathing. Inexplicably, the scent of roses was in the air. I love roses. I remember thinking it was late in the season for them.

On the hill, a soldier coughed. Another one swore. Some raucous laughter - were they drinking now? If they were to realize we were still in the courtyard, it would all be over. I know how little these men value life, even when not inebriated. Our gentlemen, so outnumbered, would be slaughtered, our ladies ~ I didn't let myself think what would happen to the ladies. If I were lucky, I would be taken prisoner. If not...I leaned close to Jean d'Aubiac's ear and whispered.

"I want to thank you for your service, Monsieur d'Aubiac."

"Happily rendered, Your Majesty."

"If this is to be the end of our lives ~"

"It is not."

"But if it is, I want you to be aware of my gratitude." I was going to say "appreciation" but I was afraid all the s's in the word would travel.

"Do not fear, my lady. We will come through." I wondered if he said "my lady" instead of "Your Majesty" for the same reason. It sounded sweet to my ear. I could feel his body radiating warmth. I felt I needed to say more.

"What I will remember most fondly about my life is my childhood, when everything was new and it seemed there was only good in the world. What will you remember, sir?"

"This," he replied, and he raised his eyes to mine. "I will remember only this."

We held one another's gaze for a long moment. All sound seemed to cease. I felt for a moment as if I were in another place entirely, another time, alone with him. The scent of roses was making me dizzy, I felt almost as if the litter were elevating. It was a moment of intensely real unreality. I wondered if he were feeling it, too.

Suddenly, the Princess sneezed. She has a very recognizable repressed sneeze, like the loud squeak of a mouse, and it is very female. On the hill, I saw movement and heard voices. A soldier mounted his horse and started down the hill. My heart sunk. The soldier was followed by another solder, and another. Surely if they got any nearer, they would spot my ladies huddled together in their carriage. M. d'Aubiac crept up to a perching position in the litter and drew his knife. What chance did he have against these soldiers, who were now drawing their pistols?

At that moment, little M. de Moley got out of his carriage and walked with great determination toward the gates. He began pounding on them.

"This is an outrage! Do you know who I am? How dare you make me wait in this courtyard when the Queen is within? Please tell Her Majesty of this indignity!"

The first soldier hesitated. Then he signaled to his men, and the three of them turned their horses and started back up the hill. Only a moment later, we could hear the sound of the hooves of many horses galloping at a goodly pace from the east, and after a moment M. de Florennes, the master of the castle, appeared in view accompanied by a healthy battalion of his men. He pulled his horse up in front of the castle, dismounted his horse, and, seeing me peering out of the litter, rushed toward me.

"Your Majesty! Such an honor! Please forgive my stupid wife for not giving you entrance! Open the gates!" His guards opened the gates, and he gestured welcome to us. I held up my hand.

"I believe the courageous M. de Molay should lead us in."

His dignity restored and flushing with pride, M. de Molay led our entourage into the castle, much to the anger and surprise of the soldiers on the hill, who I could hear cursing loudly.

I am within my apartments now, and am filled with an intense sense of well-being. It might be the euphoria of having escaped death so narrowly. It might be the warmth of the castle or the delicious sustenance that has been provided us since our arrival.

Or it might be the memory of the moment I found myself gazing into the eyes of a man I barely knew for such a strangely intimate amount of time, with the inexplicable scent of roses in the air.

It does seem likely that at the end of my life, a moment like that will be what I remember most vividly, too.

1 August, 1582 - Florennes

It occurs to me that I may have failed to write anything pertaining to the physical appearance of those closest to me on this journey. To enhance comprehension, I should like to note that Rosalind is tall and slim with chestnut hair, Maria is short and black-haired, Agatha is very freckled with hair the color of mine, the Princess has run somewhat to plumpness, the Cardinal is long and lean with a pointed gray beard, and our new lady Françoise has red hair. Molay's bulbous nose has been described already. Chevalier Salviati is short and stout and the quartermaster, whose name I have forgotten, is rather effeminate.

Jean d'Aubiac is tall and strong. His hair is sand-colored, and his beard brown but with a slightly reddish hue. His eyes are soft hazel with flecks of gold in them. When he smiles, the slightest dimple forms on his left cheek which is quite disconcerting. His arm muscles are remarkably well-hewn, as is to be expected from a man whose life involves physical labor and not preening around a court all day, but interestingly his fingers are long and tapering, a feature one associates with sensitivity and artistry.

I hope this provides a clearer picture of my circumstances.

3 August, 1582 - Florennes

Today, a gentleman appeared to us at the castle where we are taking refuge, and I challenge you to guess the gentleman's name. It was the famous Baron Von Duffel! He had returned to Dinant, heard the story about our exploits there, and had been congratulated by the town for being related so closely to the French crown, a circumstance of which he was unaware. Out of curiosity and a sudden burgeoning loyalty to France, he made the trip to Florennes to visit us. He's a ginger-haired fellow with a surprisingly large belly considering his scrawny build.

"Your Majesty, I place myself at your service. The circumstances of both your arrival and departure from Dinant sound harrowing. I trust you are now more suitably accommodated."

"We are, yes. Thank you, Baron, for being a friend to the court of France."

"I am flattered, Your Majesty, that you recall the time we met so long ago on your father's trip through Flanders. Most children don't remember such encounters."

I thought quickly. "Yes, well, you made an indelible impression upon me, Baron Von Duffel. Your noble bearing was unforgettable." The Baron seemed gratified by this. "Tell me, sir, how is it that you have inspired such loyalty within the hearts of the citizens of Dinant?"

The Baron smiled proudly. "I cured them of the plague."

"Indeed! How did you do that?"

"I'm not quite sure. Heaven was on my side, that much seems clear. I rode into town, and that very day the plague disappeared from Dinant. It seems logical to conclude that my arrival was the cause. Certainly, the citizens of Dinant feel that way, and I do not feel inclined to disagree."

"No. Logic would dictate otherwise." I glanced at the Cardinal, whose eyes narrowed in mild amusement.

"How long will you be staying at Florennes, Your Majesty? I hope you will allow me to offer my protection."

"That is very generous, but we are anxious to proceed with our journey."

"Proceed?" The Baron seemed surprised. 'Begging your Majesty's pardon, but is that wise, considering recent events?" The Cardinal and I exchanged a look.

"To which events do you refer, Baron?"

"An exchange of letters has been intercepted between Don John and the King of Spain. In them, Don John writes disparagingly of the Prince of Orange, whom he cannot forgive for becoming a Huguenot, and lays out plans to rob him of power. Learning of these plans, the Prince of Orange has sent a *peloton* of troops to Flanders to defend his interests."

"I see. Who was it that intercepted these letters and forwarded them to the Prince of Orange?"

"Why, your husband, Your Majesty. The King of Navarre."

A shock ran through me to hear his name. "My husband is in Flanders?" I felt mortified to be asking this, but had to know the answer.

"I can't answer as to that, Your Majesty. I know his emissary has been."

I have retired to my chambers to reflect upon this unsettling information. My responses are two-fold. One field of thought involves the humiliation of knowing that my husband may be here in Flanders, yet has not reached out to let me know of his presence. Does he not know of my precarious situation? Does he not care?

My second preoccupation, however, involves the fact that I have not given Henri any thought in ... Well, it has been a distressingly long time. As his wife, should I not be pining for him? Was I pining for him, at one point? I believe I was, but so much has happened since we parted. He has not written to remind me of his presence, so is it not partially his fault? True, it's been some time since I have written him, as well. But I have been distracted by the desire to survive Flanders, whereas he ~ What is his plan?

Does he intend to rescue me? Perhaps he has kept his location secret so that he can maintain the element of surprise, sweep in quickly and ~ Or perhaps he feels that things are not as bad as they seem? **After all, I am the sister to the King** of France. Would anyone run the risk of incurring his wrath by harming me? Perhaps all of this is just foolish worry on my part. I see no harm in staying here for a few days, but I'm tired of letting fear dictate my every move. I am a queen. I must act like one, and forge onward.

10 August, 1582 – Florennes

It was a glorious morning. I awoke with fresh resolve and the sense that the tide had turned. I had refused to be alarmed by Von Duffel's news; whatever wars these men were fighting had nothing to do with me. I felt strong and capable, and I had the sense that things were going to progress smoothly now. Perhaps it helped to know that Henri was nearby, it gave me the feeling that he was looking out for us.

My ladies and I were playing "Questions of Love," in which each lady in turn describes their perfect romantic encounter and illustrates it by acting it out for the others' amusement. It was Agatha's turn.

"My lover and I would meet at a grand ball. We are from warring families, and so we cannot speak without incurring grave punishment."

We all nodded, familiar with this old Italian story. "But he is overcome by my dark beauty," said Agatha, and the others tittered because Agatha is quite blonde. "He must meet me! His passions have been enflamed. And so, whilst we are dancing, he presses a note to my hand. I rush to a secluded spot to read it. 'I will come to your window at midnight,' it reads."

Now the ladies' tittering stopped, as the drama of the scene began to captivate them. "I send my nurse away early, and wait in my room that night, so impatiently. The hours pass – will he come? Perhaps he is too frightened to cross his father. But then – a noise! Someone has thrown a stone at my window! I rush to the window and look out – is it him?"

Agatha ran to the open window of the chambers and parted the sash dramatically. "There he is!" she sighed. A few of our ladies patted their hands together in excitement.

At that moment, Agatha was struck through the head by an arrow and fell to the floor, dead.

8.

"The Spartans do not ask how many are the enemy, but where are they."

— **Plutarch**

? August, 1582

I am in the woods, alone, with Jean d'Aubiac. He has gone off to hunt for food, whilst I have been charged with building a small fire. Try as I might, I cannot succeed in producing the slightest spark, and it is causing me intense exasperation. I am a grown woman, yet I cannot build a simple fire. It's not simple, actually, it is very, very difficult. Hit these two stones together, he said, until a spark catches these twigs on fire. I have hit them and hit them, and I have no idea what he is talking about. Perhaps he was just trying to keep me busy with a useless task, so I would not exhaust myself with further weeping. Perhaps he thinks it will keep me from being afraid. I'm not afraid. Whilst I write, I am not afraid. When I stop, however ...

Agatha has been killed. My sweet, dreamy, freckle-faced Agatha with her tinkling laugh, who never hurt a fly. She fell to the floor like a downed bird, the blood pouring from her head. We screamed. We wept. There was much hysteria. Mme. de Florennes locked herself inside the tower again, Cardinal Lenoncourt retreated to his brandy, the Princess had to be subdued again with her laudanum, and the general reaction seemed to be that we must barricade ourselves inside the building. I have been barricaded inside too many buildings. On impulse, I demanded my stable master be brought to me. I met him in a windowless hallway outside my chambers.

"Monsieur d'Aubiac, I want you to listen carefully to what I am about to tell you and offer your advice. Do not flatter me by saying what you think I want to hear. Just give me your honest opinion."

"Yes, Your Majesty," was his response, and I could sense his astonishment.

"Lady Agatha is dead. She was killed whilst standing at the open window in my chambers."

"When?"

"Just now."

"My God."

"I had been standing in that window not a moment before. Obviously, they thought it was me."

"Yes."

"She was the loveliest of women, so sweet and good. It was just by the most awful chance that she –" I found I was starting to cry. The stable master instinctively reached out to touch my shoulder, then instantly withdrew it. I regained control of my voice and continued. "It is the opinion of my advisors that we should sequester ourselves here until someone comes to our rescue. Do you agree?"

"Who do you expect to come?"

"Possibly my husband the King of Navarre. There's a rumor he is in the area."

"Don't you think if he were in the area, he would make himself known to you?"

"I – I don't know. He's an unpredictable man."

The stable master looked at me for a long moment, frowning in thought.

"How good a horsewoman are you?" He finally asked. "We took that short ride in Liege, but do you have the endurance for long rides?"

"Are you suggesting that I –"

"Disguise yourself, Your Majesty, and ride to safety without the retinue."

"Alone?"

"Of course not. With me. Right now, they think they have killed you, so you have the advantage of time. Soon they will discover the truth. It will take us two or three days if we ride all day. Are you up to it? You've been riding in a litter for so long, perhaps your muscles –"

"My muscles are in fine condition, Monsieur d'Aubiac. Until recently, I have been dancing every night for hours on end."

"Well then, if you feel you are capable, I believe it is your best course of action."

"And my entourage?"

"They will be safer without you. Tell them to make an extended public show of grief over the death of their princess. We must go tonight."

That is how I have come to be here, alone in this forest, trying to build a fire, and I will attest that riding a horse for eight hours is infinitely more taxing to the body than dancing.

16 August, 1582

Jean d'Aubiac and I rode night and day from Florennes. I was appareled as a man – we borrowed M. du Molay's clothing – and more than once we encountered others on horseback who did not suspect me to be otherwise. It was thrilling, truth be told. I attempted a manly swagger in the company of one group that caused Jean d'Aubiac to go into fits of laughter after we had parted. He prevailed on me to do it again and it redoubled his laughter.

"To think that this exquisite royal princess should be mistaken for a man!" He roared. I rather enjoyed being described as "exquisite."

We followed the River Meuse. Somewhere outside of Reims, we perceived – or rather, Jean d'Aubiac did, as I am rather nearsighted – that we were riding directly into the path of a troop of Huguenot soldiers. Jean d'Aubiac diverted us into the forest, where we spent the night. It was in that location that I made my previous entry. I had failed in my attempt to build a fire and had fallen asleep when Jean d'Aubiac returned with a couple of quail. I woke to find him roasting them over the fire, and I have never in my life tasted anything so delicious. It was a chilly night, and we huddled side by side under a blanket, looking up at the dazzling stars in respectful silence. I almost thought Jean d'Aubiac had fallen asleep when he suddenly spoke.

"Your Majesty, I would never challenge the judgment of a sovereign. I was raised to understand that royalty is infallible and we must not question their ways."

"Yes, yes, Monsieur d'Aubiac," I said impatiently. "Speak your mind."

"Are you quite sure that it is the safest plan to return to court, given the misconceptions they seem to have about your business in Flanders?"

"This is why I must return, Monsieur. To be on the wrong side of the crown is a perilous thing. They think I have been duplicitous; I must make them understand that all of my efforts were for the glory of the King. Or, at least, I thought they were... Yes, I'm sure they were. The Duke of Alençon would never engage in subterfuge against his own brother."

Jean d'Aubiac received my words in silence, which caused me to reexamine what I had just said.

"It is true that, in the course of history, you read stories about brothers going against one another. It's not as if the idea is entirely preposterous. But even if my brother Alençon were to have been advancing his own personal aims, I had no knowledge of it. I need to convince them of that."

"Ignorance will cause them to look kindly upon you, I suppose."

Jean d'Aubiac is very good at differing with me without literally differing with me. I tried to summon another moment in my life where ignorance of a bad situation exonerated me from my connection to it.

I remember the time when we were children and Charles became obsessed with the idea that we should have our own menagerie at the palace. I thought it sounded like a wonderful idea, and spent a good deal of effort pleading for the menagerie along with him. Mother and Father finally gave in, and soon on the castle grounds there was built a giant enclosure, with wolves, wild boars, lion cubs, a bear, and other exotic animals. We also had dogs and ponies to play with, it was an idyllic way to spend the summer. But then Charles, in one of his shifts of mood, started to kill and dismember the lion cubs, leaving their entrails all over the grounds (possibly my first clue that all was not well with Charles.) Instead of punishing him, Father punished me for petitioning for the menagerie in the first place. I couldn't have known Charles was going to take this unsettling turn, but it was I who was banished from the dining table for the rest of the summer.

"I see what you are suggesting, Monsieur. Ignorance is not always the best excuse. But I can't bear the thought that they have misunderstood my motives. I am an obedient daughter and a good person. It's important to me that they understand my motives were pure."

"And are theirs?"

"What?"

"Their motives. Would you describe them as pure?"

I became rather indignant. "You're talking about our king, Monsieur! The King of France, and his Queen Regent!"

"Of course. Forgive me. I am merely concerned for your safety."

Somewhat mollified by his response, we retreated into silence. I found myself thinking about my father, and how little I knew him. Would Charles have turned out to be a better man if Father had lived? Then I realized something.

"Monsieur D'Aubiac, I should have said this before. I am very sorry for the death of your father. He was a good man, and was in fact responsible for aiding in the escape of the King of Navarre from court. He provided the horses."

"I know. Thank you for your kind words."

"How did he die?"

"It... doesn't matter."

"Of course, it does! Was he ill?

"No. He was – executed."

"Executed!" My stomach lurched. I knew the answer to the question I was about to ask. "Why?" Jean d'Aubiac only shook his head, unable to answer. "But he – he didn't even know – I told him nothing! He was just following an order."

"Your Majesty, he knew. He knew and approved of your plan for the King of Navarre's escape. He was of the Protestant faith."

I was sickened by the realization of what my actions had done to another. "Monsieur d'Aubiac, I am so very sorry."

"Please don't apologize. You are blameless."

Tears came to my eyes, hearing him say this. I tried to repress them, but instead found myself crying audibly. The stable master reached out and touched my shoulder and I welcomed his kindness, though it seemed odd that he should comfort me for his own father's death.

"And you, M. d'Aubiac? Are you of the Protestant faith, also?"

"I am whatever faith will keep me alive, Your Majesty. Or indeed no faith at all."

"Oh, but surely you must have a faith!"

Jean d'Aubiac considered. "I have faith that the day will dawn tomorrow. I have faith that man will always be at war in one form or another, that there will always be those who are good at heart and those who are bad, and that it will be hard to tell the difference. And I have a growing faith that love might be more powerful than hate."

"And our Creator?" Jean d'Aubiac gazed up at the sky reflectively.

"I have faith that it is a mystery we will never solve," he said. Somehow, I found this a reassuring response. We fell asleep like two children, untroubled and oblivious to all but the present moment.

The next morning, I awoke and he was not there. I had a moment's panic and went to look for him. Approaching the river, I spotted a garment hanging from the branch of a tree, and a few steps further revealed him standing in the river shirtless, with the sapling that he had whittled to a point the night before, spearing fish for our breakfast. I watched him for some time.

His shoulders are very broad, and his torso is tanned a warm brown. We at court, including the men, have been given to believe that the paler we can keep our skin the more attractive it is, and the more indicative of a life of ease. Jean d'Aubiac is, I believe, testimony to the fact that sun-browned skin and muscularity of frame are not an unattractive combination on a man; in fact, it seemed rather difficult to stop looking at him. As he speared his last fish, I hastened back to our encampment so as to give him time to dress, and myself time to collect my composure.

Breakfast was, again, utterly delicious. That day we rode long and hard, and it felt enormously companionable to be riding beside this capable man. We would stop occasionally for water, or to pick some berries and eat them – he steered me away from the poisonous ones ~ and then we would set off again. I was delighted that I could keep up so well with him, it seemed that every muscle in my body was fully engaged and ready for anything.

We slowed down in the last stretch, aware that we were about to enter Paris and our journey would be coming to an end. I felt my mood sinking, but Jean began to whistle a tune.

"What is that you're whistling?"

"A drinking song. It celebrates the virtues of French wine."

"It's very cheerful. Does it have words?"

"Certainly."

"Teach them to me."

He did, and we sang it together at the tops of our lungs as we rode toward the city.

> *"When I drink of claret wine*
>
> *The world it turns and turns, my friend,*
>
> *So now, my friend, here's what I drink,*
>
> *Anjou or Arbois!*
>
> *Let's sing and drink*
>
> *And kill this bottle!*
>
> *Sing and drink, my friends*
>
> *To life!"*

I could feel my spirits soaring. I imagined myself as a laborer coming home from a hard day's work, riding beside my companion, and enjoying the simple fact of being alive. Who was to question me, riding beside this handsome strapping man? I was a man, too, a working man headed home for my well-deserved bottle of claret.

We entered the city, with its smoke and filth and noxious odors, still singing. It helped me to lose my concerns about what was to come. Past the windmills, down the narrow streets, over the river Seine, and toward the gardens of the Louvre. Arriving at the main entrance, the guards were astonished to realize that this filthy rustic singing creature was me and allowed me entrance immediately. I turned to Jean d'Aubiac.

"Thank you, Monsieur. You have saved my life."

"It has been the greatest pleasure, Your Majesty," he replied, and took my horse, ready to resume his duties as stable master.

"Be sure this man receives ample nourishment and fresh attire," I ordered, and the guards nodded.

Why didn't I then detect the change in atmosphere at the Louvre, the way the guards looked at one another significantly as they escorted me to my chambers? I suppose I was too exhilarated by my travels, and by the fact that I was now about to bathe and change my attire all by myself (it wasn't as difficult as I anticipated.) Perhaps I was reveling in the singular experience of being alone, which was wonderful but also somewhat unsettling. After a while, though, wondering why no one had yet arrived to welcome me, I opened the door to go seek my mother ~ and was stopped by two armed guards.

"Apologies, Your Majesty, but you are to go no further."

"What? I want to see my mother the Queen."

"I'm afraid that is not possible," was the reply.

"Absurd," I responded and attempted to pass, whereupon one of the guards physically blocked my exit. I was shocked at his effrontery.

"Upon whose orders am I to be imprisoned in my chambers?" I demanded.

"Upon the orders of your brother the King."

"I see. As relayed by the Duke of Guise?" They did not respond. "Where is my brother Alençon?" The guards looked at one another as though deciding whether they were required to answer this question. Finally, one of them spoke.

"The Prince is in his chambers."

"Please tell him I should like to see him."

"I'm afraid that is not possible, Your Majesty. He, too, is restricted to his apartment."

Astonished, I retreated to my rooms, pacing back and forth like a caged tiger and contemplating the situation furiously. How foolish I was not to consider more seriously Jean d'Aubiac's reservations about returning to Paris. Curse my stupidity! I recalled how, earlier in these pages, I wrote dramatically of being a prisoner after my marriage because Charles wouldn't provide me with a suitable entourage to proceed to Nérac. How could I have allowed a thing like that to stop me? Why hadn't I just procured a horse and ridden to Nérac alone, or with Jean d'Aubiac, as I have just done from Flanders?

Of course, I know the answer to that; I was a different person then. I had not yet made the acquaintance of Jean d'Aubiac, and it would never have occurred to the younger me to enlist his father in such a task. Before Flanders, my entire focus was primarily on being "in favor" with the court, maintaining my beauty, and, lastly, on being pure and good. Or rather, on being perceived as being pure and good by others. A pure and good princess does not enlist the stable master's assistance to defy her family and escape court. Yet in the woods with Jean d'Aubiac, dressed as a man, I swaggered and affected a manly demeanor, and could feel the power of that new character welling up within me, and giving me strength. Yet for all that, Jean d'Aubiac called me "exquisite." Exquisite, in a doublet and hose! I had rubbed my face with dirt to appear as if I had a beard coming, yet still, he thought me...

No. I have to focus on the current moment. This time I truly am a prisoner, with guards outside my door. There are no ladies in waiting, there is no Madame de Tournon to dress and flatter me. I am alone.

And for my stupidity, I feel as if I deserve it.

9.

"No beast is more savage than man, when possessed with power answerable to his rage."

— **Plutarch**

18 August, 1582 - Paris

I am resting against a tree in the cool of the forest, shafts of sunlight piercing the darkness here and there, dust motes dancing in the light. I am watching in fascination as they billow and eddy and listening to the singing of the birds and the babbling of a nearby brook. Jean d'Aubiac is feeding the horses and talking to them as if they are human, and suddenly one of the horses speaks back to him.

"We are grateful for your kindness, Monsieur," the horse says, clear as day. I startle.

"Monsieur d'Aubiac, did you hear that? The horse spoke to you!" I exclaim. Jean d'Aubiac turns to me and smiles. "I am glad you are finally able to hear it," he says.

I heard the doors being unlocked. I awoke to find one of the guards announcing the Duke of Guise, who strode into the room as if it were his own.

"Your Majesty," he drawled.

"*Monsieur*, I am not dressed to receive."

"This will only be a moment. I trust you are comfortable."

"I am not comfortable. I am being held prisoner."

"A bit of an exaggeration, wouldn't you say? If you were truly prisoner, you would be down in the dungeon. These guards are merely for your protection."

"From whom?"

"From what, would be a better question. From your own lecherous impulses, possibly."

"I beg your pardon?"

"I have friends in many places, Marguerite, and my friends tell me that you have been playing your husband false with Don John of Austria."

"You have been listening to lies, Monsieur."

"In fact, according to my sources, you have taken joy in the arms of almost every young man you've met in your travels. What a fool I was, to have honored your requests for restraint. If I'd known what a harlot you were, I'd have had you long ago."

"How dare you! By whose orders am I being restricted to my rooms?"

"By the King's, of course."

"Where is my mother?"

"In her chambers. She is unfortunately not feeling well. She sends her regards."

"This is absurd. Does the King really think I have gone behind his back? Or have you planted poisonous doubts into his mind?"

"Your lies to him mean about as much as the ones you told me."

"So that's what this is about. Henri, believe me, I never meant to ~"

"To what? To play me for the fool? They were all laughing at me, did you know that? My love for you was quite the source of hilarity at court. Everyone knew you had no intention of giving yourself to me. They were taking wagers as to when I would figure it out."

"I'm so sorry."

"I'm sure you are, now that your status in this court is so diminished. I'm sure you are very sorry, but it's a bit late, isn't it? The balance has shifted, Marguerite. Your brother attends to every word I say. It is I who brought you back. It is I who keep you here. I have that power now."

"Congratulations."

"It seems to me you very much owe me something, for the way you've treated me, Marguerite, for the humiliation I have endured. Would you agree?"

"I – I don't know what you –"

"What do you offer me?"

"I offer – my apologies, and –"

"Not enough!"

Guise grabbed me by the hair and pulled my face toward his, mashing it into mine in an obscene distortion of a kiss, his tongue slathering my face with spit. Astonished, I fought him off and tried to scream but he covered my mouth and forced me backward until I fell upon my bed. He pinned me down there, pulled up my gown, and reached between my legs ...

Later I was in the forest again. Jean d'Aubiac had made a cup from a linden leaf and dipped it into the cool waters of the stream. He raised it to my lips and I drank gratefully. Then we climbed on our horses and rode away.

20 August, 1582 - Paris

Alençon and I were brought before the King today. At his side was Guise, flanked by several courtiers and members of the clergy. It was the first time I had seen Alençon since before I left for Flanders. He looked pale and frightened.

Charles' appearance, however, was even more alarming. He looked wretchedly unwell and spent a good deal of time coughing. At the same time his color was high, and he appeared to be in a heightened emotional state, which is never good news with Charles.

"Well, well, well, if it isn't my traitorous brother and sister!"

Alençon responded immediately. "Charles. Majesty, we have a full explanation for our deeds which I'm sure will –"

"SILENCE!" The room went deathly still. "I have all the explanation I require for your actions. How dare you go behind my back in this way on behalf of those filthy Huguenots?"

I had to respond to this. "Brother, if I may –"

"You may not!" Roared Charles. "Women must *never* be involved in politics!" It was then that I looked around and realized that Mother was not in the room. Guise was working quickly, it seemed.

"It was not for the Huguenots, Charles, but for you, for the crown, for –" Before I could finish, Guise walked up to me and slapped me hard in the face. A gasp went up in the room. Alençon jumped to my defense but was restrained by his guards. Coolly, Guise turned to my brother.

"I trust that was what was required, Your Majesty?" Charles appeared momentarily stymied. Then he nodded. "Yes, yes, very good of you, Guise. Thank you."

I tried very hard to staunch the tears that had sprung to my eyes. Charles and Guise whispered to one another for a moment, then Charles nodded and turned to us.

"The Crown needs time to determine the punishment for your treachery. In the meantime, you will continue to be restricted to your apartments. Take them away."

"My ladies," I pleaded as they started to pull me from the room. "I require the company of my ladies. I'm sure they have arrived by now."

Charles looked toward Guise, whose gaze was black and unreadable. "Oddly enough, they have not, Majesty. I'm afraid the Princess will be alone for a bit longer." He smiled at me meaningfully.

As I was being pulled away, I saw my mother standing in the shadows behind an arras, observing the proceedings. Our eyes briefly met. Then she turned and left the room.

25 August, 1582 - Paris

Four nights have passed since my arrival at the Louvre. For three of them, I have been exposed to the grotesque aggressions of the Duke of Guise. Three nights with no one to protect me, no one to cry out to as this monster took his pleasure of me in the vilest of ways, pretending to himself that I was somehow complicit in the experience, that I enjoyed being demeaned in this way. The man harbors demons within, demons he seems to enjoy, and the shame I feel that I wasn't able to deter him is crippling. No one must ever know of this. I may burn these pages.

It occurred to me that this abuse could go on for a very long time. Rather than endure such a thing, I was contemplating the notion of taking my own life. I've heard of other women killing themselves to escape dishonor, and I examined the thought from a number of angles. On the one hand, I would not have to go through one more night of hell. On the other, by killing myself I would be going to hell anyway, since suicide is a mortal sin. Why is it a mortal sin? Does it not make sense, if one's life has become unbearable, to release oneself from this life and join our Father in heaven? How can He take offense at that? Upon reflection, however, I realized that by ending my life, I would be forfeiting the opportunity to get revenge on the devil of a man who has thus offended me.

For revenge is now uppermost in my thoughts. I had placed an andiron near the pillow of my bed, with which I planned to kill him tonight at the moment when his sickening passions rendered him momentarily oblivious. True, he might overpower me and if he did, he would certainly kill me instead, but that would be a blessing. I would be dead, but not by my own hand, and therefore suitable for heaven.

These were my thoughts. But then something strange happened. This morning there was shouting in the hallways, the sound of people running, and sobs. I banged my fists on the door, demanding to know what was occurring. A guard must have taken pity on me, for he opened the door and whispered the news. "Your Majesty, the King your brother is dead."

I was astonished. Certainly, Charles had been in ill health, but he was young; I always assumed he would recover. I felt a stab of pity for my brother but then, God forgive me, that pity was replaced by the deepest sense of relief. My torture was over. With Charles gone, the power balance had shifted yet again. Surely Guise wouldn't dare molest me now.

And indeed, tonight there was no knock on the door, no key in the lock. I suspect Guise has fled Paris to assess his altered position in the new world order. I feel shame about my relief at Charles's death, but as for Guise, my only regret is that I didn't get the opportunity to kill him.

The guards have been removed from my door. My ladies have been restored to me, and they have many stories to tell about their adventures after Jean d'Aubiac and I escaped. I listen to them, but my heart is still pounding in horror at the events of the past three days. I am well acquainted with the brutality of men toward one another, but to have survived the Flemish debacle only to become the victim of Guise; well, the irony of the situation is not lost on me. I tried to put it behind me and become interested with the stories of the ladies' adventures.

"Oh, Your Majesty, you would have been so amused! Our procession headed southwest, to give the impression that you were with us and that our destination was Nérac," began Rosalind.

"Rosalind was in your litter, Majesty, wearing your mask!" giggled Maria. "She performed a very convincing impersonation of you."

"Did she?" I raised my eyebrows. "Let's see it." The room subdued instantly. All eyes turned to Rosalind, who looked flustered for a moment – would I be angry? Then, gathering her courage, she grabbed up a mask and placed it before her face.

"Ladies, I tell you again, it is the same in love as in war. The fortress that parleys is half taken."

They all turned to see my reaction. Rosalind's caricature of me was so deft that I could not but laugh, which caused great relief. But my familiar words rang hollow; who was I to make pronouncements about love? I, who was so bereft of it myself, and had so little personal power: A husband who couldn't be bothered to contact me anymore, an ex-suitor who hated me so much that he was capable of unspeakable acts against me. I listened to the rest of the story, how they pulled the king's troops away from me as we made our way toward Paris, how my ladies were accosted by the king's guard, and when my litter was thrown open to reveal Rosalind within, the troops were so confused that they retreated to compare notes on what they thought I looked like. Finally, they realized they had been duped, and led the procession back to Paris.

I am happy to see my ladies safe and sound, although the word "happy" seems wrong; I am relieved and spent. As I listened to their stories, I felt like a different, much older person and very, very far away from them all.

I wonder what happens to the Princess of France at the end of "The Work of Love is Lost." It seemed so amusing to us at the time, but perhaps it ends badly. If it ended happily, it might have been titled "The Work of Love is Won."

27 August, 1582 - Paris

This morning my mother summoned me to her chambers. To my relief, Guise was not present, confirming my suspicions that he has fled.

"You have been informed of your brother's death. It is very sad," Mother said unemotionally. "I tried to advise Charles in the matter of your Flemish adventure, but he would not listen to me, on that or any other subject. Instead, his mind corrupted further and further as he embraced the advice of the Duke of Guise in all things. He was a weak and stupid boy, and I trust that he is in a better place. As for you, know that your actions in Flanders accelerated his demise, as it gave the Duke the perfect opportunity to sow seeds of distrust in not only his siblings but his own mother. Do you not understand, Marguerite, that only with myself at the seat of power are you allowed to thrive at all? Thankless child!"

At this point she expected me to respond, but I found that I was so infinitely weary I could not speak.

"What is the matter with you?" she demanded.

"I am sad. My brother is dead."

"That's not it. Don't lie to your mother. I advise you to take your medicine and move on, Marguerite. Self-pity will get you nowhere."

"Yes, Mother."

"Meanwhile, we have summoned your brother Edouard Alexandre from Poland. He will become Henri III and will serve much better as king here than there anyway. He is certainly healthier than Charles and has enough character not to be swayed by the subtle whisperings of a man like Guise. He will also listen to his mother, as Charles should have!"

Upon taking my mother's leave I realized I was free to move about the castle now, so I made my way to Alençon's chambers. My brother, who was lolling on his bed in his nightclothes, leapt to his feet when he saw me.

"Precious Margot!" He exclaimed and embraced me deeply. Then he looked me in the eyes.

"Are you all right, sister?"

"No, brother."

"Is there someone I can kill for you?"

"I'm afraid that would be too dangerous."

"The moment it's not too dangerous, you'll let me know, won't you?"

"Yes."

We both attempted to say a prayer for the soul of Charles, then gave it up as futile and caught up on each other's news. I suddenly remembered my anger at him.

"How could you have left me to my own devices in Flanders like that? Do you know how near I came to being captured, or killed? And why did you never tell Charles of the Flanders agenda? That was stupid, stupid, stupid!"

"Dear girl, I see that now. I suppose I wasn't thinking it through fully, but the good news is your mission was a complete success! With Don John having essentially gone mad in Namur, no one trusts Spain anymore. Now all eyes are turned toward France."

My reaction to this was complicated. It's hard not to take delight in the knowledge that one's mission has been a success. But was it worth risking one's life?

"How can you go to Flanders now, Monsieur? What of the Queen Elizabeth and your efforts there?" I asked.

"Oh, that is a sad tale. I was drawn away from Elizabeth just as things were starting to go well. She's a grand old girl and loves to laugh, but she was upset at my taking such a sudden leave. Guise forced Charles to call me home, he seems to have his hand in just about everything, have you noticed?... I say, you look awfully pale. Are you all right?"

"I'll be fine. What will happen to – him, now?"

"Guise? Well, I'd say he's been seriously demoted, wouldn't you? With Anjou coming home to be king, Mother gets back into the seat of influence. It's almost as if she planned it."

"Planned it. Monsieur... Charles' death... You don't suppose Mother ...?"

"That way madness lies, dear Margot. He is her son. It was consumption."

"Yes, of course. You are right."

Upon leaving Alençon, I walked outside and into the gardens, feeling a desperate need for fresh air. I tried not to think of the violence to which I had been subjected for the past three days, although my body kept reminding me. Realizing that there was no one to complain to, no one who would come to my aid, I had given up resisting Guise and just submitted myself to his aggressions as if dead. Which is indeed how I feel now. Did Mother know what he was doing? I can't forget the way our eyes met as I was leaving the king's chamber. Had she taken pity on me and stepped in to intervene? Impossible to know.

Amongst all the repercussions that have taken place within my soul - and they are wide ranging - there is also the practical one; what if I have been impregnated? As I walked, I remembered Mother saying, "I advise you to take your medicine and move on, Marguerite."

Take my medicine. What an odd and heartless thing to say. Yet suddenly the recipe that Madame Chauderon whispered into my ear that day at Spa came back to me – the formula for averting a pregnancy. The formula that, as a devout Catholic, I tried so hard to forget – suddenly those whispered words came back to me again, clear as day.

4 September, 1582 - Paris

I have been ill. Ill in spirit, ill in health. The good news is that I am not now with child. The other good news is that the Duke of Guise has left court, ostensibly to oversee his properties in Lorraine, but more likely to lick his wounds. Meanwhile, preparations are being made to receive my brother Anjou, who will now become King of France. Anjou, born Edouard Alexandre, is the brother who tried to drown me, but he is probably my second favorite. We used to play dress up together as children, and he always insisted on being attired as a beautiful princess. Although Anjou has renounced his early infatuation with Huguenots (if not dresses,) my marriage to the King of Navarre has caused him to take a softer line with me; he quite likes Henri. I'm hoping he'll take a softer line with the country in general.

Alençon, meanwhile, has been in quite a sulk. He's extremely resentful of his treatment at the hands of the crown, and doesn't feel that Mother has done enough to make him feel better about being branded a traitor and locked up. Upon accepting his explanation that he did intend to acquire the Flemish territories for Catholic France, no one has formally apologized to him. Of course, Charles is dead and Guise is not at court, but Alençon feels that something should be said officially to exonerate him.

Despite my illness and Alençon's wounded feelings, (or maybe because of them) Mother demanded that we three dine together tonight. She injected an artificial note of gaiety to the proceedings, so unbecoming to Mother, whilst Alençon sat there in gloomy silence.

"Isn't this nice! The three of us together." As neither of us thought it was nice, we did not respond.

"You're feeling better, are you, Marguerite?"

"No, Mother, I have in fact been quite ill, and so is one of my dogs."

"Isn't that a shame! We shall have to get you another one."

"It hasn't died."

"But when it does."

"One does not just replace one dog with another. They are unique in nature, Mother."

"Yes, all right," said my mother impatiently. "I've never cared for pets myself."

"Not only are dogs uncritical of physical failings, but they exhibit a gentleness and tenderness generally lacking in human beings," I said accusingly.

My mother spooned her soup in silence, clearly annoyed. Then she turned to Alençon brightly.

"Monsieur, after your brother's coronation, I think you should go and claim those territories in Flanders, don't you?"

Alençon brightened immediately. "Really?"

"Well, you were clever enough to send Marguerite to prepare the field, it seems a shame not to capitalize on it."

Alençon became very excited at this notion and began laying out his plan of action, with Mother nodding encouragement. Seeing him thus easily cajoled out of his depressed state of mind made me wish that I, too, could find a lightness of spirit within, but I can find no activity that will take my mind off my inner pain. I thought to go riding, but I can't face the thought of seeing Jean d'Aubiac; one look into my eyes would tell him of my shame, I am sure, and I could not bear him knowing.

10.

"Nothing fixes a thing so intensely in the memory as the wish to forget it."

— **Michel de Montaigne**

14 September 1582 - Paris

A most welcome event today – a visit from my lovely friend Adrienne, the Countess de Lalaing. I had written her of my safe arrival and apologized for not making it back to Mons as I had promised her I would. She read something in the tone of my letter, and as she and the Count were planning on coming to the funeral and the coronation, she wrote that she would like to call upon me beforehand. I am eternally grateful to her for doing so.

My ladies and I entertained her in my apartments, or at any rate my ladies did. I asked them to relate the story of our escapades in Flanders, as I didn't quite have the energy to do so myself. Adrienne was appropriately amused and frightened for us, and expressed her relief at our having finally achieved safety, but she kept throwing puzzled glances my way.

When we took a walk in the garden, the Countess and I did not speak much but listened to my lades as they chatted amongst themselves. Then she quietly asked for leave to speak with me in private. I dismissed my ladies, and we sought a quiet place that afforded some privacy.

"Your Majesty, forgive me but I sense that something has happened beyond the events of which you have made me familiar. You seem much changed."

I could not speak but felt my throat tightening and my eyes filling. I turned away.

"Someone has hurt you." I nodded. "Physically?" I nodded again. "Was it that man who accompanied you from Florennes?"

"No! That gentleman is kindness itself! No, it was...someone else. Someone who has...who had power over me."

As soon as I said this, I realized that, with the King dead and my husband far away, there was only one man who fit this description. Adrienne understood this, too. Defying the rules of court and to my surprise, she impulsively took my hand.

"My dear, I am so, so sorry. This should not have happened. You are such a good and gentle person."

With this kindness from her, I started to weep as I have never wept before in my life. We do not cry at court. It is a sign of weakness, and weakness will get you killed. But I didn't care anymore whether I lived or died. Adrienne held me in her arms until I had exhausted myself with tears. It was the deepest comfort, and something I have never known, to be held like that by another woman. She dried my tears with her handkerchief, and then looked at me meaningfully.

"I hope you understand, this is not your shame. It is his. He will have to answer to this at the end of his life and rest assured he will pay the price. You, sweet princess, are blameless."

She gently kissed each of my eyes after she said this as if to help me see myself anew, and if she hasn't entirely lifted the veil of sorrow from my eyes, she has eased my spirit in a very meaningful way.

1 October, 1582 - Paris

Charles' funeral was appropriately somber and magnificent. I could write at length about the particulars of the ceremony but really, if you've seen one royal funeral you've seen them all, and I've seen more than my share. There were thousands of people outside, wailing and beating their breasts as if they knew Charles personally; he would have been delighted at the spectacle, but repulsed by the people themselves.

I suppose times like this create a certain amount of fear within the populace; they don't know what changes are about to take place, or how those changes will affect them personally. Everyone; commoners, clergy, and of course nobility is anxiously awaiting the arrival of my brother Anjou to fill the vacant seat on the throne, but there always seems to be one imped-iment or another to prevent it. He was sent off to be king of Poland only a few months ago, but now he's behaving as if he's lived there all his life and is deeply inconvenienced at having to uproot himself. He writes Mother of delay after delay having to do with a wardrobe of clothing being unfinished, or a horse that was meant to be delivered, or the illness of some courtier who is invaluable to him. Lately, it's about the beauty of Italy, which he is passing through at a suspiciously leisurely pace.

This situation suits Mother quite well, as she is regent in his absence and can largely do as she wishes now. She has presided over a few battles, which is always amusing for her, but lately, she's decided to take the time to indulge her new passion - dance. She has devised a thing she's calling a "court ballet," inspired by a fashion she remembers in Italy. A line of women moves in synchronicity in a supposedly graceful fashion, although "graceful" is not the first adjective that leaps to mind when one watches these noblewomen flinging themselves awkwardly around the stage like injured pelicans. It is entertaining, but perhaps not on the level that Mother intended. She's having them perform before the public and tried to get me involved, but my feelings about the public have evolved somewhat since St. Bartholomew's Day; I prefer to watch from a safe distance. I will say, the crowd responded enthusiastically. (It helped to know there would be luncheon afterward.)

It was nice to have one's mind distracted from war and other hellish pursuits. It reminded me of my early dreams for Nérac; to host a salon where one could hear beautiful music, read poetry aloud, and listen to the fine minds of our time expatiate on the larger questions of life. But that was just a dream, very long ago.

15 October, 1582

Anjou has finally arrived, accompanied by an entourage of stylishly dressed and impeccably groomed young men whose extravagant manner seems to alienate certain members of the current court.

"They're all extremely aware of their appearance, aren't they?" was Cardinal Lenoncourt's dry comment upon witnessing their arrival. Others of our courtiers, realizing this was to be the new standard, immediately adapted to their mode of dress which involves towering wigs, high and starchy lace collars, and elevated heels on their shoes, as well as acquiring a new manner of behavior which involves a great deal of preening and high-pitched laughter. They're referring to themselves as Anjou's "*Mignons.*"

My mother was thrilled to see Anjou. "Precious Eyes!" She exclaimed, which is her nickname for him. He embraced her dramatically, always aware of the public effect of his actions, then said, "Mother, I'm starving. Those barbaric Poles have no idea how to eat."

Dinner that night was elaborate, plentiful, and seemingly endless, with much piercing laughter on the part of the courtiers. I had to smile at Cardinal Lenoncourt, who seemed utterly bewildered at what he realized was to be the new world order. For myself, I am more than happy to find myself at a court that has lost its masculine swagger, and so are some (though not all) of my ladies. How many evenings has one or another of them come sobbing into my apartments after one transgression or another? Many of these new courtiers seem quite nice, and infinitely more amusing. A number of Charles's more aggressively virile courtiers, however, have found reason to return to their castles or property on one pretext or another. All the better. Court feels much safer now, at least as far as the ladies are concerned.

On a darker note, Guise has come back to court. My stomach lurched when I saw him. Speculation has it he took his leave of court to vent his anger at his sudden diminishment of influence, but I'm guessing it was also to strategize with the rest of the powerful Guise clan. I don't for a moment think he left out a sense of guilt for what he did to me. Men like Guise are capable of horrendous acts followed by a four-course dinner.

Seeking an audience with the King, Guise immediately attempted to ingratiate himself, having gone so far as to acquire high-heeled shoes and a multi-story wig of his own. He looked like an idiot, and I am happy to report my brother appears to be onto his tactics. Anjou has a habit of staring blankly at a person as they blather on about themselves and their agenda, and then waving them away as if he hadn't heard a word, or suddenly declaring, "I need a fuck! Anyone?" The shock on Guise's face the first time he did this was gratifying both for myself and for Mother. It's one of the few times Mother and I have exchanged a look of affinity.

I ask myself how I am able to behave in my accustomed fashion after what Guise has done to me, but I am finding that I have more inner strength than I earlier suspected. I have not forgotten, far from it, and I may be powerless now, but I am biding my time. I watch Guise closely when he's not aware, to gauge where he is weakest. Someday, my moment will come.

Guise may find his influence considerably lessened, but it's not as though Mother can claim victory. If she had envisioned Anjou kneeling adoringly at her feet, she must be sorely disappointed. Anjou has grown away from Mother these past years in more ways than one. The only people he's trying to impress are his Mignons. Mother's going to have to work hard to reestablish whatever hold she had on him previously, and although Anjou may have unconventional tastes, he has proven himself to be ferocious on the field of battle, and has strong convictions of his own. Still, for Mother, he's an improvement over Charles, rest his tortured soul.

Anjou has brought back some interesting inventions from his time in Poland. He is requiring us all now to eat our meals with a new four-tined metal implement called a "fork," which is more useful than you might think. He, too, seems quite interested in the convention of more frequent bathing. To that end, he has ordered the installation of tubs in the castle, which will have separate taps for not only cold but hot water as well. It's a new era of modern conveniences, and why not? I have completely dispensed with the notion that bathing invites plague, as I have dispensed with a number of my earlier preconceptions about life, such as that people are intrinsically good.

The coronation is three months away. I can just imagine the spectacle Anjou has in store for us, because it is Anjou, with a few of his more creative courtiers, who has decided to orchestrate the event himself, right down to his peacock feathered coronation robes.

20 October 1582 ~ Paris

Anjou ~ or rather, the King summoned me to his chambers today. It is the first time, since our quick embrace at his arrival, that we have had the opportunity to speak directly to one another. He was magnificently attired in black velvet, his face framed by an enormous lace collar. From one ear dangled a large pearl drop earring. His coiffure was ornamented with a peacock and pearl brooch, and he wore long strands of pearls along with a bejeweled gold belt. He has set a new fashion for the wearing of a mustache and goatee, which all of his courtiers have quickly adopted. I must say, he looked very impressive. I had done my best to appear presentable but with considerably less enthusiasm.

"Margot," he said, looking me over critically, "I perceive that you are sad. You are still beautiful, but you carry around with you a cloud of darkness that is most unattractive. Are you aware of that?"

"Yes, your Majesty," I replied.

"Oh, for God's sake, it's just us. Remember when you used to call me Eddie as a child? It was adorable."

"You tried to drown me as a child."

"You see, this is what I mean, so gloomy. What are you still doing here at court?"

"What do you mean?"

"You're married now. You should be with your husband."

"Well yes, of course, but mother ~"

"Mother's lovely ~ well, not lovely, she's often horrible ~ but Mother's thinking can be quite parochial sometimes. She holds onto ideas sometimes long after their usefulness has expired. In Poland, I passed an edict for religious toleration and everyone was very pleased with it. I don't see why we shouldn't have the same thing here, do you?"

I looked at him, surprised. "No, uh, Eddie."

"To that end, I have invited the King of Navarre to my coronation. Will that brighten your lugubrious spirits?"

"Oh! Brother, I hardly know what to say!"

"I should think 'thank you' would be a nice start."

"Thank you! And ~ if I might ask, may I return with my husband to Nérac after the ceremony?"

"I don't see why not. Although it might be nice for him to stay here with us for a while afterward. Henri is so very handsome; my courtiers will adore him!"

I didn't know what to say to this, but thanked my brother again profusely and was about to take my leave when I had another thought.

"Your Majesty. Eddie. The man who rode with me from Florennes, Jean d'Aubiac, saved me from great peril. Without him, I'm very sure I would not have survived the experience. Would it be possible to knight him Chevalier?"

"Certainly! Who did he kill?"

"He didn't kill anyone."

"But he did battle?"

"No. But he guided me home, hunted for food so that we would not starve, and protected me from peril during the night. I have no sense of direction and to my shame cannot even build a fire. At one point we almost rode into a troop of Huguenots who would surely have taken me prisoner, but Jean d'Aubiac diverted us into the forest, and - "

Anjou cackled with laughter. "Margot. I cannot knight a man because he ran from the troops."

"That's not how it was."

"A man has to provide heroic service in battle to be knighted Chevalier."

"To me, it was heroic service. Why does it have to be battle?"

"It just does. But he will be recompensed. I'll see to it that he receives a bit of gold."

"Thank you, brother."

I took my leave, knowing I should have felt nothing but elation, but it bothered me. A bit of gold, for my life. Jean d'Aubiac deserved far greater thanks than that. I decided I had been avoiding the moment for too long. After some thought and preparation, I went outside to the castle stables, where I found Jean d'Aubiac. His face brightened to see me, but he also appeared flustered.

"Your Majesty, I was not informed. Was I meant to prepare the horses for a ride?"

"No, Monsieur. I have just come to thank you. You saved my life, and I have not properly acknowledged it."

"Your Majesty, that is not necess ~" He stopped, as I had put my finger to his lips. I then produced a scroll and read it to him.

"This is to acknowledge meritorious service above and beyond the command of office, by decree of Her Majesty Marguerite, Queen of Navarre. Monsieur d'Aubiac, would you kindly kneel?" Raising his eyebrows questioningly, Jean d'Aubiac knelt, whereupon I revealed one of our new eating implements and doffed him on both shoulders with it.

"I hereby pronounce you Chevalier d'Aubiac, the first Knight of the Secret Realm of Valois. Arise, Chevalier!"

Jean d'Aubiac arose, flushing with pride and amusement. He took the implement out of my hand and examined it appreciatively.

"What is this?"

"It's called a fork. It's meant for eating food. The King brought them back from Poland."

"Very finely wrought."

"It is yours. I'm sorry I don't have a sword."

"I quite prefer this fork. I will treasure it always." We regarded one another for a length of time, neither of us sure what to say next. It was intensely enjoyable, which caused me a sudden sensation of guilt. As a result, I laughed nervously, which broke the spell, and I instantly regretted it. Then I compounded my error by saying, "The King of Navarre is coming for the coronation, after which we are finally going to make our way home to Nérac." Perhaps I said it to observe his reaction; I don't know why I said it. We could have continued gazing at one another all afternoon and it would have been a day well spent.

"Indeed, Your Majesty. I wish you much happiness," was his only reply. He appeared to be mastering his features.

"I was thinking you could lead our procession to Navarre and join the household there. If you'd like, I'll petition the King to release you from service here."

Jean d'Aubiac winced slightly. It was as if I had taken the fork and stabbed him with it.

"I serve at Your Majesty's pleasure. It is not for me to express a preference, but the Queen your mother has told me she will require my presence to lead her party to Normandie after the coronation."

"I see," I said, wishing desperately that we could go back to the previous moment. "My mother of course takes precedence. But please know how very welcome you are in Nérac. You are ~ you are an excellent man in all ways."

I retreated awkwardly, feeling enormously stupid, and returned to my apartments so that I could pace the floor cursing myself for a while. Then I sat down to write to Henri of the good news about being invited to the coronation. I arranged the paper on my writing desk, filled my quill with ink...

Yet I haven't written to him. I'm writing this instead, which is curious. The problem is, it's been so long since Henri and I have had any meaningful correspondence, I'm not sure exactly what tone to take. I can't write him with the breathless enthusiasm of the new bride; so much has happened,

I'm guessing to both of us. I have heard much of his heroism in battles across the country and it's marvelous that he seems never to have been seriously wounded, but why does he never write? I never did learn whether he was in Flanders when I was. I'm hoping he was not, because I don't want to harbor resentment against him for leaving me to fend for myself. I would so like to just pick up where we left off. Is that possible? I will attempt a letter that causes him to understand my joy that he is being invited to the coronation and my hope that our life together can now continue unhindered. That should be easy enough to accomplish... yet my mind drifts to other things...

I wish I had just knighted him with the fork and taken my leave.

10 November 1582 - Paris

Henri has written me back.

Henri, by the grace of God King of Navarre, to his beloved wife Marguerite, by the grace of God Queen of Navarre, greetings and affection.

It is with the greatest pleasure that I learn of the softening of sentiments on the part of the Crown toward not only myself but my Huguenot brethren, and have most willingly and in good faith accepted the invitation to attend the coronation of your brother who shall be Henri III. The months since our marriage have been long ones in which I have thought of you without cease, anxious for you to join me in Nérac, site of so many happy memories for us both.

I trust the intermittent time has not been too trying for you, and that our lives together may now begin in earnest. It is also my fondest wish to produce many children with you to further burnish the reputation of the House of Navarre. I trust that you are in fine health.

Sincere affection. Etc.

I have read this letter many times, and each time I read it I see something new and feel something different.

The first time I read it I scanned it hastily, looking for the keywords that would exemplify his feelings. I saw "pleasure," "most willingly," "thought of you without cease," and "fondest wish," and breathed a sigh of relief. Then I read the letter more carefully and was struck by the formality of it. Not one word of endearment, other than that which is required. I suddenly wondered if he had dictated it to someone else, and indeed when I went to retrieve his previous letters, this one is in another's hand. That is fine, of course. He is a king, he is busy, and it wasn't a love letter, it was a letter of confirmation. Then I asked myself, why wasn't it a love letter? We are to be reunited, doesn't that call for a love letter? On the other hand, I did not write a love letter to him, so perhaps he did not think one to me was required. (I did, however, write my letter with my own hand, which should count for something.) I deliberated over every word of my letter carefully; this letter did not sound as if Henri deliberated over it at all, it sounded as if he dictated it in between orders to his tailor and his squire. Did he really think of me without cease? It seems to me he spent a lot of time killing people, I hope he wasn't thinking of me during that activity.

It occurred to me I was being too judgmental, so I read the letter again. "Nérac, site of so many happy memories for us both," that part was certainly true. Now I came to the line that I had skipped over several times, trying not to think about. "It is my fondest wish to produce many children with you."

I know this is required of me. Of course, it is. When two houses join together, it is the children that cement the union and make the house strong. But "many children?" Is that really necessary? My mother had ten children, but only seven lived and look how most of them turned out. Is it not possible to have one perfect child, and then be done with it? A male child, of course, Salic law being what it is, although I would much prefer a little girl. Then again, if Mother had had only one son, we'd have been banished from court many years ago. But still...I dwelled on this for a while, then concluded that I should think of it simply as something one says as a matter of course. "I wish to have many children with you," as blameless a phrase as "I hope we have many years of happiness." Would I respond, "Is it really necessary to have many happy years?" No. Of course not.

Reading again, my gaze lighted on "I trust the intermittent time has not been too trying for you." If only he knew. He would never touch me again. He hates Guise, who is responsible for the deaths of Coligny and so many of his kinsmen. If he thought anyone else had touched me it would be calamitous, but Henri of Guise... He must never know. I have a strong box for these papers now. No one must ever know...

I felt my heart racing. No. I was going to a dark place again. I closed my eyes, summoning my muse of lightness, she who can keep me from dark oppressive thoughts. After a time, I opened them again and felt better. It is good enough to know that Henri is eager to rejoin me and resume our marriage. That is good enough.

7 December, 1582 - Paris

Henri is here, at long last. He looks older and bears a number of scars on his body, but he is still very handsome. My ladies think the scars have rendered him more handsome, but I don't know about that.

We received one another with all due ceremony, then retired to our chambers and immediately had sexual congress. I believe it was successful for Henri, he went straight to sleep afterward, and hours later arose declaring himself much satisfied. Then he asked me to give him all the news at court so that he could better understand its current inner workings. I'm afraid I wasn't very useful in this regard. Though the King sees the idea of my reuniting with Henri as something of an appeasement for the Huguenots, he clearly doesn't feel comfortable sharing his thoughts about war at the dinner table. As ever, I am uninformed and distrusted by both parties.

Henri and I have not yet managed to recover the playful ease we had with one another following our wedding. I have employed my happy laugh numerous times, and my amused laugh, but even to my hearing it rings hollow. As for Henri, he, too, seems preoccupied with other thoughts. I believe we both wish to find a mutual accord, but it is as if we are extending our hands toward one another from a great distance. I pray that distance will begin to close.

11.

"And he used to say that sleep and sexual intercourse, more than anything else, made him conscious that he was mortal, implying that both weariness and pleasure arise from one and the same natural weakness."

— **Plutarch** on Moralia

1583

13 January, 1583 - Paris

Mother has procured a bride for Anjou. She is Louise de Vaudémont, a princess of the house of Lorraine. She is quite small with enormous eyes like a child, and looks utterly terrified, as if they pulled her in off the street for a public execution. I wonder if she and Anjou have even properly met yet. They are to be married at the same time as the coronation; it's always good when you can get two major events out of the way at the same time, especially since we all had to endure Charles's funeral so recently.

I can tell that Henri is uneasy about being at court. I suppose he's wondering if they have plans to hold him prisoner again. To my knowledge, they do not, but I completely understand his trepidation. He startles at the slightest disturbance, and will never allow himself to have his back toward an entranceway. I sympathize, as I am suffering from a jumpiness of my own, particularly when Henri and I are near the object of my hatred, Guise. I may be imagining it, but he always seems to be looking at us with a gloating look on his face. Is he reveling in the fact that he has "had" his enemy's wife and his enemy doesn't know it? Even the limited conversation Henri has had with Guise seems charged with Guise's smug self-satisfaction. He sidled up to us at the ball that was held the other night.

"Your Majesty, how good to have you with us. Your reconciliation with the crown means the world to us."

"I would call this more of a detente."

"Of course. For your queen, however, it must provide great ease of mind. She's been so very active in your absence! Now she can relax and enjoy the benefits of being queen of her domain. When do you travel to Nérac?"

"Immediately after the wedding."

"Navarre's gain will be our loss. Your queen is much loved around this castle. Much loved." At this point, Guise looked at me meaningfully, and I honestly thought I might start to scream.

But I didn't, of course. I'm a queen. All of my screams take place inwardly.

13 February, 1583 - Paris

The coronation was a magnificent affair. My brother, in full peacock regalia, entered Reims Cathedral to much singing to be met by the archbishop. A prayer was said, and then a few more hymns were sung. The Abbot entered, accompanied by four monks bearing a silk canopy over his person. The Abbot had the Sainte Ampoule hanging from a chain around his neck, and he and the monks proceeded to the altar where the archbishop was waiting, and there followed a great deal of inexplicable but reverent bowing. Then Anjou spoke the coronation oath in the new lilting voice he has acquired, and the Recognition took place followed by the singing of the "Te Deum." Then I think they had yet another prayer, after which the buskins and spurs were placed upon Anjou's feet and he was girded with the Coronation Sword. You could tell he quite liked this look. Then there was more prayer, by which point I was restlessly thinking of ways I could describe this in writing without provoking great boredom.

After that, it became more entertaining. Anjou removed his coat and other outerwear, and the special silver latchets on his silk shirt were opened to expose his chest, upper back, and the joints of his arms. I noticed the courtiers all exchanging appreciative glances during this bit. The archbishop took the Sainte Ampoule from the abbot, and with a small golden stylus he removed a particle from the contents and mixed it up with something I couldn't see to make an ointment. He then applied the ointment in the form of a cross on the top of Anjou's head, on his naked breast, between his shoulders, and on the joints of both arms, each time saying: "I anoint thee King with holy oil in the name of the Father, and of the Son, and the Holy Spirit." The Mignons leaned in to appreciate every nuance of this vaguely carnal ministration.

During the ceremony, I spotted the Countess and Count de Lalaing in an aisle near me. I caught Adrienne's eye and she smiled at me warmly, nodding approvingly at seeing Henri standing next to me. I smiled back, hoping to convey the conviction that I was now fully well and restored to a happy situation. As, of course, I am.

20 February, 1583 - *En route*

At long last, we are on our way to Nérac. The minute we left the castle, Henri seemed to recover his zeal for life, indeed he finds it necessary to ravish me in my litter at least once a day, often more. I keep telling myself that I am delighted to accommodate him, as it seems to engender bursts of good feeling within him, and when Henri is in good spirits, he is the most charming of men. Additionally, I am very glad to finally be free from my mother's influence, the dictates of court, and the cold, cold castle even though the current weather seems even colder with a bone-freezing wind, and the scenery so gray and sere. But what matter, when one is finally with one's rightful husband? Such joy.

Despite all this joy, I find myself mostly sleeping between the plentiful furs that have been provided me. I have missed many meals, and I have slept a great deal. But of course, I am joyful. This is what I always wanted. I am going back to Nérac with my husband, as I have dreamed.

Anyone would be so happy.

28 February, 1583 – Nérac

We have arrived at the chateau in Nérac. I shouldn't have been surprised, but somehow was, to see it looking very different in the dead of winter than it did that magical blooming spring two years ago. Of course, that is true of any place with changing seasons, so there's no reason to be anxious about that.

Henri was excited to be home and showed me all around as if I'd never been here before, which feels almost true. The first thing I wondered was who is in charge of the housekeeping; the place is not clean. Henri lined up his household staff to receive me, and I must say I have experienced warmer welcomes in my time. I understand there is distrust, that these people are undoubtedly worn down by war, and that having a Catholic queen to serve at this very moment in time is not a prescription for their well-being, but they don't seem very good at masking their emotions (and it goes without saying they don't know how to manage the affairs of a castle.)

It is hard to ignore the fact that the atmosphere is much different from that beautiful time two springs ago, with ladies Rosalind, Maria, and Agatha making everything so entertaining. Agatha – my heart still aches about her. Rosalind and the Duke of Biron are to be married, so she is naturally much occupied with those preparations. Maria and Françoise disappeared mysteriously from court a week ago, with no word as to where they have gone. I did overhear them expressing fears about being away from the Catholic state but surely, they would have told me if they wished not to accompany us. I miss also the Countess de Lalaing, who has returned to Mons; Madame de Tournon, who never recovered from her daughter's death and lost many of her mental faculties; and Madame de Brezé, who was not well enough to travel.

Henri has provided me with a new maid *de chambre*, Fosseuse, who is extremely young, quiet, and intimidated by me. He has also ordered the construction of a chapel in the Parc de la Garenne for me and my courtiers to worship privately. This was part of the arrangement with the crown for my release, and I am grateful for it. The chapel will be small, very small; I'm sure the Cardinal feels the indignity of how small it is going to be. But he will be allowed to conduct Mass for our small party, which will introduce a note of normalcy into our lives.

It's bewildering to me that, even with Anjou's new declaration of tolerance, there are still so many wars raging. I had thought Anjou's new policy of tolerance coupled with my presence here in Nérac would signal a new era. Far from it; it seems Henri's men are rushing off to battle someone at this very moment, I don't even know who. It's quite disheartening.

I'm here, however. I'm finally here. I will count my blessings.

But first, I must sleep.

March 1583 - Nérac

I have not found time to write because

13 July, 1583 - Nérac

It has been four months since I have picked up a quill. I have not been well; I have been sick in body and spirit. But for reasons which I will here relate, I have come back to myself.

The first time I saw Nérac more than two years ago, we were barred from the castle because the men were training for war. How easy, when one is consumed with one's own agenda, to overlook a clear indication that one should go no further. My mother didn't care about their preoccupation with war; she grew up with it. My ladies took it as an amusing challenge. Even my friend M. Shakspere found it to be the grounds for a comedy, although he turned his characters into men of study, which makes much more sense. Men of war giving up their violent sport for the company of women? I think not. War is in most men's blood, as is brutality, and there is no way to make a comedy out of it.

My chapel was completed in March. I liked to go to it for prayerful meditation, even when there was not a Mass. I have been deeply troubled in spirit by the events of my life thus far, but I find great relief in my little altar.

After a few weeks, I began to notice a clutch of townspeople standing at a respectful distance during the Mass, and realized they were Catholics who had been denied their own opportunity to worship. I gestured for them to come closer. With hesitation, a few of them did, then some others until we had about twenty people, most of them too timid to come in but hovering outside the door to pray along with us. It was gratifying to be able to provide these people I didn't know a place to pray to our God. Singing, of course, could not take place, and even prayer was spoken in low voices, but the sense of community was novel and welcome.

Someone spotted our new congregants, however, and that person went to apprise my husband's secretary, a loathsome little man named Le Pin. The following week we had a slightly larger number of worshippers, which filled me with delight. We were on our knees in joyful prayer when, all of a sudden, we were descended upon by the King's guards.

"Infidels!" they shouted and, right in front of me and the Cardinal, proceeded to beat my worshippers brutally, even the children! We begged them to stop, but they would not. Instead, they dragged the unfortunates off to prison, whence I'm told they would not be released until they paid an exorbitant fine. Cardinal Lenoncourt was so upset that he became ill, and took to his bed.

Horrified, I demanded to know who was behind this unconscionable act. Learning that it was this Le Pin, I went to Henri and demanded, in front of the weasel-faced coward, that he be dismissed.

"These are innocent people! They do not deserve to be punished for coming to my chapel to hear Mass. I welcomed them!" To my astonishment, it was Le Pin who replied.

"Your Majesty, this is not something that the King should be troubled with. What was done was right and proper. You should be satisfied with being permitted to have Mass said to you and your servants."

I was speechless. Henri saw that this was a deeply offensive and inappropriate response, and he ordered the man from the room. Chagrined, Le Pin retreated.

"I'm sorry, Marguerite. Le Pin is not accustomed to having a queen to answer to. He becomes very zealous on matters of religion, but he's a good man."

"He must be dismissed."

"I will censure him severely."

"My mother would have had him killed."

"We are not, fortunately, in Paris."

"Henri, if you do not have him dismissed, I will write to my mother and Charles about this unthinkable offense. I will tell them about the innocent Catholics so brutally beaten and lying in your dungeon at this very moment. I do not think they will take kindly to this information. On the contrary; I predict you will find a thousand troops at your door."

I had never spoken to my husband in this manner, and he was greatly surprised. Realizing the untenable nature of his position and with great reluctance on his part, he dismissed Le Pin and ordered the prisoners released. That was in March. From that moment forward, Henri's attitude toward me changed; he became distant and abrupt and came less often to my bed. The incident, however distressing, had a beneficial effect on me, however. It was on that day that I awoke from the mental slumber of the last months and found my voice. I am able to see my surroundings now, and what I have seen is not good.

This chateau is not my home. It is not even Henri's home. It is Jeanne d'Albret's home. It resonates with her stoicism, inflexibility, and her rigid adherence to dogma. There is no joy, no music, no poetry. There is only religion, war, and sex.

As to sex: Henri is not faithful to me and makes no pretense about it. His passion for one young woman or another is always on plain display, and I am meant to ignore it. In a way, it is a relief. He has a vast appetite, and my body is simply not able to accommodate his constant needs. These women who do the job for me have only my compassion, although I will admit to some jealousy when he dotes on one of them too extravagantly. There was a Mademoiselle de Rebours who fit that category for a while, also a Mademoiselle de Dayelle, but soon each passion dies out and is replaced by another. He is in love with someone else now, I'm not sure who, but I recognize the symptoms. Henri does still visit my bed occasionally, as he is fixed on the idea of our having many children. But it is perfunctory work, and then he is off to the next liaison. His targets are most often women of low birth, I suppose to inflict less offense upon me. Henri is nothing if not considerate.

For myself, I have had enough of this stifling Calvinist atmosphere. The episode with the chapel has caused me to understand that I have some leverage within this household, earned both by our recent confrontation and perhaps by my indulgent response toward Henri's infidelities. I shall now set out to alter the ambiance of the chateau. I am determined that this shall be a place of beauty and enlightenment. We shall have magnificent balls, poetry readings, and dramatic performances. We will invite and listen to the thoughts of the great thinkers of our time, and there will be joy and a celebration of life. Nérac will be a shining beacon for art and intellectual discourse and in the course of these activities, people will begin to see and understand one another better, which will lead to an era of peace and tolerance. That was my dream so long ago, a dream that I relinquished for a number of reasons. I now intend to revive that dream.

15 October, 1583 - Nérac

The mildness of the weather in this part of the country has allowed us to have outdoor staged events well into autumn. I have made it known that, within this chateau, there will be no discussion of politics or religion; Huguenots and Catholics shall mingle freely and direct their conversation on a higher level. Henri was resistant to the idea at first but has soon come to see the benefits, as there are often a good number of attractive Catholic ladies at my events. In addition, I believe his health has been sapped somewhat by constant war, so he is happy to relinquish the conduct of the chateau to me. It has been given a thorough cleaning.

On Sundays, Henri and his sister Catherine (whose name doesn't suit her, she giggles rather more than I find bearable) go with their retinue on one side of the castle to hear the preaching of their very dull religion, whilst my party goes to the chapel in the woods to hear Mass. Then, we all meet together and have a promenade along the river in the park, which I have caused to be planted with beautiful cypress trees at a length of three thousand feet. It is a pleasant walk, filled with gay conversation on every topic except religion and war. In the afternoon, there is generally a ball, followed by a performance of some sort. Catherine is an enthusiastic advocate of dance, and usually organizes a recital for the evening. We also have a theatrical piece. but not, unfortunately, "The Work of Love is Lost" because that work of love is, in fact, lost. Its translator, Madame de Brezé, died of her illness, and in his grief, her husband either lost or destroyed the manuscript. It's unfortunate, I was looking forward to learning how the play ends. I can only hope M. Shakspere gets an opportunity to have it play in England.

Although battles continue to take place throughout France between the Catholics and the Huguenots, Nérac has become acknowledged not only as a delightful destination for lighthearted entertainment and edification of the spirit but as a neutral zone where war is temporarily forgotten. I'm quite proud to have carved out an oasis of this nature. I feel as if I have made a contribution to civic discourse. It is true that I no longer have the undivided love of my husband, which I suppose makes me sad. I do, however, enjoy the attentions of many gallant courtiers, which lulls me into thinking I am loved. Thinking you are loved is almost the same thing as being loved, is it not? Many women have gone to their graves with less.

30 November, 1583 – Nérac

It is odd how something can be right in front of your face, yet you don't see it. Perhaps I did see it, and didn't want to. At any rate, it probably comes as no surprise to anyone else residing in the chateau that my maid *de chambre*, Fosseuse, is with child. When I finally noticed and spoke to her of her condition, she broke down in tears and refused to tell me the name of the father. Then she revised her story and said it was a gallant soldier who had died in battle, whose name she did not wish to reveal. Of course, I know full well who it is. I'm fairly sure Fosseuse was assigned to me by Henri as a reward for receiving his attentions. I find it hard to hate Fosseuse, as she seems to be barely more than a child herself. She is also meek as a mouse and somewhat dull. Though she is flattered and thrilled by Henri's attentions, she has the good sense to behave at all times respectfully with me. She is doggedly sticking to her story of the heroic soldier, but court gossip has already grasped the situation fully. I dare not speak to Henri about this; he will only deny all. In a way, it's rather amazing there are not more pregnant women wandering around the chateau. I do feel sorry for this one, though. She seems so lost.

It's odd that I should feel so little regarding this incident. There was a time when news of this sort would have devastated me. Am I becoming hard, losing the ability to feel things? I look at Henri now, and all I feel is pity for a man who is such a slave to his bodily urges, who thinks of only two things; proving himself on the field of battle and conquering women. He's beginning to take on the semblance of a willful child in my eyes, and children don't interest me.

It is distressing to me, however, that I have been here these months and never guessed that Henri and Fosseuse were lovers. I thought by now I'd be more perceptive about things like that. What else am I blind about? It frightens me that I don't know.

15 December 1583 - Nérac

Mother has come to court. She made the journey ostensibly to nego-tiate another one of these tentative and so easily broken truces between the crown and the Huguenots, but also to spend Christmas, thus asserting her Catholic domination over the celebration of our Savior's birth. I'm sure it will all be terribly awkward.

At the first available moment, she pulled me aside and demanded, "Marguerite, why are you not with child?"

I have acquired her art of masking my features, so I responded calmly. "Alas, Mother, God has not yet seen fit to reward me with such happiness."

"Don't prevaricate, *mademoiselle*. You have been here almost a year. Rumors have reached the court, and I think you know about whom. Are you going to let this person rob you of your entitlement?"

"No one is robbing me of anything, Mother. Henri will never acknowl-edge those rumors, and neither will the person in question."

"Are you and your husband having relations?"

"Of course."

"And there has been no result? Not even a late menses?"

"No, Mother."

"It may be that your anatomy is ill-constructed, it is a trait that some-times occurs in this family. I will give you instruction on how to bear your body during the conjugal act."

"I already know about that. I met your friend Madame Chauderon at Spa."

Mother looked stunned. She stammered, "Juliet – Mme. Chauderon is still alive?"

"If she's not, I spoke to a very convincing spirit." Mother's eyes wid-ened in what almost seemed like fear. Did she not realize I was jesting? "She claimed you and she once shared accommodations at a convent. She seems to think you were a charming songbird."

To my astonishment, the quickest flutter of a shy smile came to my mother's lips. I believe it did, anyway. It appeared and vanished in such quick succession I could scarcely believe what I saw.

"And – and she spoke to you of these matters. Did you follow her directions?"

"Not yet."

"Why ever not?"

"I suppose it did not occur to me until this moment that I might share your anatomy in that regard."

"What did she look like?"

"I don't know. Your age." From the look on Mother's face, I saw that this was not enough. "Wild graying hair, as if it had a life of its own. Overly large eyes."

My mother nodded, absorbing the information deeply. "Yes, that is she."

She turned away and walked to the window as if she were suddenly alone. I was fascinated by the strange mood that was in the air and dared not break it. A moment passed. But then she abruptly collected herself and turned back to me, a suspicious look in her eye. "Did she speak to you of any other of her remedies?"

Of course, I knew what she meant. I returned her gaze as blankly as I could. "Other remedies? Do you mean for the relief of arm pain? No, the waters eased those symptoms remarkably. Thank you for asking." My mother and I shared an extended locking of the eyes, a gambit that I am happy to relate I won. Mother turned away in disgust.

"Marguerite, you are a clever girl but you thwart me at every turn, when all I've ever tried to do is look out for your welfare. I don't think you realize how much I've done for you."

I felt suddenly guilty because actually I do realize; I just prefer not to think about the body count.

I have often wished that my mother were an affectionate person, with compassion in her heart for others. I wish she were still that gay songbird, if indeed that remarkable story is true. But if she were, it's very possible I would not be alive to relate this story.

Mother did not have a happy childhood. Her parents died the month after she was born, and she was passed around from relative to relative and sent to a series of convents as the Medici wealth and prestige waxed and waned. If her great uncle, Pope Clement VII, hadn't orchestrated her marriage to my father, God knows what would have happened to her. There are people who have wanted her dead all her life. I don't believe anyone ever loved her. My father was passionately in love with his mistress, Diane de Poitiers, for many years; it was Diane who rode by his side in processions, while Mother suffered the indignity of trailing behind like a servant. In my more trying times with Mother, I try to remind myself of these things.

To assuage my guilt, I spent the rest of the afternoon demonstrating great interest in Mother's work in the negotiations with the Huguenots, and that evening we had a ballet performance that brightened her spirits.

After that event, weary of the company of others and, I will admit, dispirited by this whole Fosseuse situation, I took a walk on the grounds outside the chateau. The River Baîse runs right beside the chateau, and it is a great delight to watch the lights of the town reflected in its dark waters. The night was black and moonless, the stars were crystalline in the sky. All was silent until I heard the snort of a horse. I turned and saw Jean d'Aubiac standing outside the stables, currying one of the horses. My breath caught, and my feet brought me toward him before I knew I had told them to. I wanted to confirm that I was not imagining him.

"Monsieur d'Aubiac." He looked up from his work, and his hand arrested in mid-curry. He straightened immediately and smiled.

"Your Majesty."

"I did not realize you were conducting my mother here. I am happy to see you."

"The greater happiness is mine, Your Majesty."

"Would you ~ would you mind very much not calling me Your Majesty? I feel as though we have been through so much together, we should be friends."

"What would you like me to call you?"

"My name is Marguerite."

"I ~ I don't know how I could possibly ~"

"Just once. Just now. Could you just... try it out?"

"Very well...." He took a breath. "Marguerite." It sounded so beautiful to my ears, and just the way I had heard it in my reveries.

"Are you quite well, Monsieur d'Aubiac?"

"Ah, surely now that we are familiar you must call me Jean," he replied.

"Are you well, Jean?"

He smiled. "I am very well at the moment."

"I am glad. Did my mother say how long she intends to stay?"

"She said until these negotiations are complete."

"I see... I was thinking of taking a walk along the canal. Would you like to join me?"

"I would, but I must finish with this horse."

"I'll help you."

He grinned at this, and allowed me to help in my inept way. We closed up the stable and proceeded to walk side by side along the river, neither of us saying a word. I could tell Jean was feeling enormously ill at ease, and I felt bad about that, but the joy of having him by my side outweighed all other considerations. To set him more at ease I asked after the journey here. He told me it was fairly easy except that one of his horses threw a shoe.

I coaxed him into describing for me in detail the process of replacing a shoe on a horse (there are more steps to the process than you would imagine) and by the time he had ended that narration, he was much more relaxed. Our shoulders touched now and again as we walked, or rather my shoulder did against his upper arm, and I had the sudden mad thought that he might take my hand, but he didn't. I told him the story of one of the comedies that was recently presented, and he laughed. He has a wonderful deep laugh that fills me with a sense of well-being. I remembered the way he laughed when I practiced my manly swagger in the woods, and I was thrilled to hear it again.

We got to an impasse where we would have had either to climb an embankment or turn around, and we stood there indecisively for a moment. He turned to me, and impulsively I put my hand to his face. I saw his expression soften, and his face moved toward me. I felt sure he was going to kiss me. The moment was so perfect for him to do so. But he didn't.

"Marguerite," he said softly.

"It's all right," I whispered. "I want you to."

"I can't," he said.

"Because of the difference in our states? I don't care about titles, I have never met a man like you, Jean. If it's the fact that I'm queen ~"

"No. It's the fact that you are married."

For a moment I had an impulse to laugh.

My empty marriage is not unique in our circles; in fact, it is the unusual marriage that is not designed strictly for the purpose of cementing two houses together. As a result, infidelities are the rule of the day at court, and though my husband perhaps takes his infidelities to a new and remarkable level, one's married status seldom, if ever, stands in the way of one doing what one pleases, as long as one is discreet. I wondered at Jean d'Aubiac's scruples; where did they spring from? He as much as told me he is not religious. Is he worried for my welfare? It's true that there are laws against adultery which are generally only enforced against women, who often have their noses or ears cut off. I have never heard, however, of a queen having her nose cut off - how inconvenient for the portrait painters! It is true that at the Castle Puymartin, not far from here, a Therese de Saint-Clar was imprisoned by her husband after he discovered her in the arms of another man, and she stayed up in that tower until her death fifteen years later. But I would never put up with that kind of treatment, and feel quite sure I would find a clever way to escape. Jean's face told me he was deadly serious, and so I became serious, too, to honor his feelings.

"I understand," I said.

We turned and walked back along the canal, a million emotions pin-wheeling throughout my body. But my only thought was, I love this man.

26 December 1583 - Nérac

I am trying to delay Jean's departure as much as possible. Every time Mother thinks she and the Huguenot tribunal have reached an agreement, I say something to Henri like, "Is it fair for Biron to surrender Guienne, when he gets so little in return?" Thus, they find themselves back at the table. But there were only so many objections I could make before Henri started to regard me with an odd expression. I have ceased trying to complicate matters, and am very worried a new peace will be announced soon.

Jean and I go riding or walking as often as possible. I pray God will not judge me harshly, but I have succeeded in getting him to kiss me. It *was wonderful! His lips* were warm and searching, and tasted like roasted chestnuts – is that strange? That's the comparison that sprung to mind. Fortunately, I love roasted chestnuts. He was racked with guilt afterward, but I felt as if my heart would fly from my body, and the fact that he felt so guilty made me love him all the more. I have tried all my life to be so good, but less and less does that seem like a fruitful use of my time. When I am in Jean's gentle arms, I am happier than I have ever been in my life.

Alençon has arrived at Nérac. He's here to complain to Mother that her promise to allow him to take Flanders has not resulted in a provision of troops. Mother had initially thought it was a good idea, but she met with some unexpected resistance from Anjou, who continues to be less pliable a king than she had hoped. "Exasperating" is a word I hear her utter frequently regarding him.

Alençon has always been able to read me well, and though I try to guard my emotions he is a keen enough observer to detect a change in me. He cornered me the other day in a hallway.

"Who is it, dear Margot? Brother wants to know."

"I'm not sure to what you refer."

"I refer to the bloom in your cheeks, the spring in your gait, the unexpected laugh that emits from you in moments that are not particularly hilarious. Who is the suitor? Is it Montmorency? Bussi? LeCocq?"

"You are imagining things, brother," I retorted, and bolted from the room in a very guilty fashion. Because the fact is I can't hide it, it's as if my life has suddenly gained color and definition. I can see the world around me more clearly, as if before this I had been holding a distorted piece of glass before my eyes. I live for the moment when I can be with Jean again. We have not had sexual congress; for Jean that is a line he will not cross. But I don't care; in my life, the act of sex has only been something to be endured. Nothing can compare with the simple act of holding Jean's hand. These intense feelings bursting forth from me render it impossible to return to the pallidly dissatisfied creature I was before. I am amazed that the entire court doesn't note the change in me, but they don't. Not even Henri notices any alteration. It's extraordinary that one can be a changed woman and no one notices.

31 December 1583 - Nérac

It had to happen eventually; Jean has taken his leave, along with Mother and her retinue. I ache with loneliness for him, it feels impossible that our bodies should be wrenched apart. Each moment that we spent together was so precious that I was tortuously aware of the fleeting nature of the experience at the same time as I was relishing it. His arms, his chest... All of him.

When Mother and the Huguenots finally came to terms (whatever those terms are; at this point, I don't care) my heart sank, knowing our time together was coming to an end. Mother stayed just long enough to ruin the nativity feast for everyone, and today they have gone. Jean and I did get the opportunity to say goodbye. As soon as the terms were settled, I ran down to the stables and threw myself into his arms, crying.

"Ah, my little girl," he said. He calls me his little girl, and I adore it. "Don't cry. This is not the end; it is just an intermission."

He wiped my tears, and I made an effort to smile, wanting to believe that. We stood outside for a while after I had calmed down, discussing the options, and we were about six feet apart, I think. I'm trying to remember exactly how far apart we were. We weren't touching in any way, I'm sure of that. I'm trying to remember exactly, because suddenly Mother came out onto the balcony. I believe I flinched. I may have taken a few steps back, but then I quickly rallied and said loudly,

"My mother the Queen will be leaving soon, Monsieur D'Aubiac, so make all necessary preparations for your departure," at which Jean, sensing the situation, replied, "Yes, Your Majesty," and immediately retreated into the stables. I then made as if to go into the chateau, and stopped upon "seeing" her.

"Oh hello, Mother. I was just speaking with the stable master about your coming departure."

"So I see," was her unreadable reply. "Eager to rid yourself of me?"

"Mother," I said in a wounded tone. "I'm merely trying to be helpful."

"Normally not one of your more salient characteristics," said Mother. "Then again, it is Christmas." She went back inside. I was terrified that she suspected something, but when I went back in, she behaved in her accustomed fashion; none of her piercing looks and no more accusations about my childless state.

Alençon departed with her. Mother's Christmas gift to him is a promise to lobby the King on his behalf for the taking of Flanders; he's going with her to make sure that she follows through. He was very excited about the prospect; he feels that this will somehow cause everyone to forget his failed efforts elsewhere. Despite his attempts to keep the flame alive with letters of love to Queen Elizabeth (for whom he had a deep affection despite the difference in their ages,) efforts to create an alliance there have failed due to resistance within her government. Alençon says Elizabeth is most dismayed by this; he displayed to me a poem the Queen wrote to him. The paper was tear-stained, whether from the Queen's tears or his own, I didn't dare ask, but he allowed me to copy it.

> I grieve and dare not show my discontent,
>
> I love and yet am forced to seem to hate,
>
> I do, yet dare not say I ever meant,
>
> I seem stark mute but inwardly do prate.
>
> I am and not, I freeze and yet am burned,
>
> Since from myself another self I turned.
>
> My care is like my shadow in the sun,
>
> Follows me flying, flies when I pursue it,
>
> Stands and lies by me, doth what I have done.
>
> His too familiar care doth make me rue it.
>
> No means I find to rid him from my breast,
>
> Till by the end of things it be supprest.

Some gentler passion slides into my mind,

For I am soft and made of melting snow;

Or be more cruel, love, and so be kind.

Let me or float or sink, be high or low.

Or let me live with some more sweet content,

Or die and so forget what love ere meant.

I found myself getting terribly emotional as I read this, and could not restrain my tears. Alençon thought it was compassion for him and was touched by my sisterly loyalty. He's off now, eagerly looking forward to his glorious Flemish reception. They've all gone. The castle has never felt so cold.

1584

February, 1584 - Nérac

Fosseuse is very near her term, and I am concerned for her. She has been querulous and unhappy lately, undoubtedly because my husband is not doting on her as once he did. Yet despite her condition being an open secret in court and many whispers and jokes being made about it, she continues to insist that the father belongs to an unnamed war hero. I spoke to Henri about the situation, without actually accusing him. He feigned ignorance and changed the subject. Fosseuse is a small woman with a narrow pelvis, and I know enough about childbirth to know that it is not a propitious condition for delivery.

I approached her a few weeks ago. "Françoise," I pleaded." Her full name is Françoise de Montmorency-Fosseux. "Tell me the truth about your condition, and I will do everything possible to make your situation easier. There is an influenza going around court; it would be easy to use that as a pretext for leaving the chateau and going to Mas-d'Agenais, where the King has a house in a very private location. I would be happy to take you, and anyone else you wish. The King will announce that he's going hunting, and I swear I will see you through this delivery. Meanwhile, we will put a stop to all these scandalous rumors, which hurt you more than me."

To my surprise, Fosseuse became furious and screamed, "How dare you call me a liar? You're the one spreading these ugly rumors, I am innocent!" She flew from the room in a flood of tears and hasn't spoken to me since. I began to worry; why is she holding so firmly to this soldier story? Was I wrong about Fosseuse, or has Henri given her instructions of some kind? It seemed a given amongst all the courtiers that she is Henri's mistress, and indeed I have seen much evidence myself in the past, when Fosseuse was a carefree maiden with nothing to worry about but her own pretty appearance. But I shall drop the subject.

18 February, 1584 - Nérac

It was the middle of the night. Henri and I were asleep when the physician arrived at our door to announce that Fosseuse was in labor. Henri was embarrassed and angry. "Why do you tell me this?" He demanded. The physician replied that he had been instructed by Mlle de Montmorency-Fosseux to do so. He added that Fosseuse had a fever, and that it was a concern for the pregnancy.

"No concern of mine." Henri snapped, "Do what you usually do in these situations."

The physician left, but now Henri became agitated and started pacing the floor back and forth as if wrestling with himself. I feigned sleep but was actually wide awake, thinking how stupid men are. Finally, he came to my bedside and gently "woke me up."

"My dear, something has come to my attention that I think I should tell you about. This woman Fosseuse, I believe she may be with child on my account."

"Is that so?" I replied.

"Yes. I'm very sorry, and I hope we can speak no more about the subject. Would you please go to her and oversee the delivery, as you do with all our maids of honor?"

"Henri, I have offered to assist with her delivery. She took great offense."

"Yes, but if you don't go now, it will look very bad. You know how court gossip is."

"I do have some idea."

"Please, my dear. It's important to me," said Henri, and I suddenly realized he was in love with that placid, docile little creature. It also gave me a sudden window of understanding of why he was no longer enamored of me; I am not the wide-eyed guileless creature I was when we first met. I couldn't help but feel sorry for him, as he looked utterly miserable.

"Yes, of course I will go. It's almost morning. Why don't you go hunting? I don't think it will do for everyone to see you so anxious."

Vastly relieved, Henri kissed me with more fervor than he has in many months. I arose and left our bedchamber.

I found Fosseuse, who was flushed with fever and already weak with pain, and moved her into a more private chamber. I called the physician and enlisted the help of some of our more experienced women. It was a long, agonizing delivery, some thirty-six hours or more. I never saw anyone in more pain. She kept crying that she wanted to die and finally, finally she cried out,

"Henri! Henri, where are you?" I took her hand and told her that Henri was not there but that he loved her and was eager to see the beautiful child that she was about to bring into the world. This seemed to bring her momentary relief, although I don't think, at that point, she even knew who I was. She was all alone in a world of pain.

Then it was over. She gave birth to a beautiful baby girl.

It was dead.

Fosseuse fell unconscious. I did not want to be there when she revived and learned the tragic news, so I left the room, went into my bedchamber, and cried for a very long time. I cried for the child who would never see this world. I cried for Fosseuse, who may now very well have lost her allure for Henri. And I cried for myself for living in a world where women have to suffer in this way.

17 March, 1584 - Nérac

Henri and I had a long talk yesterday. He has been moribund since the death of his child, and, as I suspected, finds he cannot even look at Fosseuse, who is herself grief-stricken. My heart breaks for the girl, but what can I do? Henri, ever resilient, has lately become attracted to one of my other ladies, Charlotte de Sauve, a much sought-after beauty who has up to this point deferred his attentions. Since he and I have become more friendly lately, Henri started to speak to me about Charlotte's many virtues. Extraordinary that he would think I'd find this interesting subject matter. Are men just essentially stupid? It gave me, however, an idea for how to use his needs to achieve my own ends. We were walking in the Parc de la Garenne on a cold morning when he once again brought up the subject of Charlotte de Sauve's seeming indifference.

"Henri, it occurs to me that my presence here might be something of an impediment to your romantic pursuits. Charlotte is a close friend; it may be that she feels a liaison with you would be a betrayal of our friendship." Charlotte and I don't like each other very much, but the fact did not seem particularly useful at the moment. Henri looked at me in surprise.

"I never thought of that," he said.

"You and I don't make very good lovers," I continued. "Oh, I appreciate your efforts on my behalf, and of course, the fault lies within myself. But I rather feel we make better friends than lovers, don't you? I propose that I take some time away from court, perhaps go to Paris for a while. I'm not at all convinced that Alençon has the wherewithal to convince the King of the necessity of his taking Flanders, and Mother's efforts on his behalf seem half-hearted at best."

"The King is wrong. Flanders would be a good move for France."

"Of course, but Anjou is still worried that Alençon might be in league with you. You are very good friends."

"If he had seen the battle I just had with Alençon over who will win Charlotte, he'd be convinced otherwise. Fortunately, your brother conceded the field to me."

"Decent of him." Sometimes I could just kick Henri in the head. "But all Anjou knows is, that you and Alençon spend a good deal of time together; it can't be a balm to his fears. As next in line to the throne, Alençon is a constant threat to Anjou. I think I should go assist him."

Henri brightened. Seeing the idea presented to him in the context of political expediency distanced him from his personal obsessions, and allowed him to gallantly agree that some time away from the court of Nérac would be good for me. It's lovely to have formed this new relationship with Henri, free of mutual accusation and resentment, even if he is a thoughtless dolt whom I would occasionally like to shove down the stairs. Such, I suspect, is the nature of marriage.

But more importantly: It seems, incredibly, that I am at last free to go to the man I love. And go I shall.

3 April, 1584 - Paris

After a three-day journey that felt more like three months, our procession finally arrived back at the Louvre. As he was in charge of receiving the horses, Jean was one of the first persons to welcome me. I could barely control my excitement at seeing him, but as it was a public reception, I was forced to give him little notice as he helped me out of the litter.

"Your Majesty!" he said, less skilled at concealing his delight.

"Monsieur d'Aubiac," I replied with more professional *sang-froid* and coolly walked into the Louvre, my heart pounding wildly.

The first person to intercept me was the Duke of Guise. It was nauseating to see him, I actually felt faint for a moment, but I have been giving it great thought and there is nothing to be gained by letting him know how deeply I detest him. If he is to be useful, he needs to think the opposite.

"Your Majesty," he drawled. "How delightful to have you with us. Your time away has only heightened your beauty."

Incredible. Not the slightest glimmer of unease at being in the presence of a woman he has repeatedly violated. I swallowed the bile that was rising into my mouth.

"Henri," I replied warmly, and his eyes glimmered at having his given name spoken by me. "You're looking well yourself. Congratulations on your recent victory in Bourges."

His eyes widened in satisfaction. "Ah, you heard of my campaign! Yes, yes it was a challenge, but we vanquished the foe handily. To what do we owe the pleasure of your illustrious company here at court?" inquired this monstrous demon from hell.

"I find myself in need of a change of venue. Nérac is, of course, enchanting, but even a garden of delight can become wearisome if you have spent too much time there."

"As the Bible tells us," responded Guise, who I am quite sure has never read it.

"How fares my brother Alençon?" I inquired. "Is he in preparation for his triumphal march to Flanders?"

For the first time, Guise looked slightly uncomfortable. "Alas, no. I'm sorry to inform you that your brother will not be making that march."

"Whyever not?"

"He is unavailable for such a mission. In point of fact, he has been imprisoned."

Imprisoned! I had been worried for him but had not expected Anjou to take so drastic an action. I begged Guise to make my request for an audience with the King, and as things were now so seemingly friendly between the two of us, I was given one straight away.

When I entered the king's chambers I stopped and had to gather my wits.

King Henri III was wearing women's attire; a bodice opened at the throat in such a way that it exposed his bare chest. He wore a flowing skirt of maroon velvet and the highest of platform heels. His crown nested upon an elaborate periwig punctuated with pearls; his cheeks and lips were stained with rouge, and his fingernails were long and painted. If he weren't my brother, I would have said he was a stunningly beautiful woman. Mother, who was in attendance, came to give me one of her perfunctory embraces, and at my questioning look she gave the slightest shake of her head. Guise was also in attendance, as well as some deeply uncomfortable-looking members of the clergy.

"Margot!" Exclaimed the King. "How well you are looking. A vast improvement from the last time I saw you. Married life seems to be agreeing with you."

"Indeed, Your Majesty."

"How fares your husband, the handsome Navarre? Is he busy laying plans to overthrow the country?"

I laughed. "Hardly, Your Majesty. He is delighted at this new peace attained by your grace with the aid of our good mother, and asked me to extend his heartfelt gratitude and respect."

"Oh, now nice. I've always liked him."

"Your Majesty, I wonder if I might speak to you about the current status of our brother Alençon."

"I knew you were going to bring him up. Abandon the subject, Margot. I'm willing to believe you were an unwitting participant in his plans to snatch up Flanders for himself, but the fact is, Alençon is a traitor and a threat to the crown. He's lucky he wasn't executed for his crimes."

"I wish I could convince you otherwise, brother. In the time I have spent with Alençon, he has spoken of nothing but the desire to earn your respect. If you could only have seen his eyes shine at the thought of winning your approval, you would be so moved. Even as a child, all he wanted was to be like you."

"I can hardly credit that."

"It was hero worship, brother. Perhaps the same way you wanted Charles to like you." I saw Anjou reflect upon this. "In the time I spent discussing the issue with the nobility of Flanders, Alençon's name was barely mentioned. Every noble spoke only of you."

"Why me? Charles was king when you were in Flanders."

How stupid. I cursed myself. It had been a long journey and I hadn't fully collected my wits after seeing Anjou in his new Henri III persona.

"Charles, yes, but it was common knowledge that Charles was quite ill and that you were next in line. So many of them spoke, with great discretion of course, of their expectations of you as a great leader, when the time came."

At this moment I glanced meaningfully at Guise. He received my meaning, digested the pros and cons of my unspoken plea, and chose to speak.

"It's quite true, Your Majesty. I had letters following the Queen of Navarre's return from Flanders, from nobles expressing their loyalty and admiration specifically for you. I believe they perceive the Duke of Alençon to be merely your representative."

I saw Mother tracking this exchange. Her eyebrows raised, and she gave me a look that I could have sworn was tinged with respect.

The King was silent for a moment. Then he gave his dress an impatient flounce.

"Oh, very well, release him. But advise him that the crown is observing his every move like a hawk."

Elated at my success, I made my way to my chambers, had my ladies bathe and dress me in my loveliest new gown, and hastened to find Jean d'Aubiac.

As if anticipating my every move, however, Guise intercepted me in the courtyard, saying "That was very well played, Marguerite. But then you have always had a convincing ability with words."

"Thanks to you, Henri, for giving support to my statements, which were nothing more than the truth."

"Of course. I believe you and I have much to catch up on. Might I visit you later in your apartments, Madame?"

I recoiled inwardly at the thought of ever having him near me again. "I should be delighted," I replied, "but confess I have been much wearied by my journey and need to rest. Perhaps another day?"

"I am at your service," replied Guise with a bow, and I thankfully escaped to go in search of the man who is at the center of my heart and soul.

3 May, 1584 - Chenonceau

Mother enjoys collecting castles. She's a collector of many things; tapestries, maps, sculpture, fabrics, furniture, china pottery, and portraits. But castles are her passion, and the one that I think is the most beautiful, and remember very fondly from my childhood is Chenonceau in the Loire Valley. The Tuileries Palace is nice, Fontainebleau is grand, Montceaux, Saint-Maur, and Hotel de la Reine; all are very imposing. But Chenonceau is the only castle that feels like it is built for a woman. And so, it is Chenonceau where Jean and I have come.

Paris was becoming impossible. Guise was relentless in his pursuit of rekindling a fire that had never been there in the first place. He seemed oblivious to the fact that our sexual encounters had not been consensual, or else conveniently forgot, and could not understand why I persisted in having my ladies with me at all times. It became my strictest order that I must never, ever be left alone with him and my ladies were vigilant in acceding to my wishes.

"Are you not concerned, Your Majesty, that the Duke might soon take offense?" Rosalind asked once, and indeed I could sense his growing exasperation at always "just" missing the opportunity for a private audience. I didn't care; in fact, I enjoyed punishing him in that way. But matters were becoming uncomfortable; I felt as if we were being watched at all times, and opportunities for meeting with Jean were fleeting. Perhaps it was nerves, but I developed a racking cough that seemed ideal for convincing the King that I should remove myself from the damp and polluted air of Paris for my health. Jean and I journeyed here alone together for privacy, along with perhaps fifty other essential people.

It has been transformative. Not only is the weather glorious, (the Loire Valley in springtime is something that no one should miss) but to experience this kind of freedom with the man I love is a privilege almost undreamed of. During the day we go riding or hunting or, what I enjoy better, hawking, a more ladylike activity. I took it up after the trip to Flanders, where I saw a beautiful tapestry featuring a woman and her trained hawk, and decided a similar bird would look enchanting on my wrist. I use a female merlin; she's very well-trained and I love to hear the bells on her legs tinkle as she goes after her prey. Jean uses a quite imposing-looking falcon, which he is training himself. We are most comfortable when we are out in the country by ourselves. It reminds us of our flight from Liege on horseback, the adventure, and also the silliness in which we indulged whilst in the woods. It was there that I discovered I do possess a natural laugh after all, which springs entirely from mirth.

The afternoons are for pleasurable indoor activities, and in the evening, we always have the reading of poetry and the performance of song and dance. Jean, after some tutoring, has turned out to be an excellent dancer. How I love watching him move! Whether it's dancing, riding a horse, or making love, he has the ease and grace of the finest nobleman. In another life, he could have been a king. But in this life, he is not, alas, and that is why I have selected only my most faithful companions to accompany us here.

My husband and I have exchanged letters; he seems to be making headway with Charlotte de Suave and is very grateful to me for making his courtship of her easier. Fosseuse has gone back to her people, which removes that emotional burden. I feel deeply sorry for her and have arranged to have funds sent to her family to make their lives more comfortable. I have not, of course, told Henri anything about my own situation. He wouldn't mind if I had taken someone from our circles for a lover but I'm afraid the notion of his wife with the stable master (or First Equerry, as I've arranged to have him designated) would not be received as well. Men do have their pride.

Jean has completely overcome his initial resistance to being with me now that he understands how things are done at court, and it causes me the greatest joy to watch him relax in his new circumstances. Upon occasion, I also mark a certain uneasiness, particularly in conversational settings with others. He does not have the liquidity of tongue that so many of our wittier courtiers do. Oh, but when we are alone...

How beautiful life can be!

12.

"The fact is that men who know nothing of decency in their own lives are only too ready to launch foul slanders against their betters."

— **Plutarch**

27 May, 1584 ~ Chenonceau

I have finally experienced it. The state of being my ladies have always referred to as "*le petit mort*" is one that I now understand. In the past, I always feigned knowledge of it, laughed at their little jokes, nodded wisely, and assumed it would never happen to me. But it has happened, more than once, and now I understand all. It's not like a little death, if anything it's like being more alive than ever. It's as if one is extending one's being to the furthest stars, dancing amongst them, and then returning to earth. It is the most delicious thing!

Adrienne, Countess de Lalaing came to call a few days ago and I was overjoyed to see her. I introduced her to Jean, and Adrienne is so good at putting people at their ease that before long they were conversing as if they had been friends for many years. She told me privately that she is delighted to see me so happy, that Jean seems like the best of men. I'll vouchsafe she is correct about that.

On a walk along the river, Adrienne surprised me greatly with a story about her daughter, Christine, who is nineteen years old and not long ago married to the Prince of Espinoy, who is also the governor of Tournai. The Prince has taken the side of the rebels against the King of Spain, and one day he was called north to lead the attack against Gravelines, near Dunkirk. It seemed safe to do so, but shortly after he left, Tournai itself came under siege.

"Under siege!" Repeated the Countess. "Leaving the city in the hands of only my daughter, and one inexperienced lieutenant. Can you imagine?" I could not. Adrienne went on to recount that Christine led the troops brilliantly, bringing down many men with her very own hand using her husband's bow and arrow, and making an inspirational speech that inspired her troops to commit great feats of courage. Christine herself was injured in battle but recovered.

"Thanks to the bravery of my daughter, Tournai is saved!" exclaimed Adrienne.

I watched her face as she told this story. She radiated such love and pride in her daughter that it inspired an emotion within me that I came to recognize as jealousy. Deeply profound jealousy. It is unbecoming of me, I know, but at that moment, I wished it had been me at the parapets, shooting down the enemy, making the stirring speech, and causing Adrienne to glow with such pride. Of course, I am not her daughter, so that hardly makes sense. But I thought back to the time in the garden when Adrienne held me in her arms and let me cry. It was as near to experiencing the warmth of maternal affection as I have ever known. Now, listening to her proud reflections on her brave daughter, I felt as if I had been demoted in her eyes, and it made me feel angry, sad, and foolish for living this life of leisure whilst young women like Christine are doing courageous things. I know it was an irrational reaction, yet I feel the need to commit it to paper. This journal is for all thoughts, rational and otherwise. (As is the confessional, of course, but I find it difficult to unburden oneself when one knows one's confessor is fully as sinful.)

I have decided this might be a good time to take up the bow and arrow.

The final moments of Adrienne's visit, however, changed the afternoon entirely. As she bade me farewell, the Countess hesitated, then reached into her reticule.

"Your Majesty, I am loath to interrupt your well-deserved happiness, but I'm afraid I must share this with you before I leave."

She handed me a thin pamphlet with a rudimentary sketch of a woman who bore a slight resemblance to myself on the cover. Inside, and printed on all four pages, was a diatribe of the ugliest nature written specifically against me, describing me in utterly loathsome terms. It claimed that I was a woman of no morals who began a life of sin at the age of eleven, that I had taken scores of lovers –including three of my brothers! – that I betrayed my husband, the faithful Prince of Navarre, at every turn, and was the shame of the court. It wrote that at one time I had been in love with and affianced to the Duke of Guise, but that he had rejected me because of my licentious nature, for which my mother and brother beat me severely. It even said more but, feeling ill, I could not bear to read further.

"Where did you obtain this?" I asked.

"My husband brought it to my attention. They are being widely distributed in Flanders, mainly in the rural areas. I'm guessing it's the work of the Huguenots."

"But why?"

"Christine tells me your visit to Flanders provoked a negative reaction in some segments of the population. It's an attempt to discredit the French crown."

"Surely no one will believe this poison."

"It's hard to say. Simple people who see something written and repeated often enough tend to believe it. I'm so very sorry, dearest. Now that you've seen it, we must burn it. I did not mean to ruin our lovely day but felt it was something you should know so that you can prepare yourself for every eventuality.

"You don't think this obscene pamphlet has made its way to Paris?"

"I doubt it," replied Adrienne, "but there's no way of knowing."

I will not sleep well tonight.

30 June, 1584 - Chenonceau

Two messages arrived today, one from Alençon and the other from my mother. I of course read Alençon's first:

> *Francis, by the grace of God Duke of Alençon, to his beloved sister Marguerite, by the grace of God Queen of Navarre, greetings and affection,*
>
> *I am pleased to inform you of the commencement of our Joyous Entry to Antwerp, as invited by William of Orange, for the glory of King Henri III and to take my seat as Lord Protector of Flanders. With the leadership of the King, the wisdom of our honorable mother the Queen and the Duke of Guise, and your blessed assistance, dear sister, we have secured the enthusiastic endorsement of the most significant nobility in the region, the results of which will bring Flanders once again under the protection of France for evermore. My delight at long last in bringing this mission to fruition, as well as my gratitude to you, can scarcely be expressed in words.*
>
> *I remain your loving brother, etc.*

The uneasiness that I felt seeing my name grouped with Guise and my mother was counterbalanced by the happiness I felt for my brother. At long last, a true accomplishment for Alençon! After the failure of his peace treaty and the aborted courtship of Queen Elizabeth, he was starting to be mocked as ineffective and weak. This is a much-needed victory for my brother and, once he is established in Flanders, Jean and I intend to visit him there to celebrate the fruits of his labor.

The letter from my mother was as follows:

> *Catherine, by the grace of God Queen Regent of France, to her honorable daughter Marguerite, by the grace of God Queen of Navarre, greetings and affection.*
>
> *We are not insensible to the services you have rendered your brother and trust that your time in Chenonceau has been felicitous to*

*the resurrection of your health. Know that as your mother I am always
protective of your welfare and though your actions in Flanders may
not have been fully authorized at the time, I take pride in the wit and
discretion demonstrated to produce such felicitous results. Joy be to the
crown with this accomplishment.*

Usually with my mother's letters, I have to study them carefully to
discover their true portent, but this one seemed miraculously free of inner
meaning. It feels unusual and strange to be on good footing with her, but I
am more than grateful to be so. In fact, it has caused me to feel a lightness
of spirit I have not experienced in a long time.

We are very much enjoying this beautiful summer in the Loire Valley.
As time has passed and Jean has become more accustomed to his new role,
so also has our company expanded. My lady Rosalind has returned to me
for the summer, and we have now been joined by others, such as Henriette
de Cleves, Duchess of Nevers, Jacques de Harlay, my lady Maria, and her
beloved Françoise. We are having balls and entertainment much the way
we have before. Adrienne came to us again, this time bringing her daughter
Christine, who is tall and broad-shouldered, with bright perceptive eyes and
a boisterous laugh that rather takes one by surprise.

"I am very happy to meet you, Christine. Your mother has told me
tales of your recent heroism in Tournai. Your courageous battle fairly took
my breath away."

"I was only doing what I had to do, Your Majesty," she replied. "My
husband chose that moment to be away."

"But weren't you afraid?"

"I was terrified. But I was afraid of being raped and murdered more."

I was shocked by her forthrightness; women do not generally speak
publicly of rape, although it happens all around us and to us. Christine
seemed like a new breed of woman to me, and oddly I found myself seeking
her approval.

"You should know that after some fruitful negotiations on my part, the Duke of Alencon has graciously offered to place Flanders under French protection, once Flanders frees itself from Spanish tyranny. You will be well protected then."

"Begging Your Majesty's pardon, but the only one who can truly protect Flanders is Flanders itself."

The Countess stepped in at this moment. "But, of course, Christine is more than grateful for the Prince's interest, isn't that correct, Christine?"

Mother and daughter exchanged one of those glances with which I am quite familiar. But then Christine did something that I have never done. She issued that boisterous laugh, which said far more than the words that followed.

"Yes, of course. Most grateful, Your Majesty."

From this, I received the impression that Christine found our leisure entertainments frivolous and was eager to be back in Flanders hunting or maintaining the barricades. Later, Jean was able to engage her in a conversation about horse colic, which seemed to hold their interest for an unusual length of time. It never occurred to me to introduce the subject of horse colic; I'll look for the next opportunity to do so. Though I found Christine to be rather masculine and certainly not your average beauty, I watched her all evening and marveled at her ease, her confidence, and that completely uninhibited laugh.

July 1, 1584 - Chenonceau

Jean comes from a happy home. His father and mother loved one another dearly, and his brothers and sisters made no attempts to murder one another, not even once. I find this so extraordinary, and am constantly asking for further stories of his remarkably fortunate childhood. His mother used to read to him, and also to sing! He has a clear recollection of lying in her arms whilst she sang to him. (Lying in her arms! I remember once my mother touched my cheek, but I believe it was to check for fever.) The family stayed together for an abnormally long time, voluntarily, before the sons went out to seek their fortune. It is extraordinary tales like these that give me hope for mankind, and make me love Jean even more.

I have been encouraging Jean to relinquish his position as First Equerry whilst in Chenonceau; we have others who can fulfill those duties. But maintenance of the horses which are, after all, the measure of an army's strength, is work that Jean has known all his life and he is loath to relinquish it. "My friends," is what he calls his horses. Indeed, there are times when I see a certain expression cross his features that makes me wonder if he is missing his position in Paris, where he functioned in a larger arena and answered directly to the King. I have tried to make his life here as comfortable as possible; he wants for nothing, and when asked will always say that he is perfectly happy. But I understand that men need to go out from time to time and perform acts that make them feel their masculine importance. Perhaps he should take up bear hunting.

We have a lively entertainment planned for this evening, and then I intend to catch up on my reading. Hélisenne de Crenne's translation of Virgil's Aeneid particularly interests me. A female published author - so exciting! Is the world finally changing for women? I understand that she concludes the book with Dido's abandonment and suicide and erases all of Aeneus's later triumphs. Completely appropriate, in my opinion. Once Dido dies, I don't care what happens to Aeneus.

13 July 1584 ~ Chenonceau

A message has come from the King requiring Jean's presence at the royal armory to serve as advisor on the subject of the breeding of the King's horses for jousting purposes. This is a topic on which Jean has strong opinions, and I could see the excitement in his eyes as he read the message. I know I have to let him go; it's unthinkable to say no to the King, particularly when we have his and my mother's good opinion, but it is breaking my heart. Jean has assured me he will be back in a fortnight, but I have grown so accustomed to having him beside me that I'm sure a fortnight will seem like an eternity. We do have several merry entertainments planned for the interim, which will hopefully take the sting out of having him gone.

The two of us had a long and pleasurable goodbye. As I was embracing him, I felt something sharp in his breast pocket. It turned out to be the fork I gave him when I dubbed him Chevalier. He says he never travels without it.

I think it will be good for him to feel himself valuable to the King. Having him back again will be all the sweeter.

16 July, 1584 - Chenonceau

A letter arrived for me from Adrienne, and it chilled me to the bone.

My dear friend,

I write this in haste without formalities. More hateful litera-ture is being disseminated throughout the countryside, and they now reference your friendship with M. d'Aubiac. In addition, my husband has discovered who is behind its printing and dissemination: It is the Duke of Guise. The likelihood that the court has seen these tracts is increasingly certain. Please take all necessary precautions.

I am terrified. Why did I let him go?

28 July, 1584 - Chenonceau

It has been a fortnight. Jean has not returned. I have written many messages imploring him to return to Chenonceau, but have received no response. I am too frightened to return to court myself. Something terrible has happened, I know it. Oh please, Blessed Virgin, protect Jean from any evil that may lay before him and lead him back to me safe and sound!

1 August - 1584

He is dead! They have killed him. I cannot live.

29 August, 1584

They have taken everything from me. Everything. I

13.

"You too, then, are as able as any man to revive this chilled portion of your life and restore it to warmth: you need no further resources; it is enough to use wisely those you have."

— **Plutarch**

24 December, 1584 - Nérac

I vow before God and the Virgin Mary I will have my revenge. My heart is now cold. I have seen the face of evil, and now I know - this playful world that I have lived in has been nothing but an illusion.

Five months have passed, and I find I must commit these atrocities to parchment so that others may know of them in future and forever curse the names of Catherine de Medici, Henri III of France, and most particularly the vicious and brutal Henri, Duke of Guise. I will never recover from the blow they have dealt me, never be the same person. But sick at heart as I am, I force myself to write this down, if only as a way of preserving my sanity.

It was a trap. The flattering letter from my mother, the announcement that Jean's services were needed in Paris ~ all a trap. As soon as Jean arrived at the palace, he was imprisoned. Anjou reportedly thought imprisonment to be a sufficient punishment; it was my mother - my mother! ~ who insisted he be drawn and quartered. Drawn and quartered! Dragged through the streets by horses, hung from a scaffold, and publicly disemboweled before a crowd of people whilst alive! The most barbarous legal practice this court has ever inflicted upon another human being. Mother, in a rage having seen the pamphlets and heard all of Guise's poisonous lies, wanted this atrocity to be committed *before my eyes*, but the King felt that the knowledge of Jean's death was enough of a punishment for me. My mother wrote me a letter which I shall not reproduce here except for this sentence:

"I was willing to let it continue as long as you weren't foolish enough to let it be discovered. But you have, and this is the price you must pay. The family name is at stake."

What kind of monster is my mother? How have I not understood the depths of her depravity until now? Wild with grief, I fled Chenonceau with my retinue. I could not return to Paris, as I was certain to be imprisoned again. Alençon was no longer in residence at his castle, as he was preparing for his Joyous Entry into Flanders. There was only one destination that seemed possible to me, so I sent a message ahead to Henri that I was returning to Nérac. If the court knew about Jean it seemed likely that he did, too, but I saw no other option.

I was prostrate with grief the entire first day of travel, but eventually a dead calm came over me as I reflected on how events had come to pass. I thought of the many times in Paris Guise had tried to manipulate me into situations where he could be alone with me. I thought of the pleasure I took in outmaneuvering him. Indeed, and painful to recollect, my ladies and I laughed about it at the time, but I wasn't considering his tremendously bloated sense of self-importance or the price of repeatedly insulting it. Guise is a sadistic man; witness how gleefully he brought about the horrendous death of our friend Coligny, how he violated me. I cursed my stupidity for having been so cavalier about crossing a brute. I should have known he would find a way to make me pay.

I spent most of the journey reading Plutarch, my great comfort. The section "On Exile" was enlightening. By the time we arrived in Nérac, I was composed enough to comport myself with seeming calm. I was taken to my apartments, where I sat. I desired to sit in that room in complete silence for the rest of my life. My days of happiness had come to an end, and there was nothing more to do but stare into the abyss and wait for death to finally take me.

But eventually, a servant arrived with word that Henri would now see me. I rose stiffly and was led to his chambers. He was standing by the hearth, and I was amazed at the change in his appearance. He had lost weight, his hair had thinned, he was ill-shaven and very pale.

"My lord, are you quite well?" I inquired. He brushed off my concerns, offered me a goblet of wine, and, to my surprise as we spoke, appeared to know nothing of the recent horrors of my life. We sat opposite one another, sipping wine.

"I'm glad you are here. We need to make a child," he said.

"Now?"

"Yes now, when else? I have no issue, and the subject is becoming of more and more vital interest."

"And Charlotte de Sauve?"

"She has left me for another."

"I'm sorry."

"It is of no consequence. We need to make a child."

"You may feel differently when you hear the circumstances of my arrival," I replied.

"I don't care about the circumstances."

"My lord, let me speak," I said quietly, and I proceeded to detail the events of past weeks. He sat there listening to me impassively but became confused when I got to the story of Jean's barbarous execution.

"Why would they do that?" he demanded. "Who was this man?"

It was at this point that I was forced to reveal Jean's identity. The blood rose in my husband's face.

"The stable master?"

"The First Equerry. His father was my father's - "

"THE STABLE MASTER?" He bellowed, and his voice could be heard all over the chateau. He arose and started toward me in anger. I felt sure he was going to strike me, but suddenly something stopped him, and he started to twitch in an alarming way. Convulsing, he sank to the floor, and I called out for aid. We helped him to his bed, whereupon he collapsed into a feverish state. I did not know what his condition was, but I nursed him as best I could. It looked very much as though we might lose him.

I never left his side, never let anyone else do any of the duties a queen might shrink from as distasteful, but took them upon myself with gladness. I did not know whether he had been poisoned or whether it was an infirmity that lay within himself, but it seemed essential that I and only I come into contact with his body. Fortunately, there was no new mistress around, or if there was, I didn't see her.

Weeks passed, and he lingered in a semi-conscious state. Sitting by his bedside suited me, I could stare out the window and cause my mind to go blank if I were lucky. If I were not lucky, I would end up sobbing quietly for hours, thinking of Jean's smile, his touch, the way he had of looking at me as if seeing into my soul. I'm the reason he's gone. I brought this upon him. He was the one with the scruples, the hesitation to engage in intimacy with a woman so far above his station. He was goodness itself. I am not a good woman. But thoughts like these started to drive me mad. Constantly reflecting on one's pain is the gateway to hell. After a while, I trained myself to focus entirely on the present moment.

It was useful, having this time to myself as I cared for another. Slowly as the days and weeks went by, Henri began to revive (I suppose we both did,) and as he came back to health, he appeared to have totally forgotten his earlier rage with me and was filled instead with gratitude for my ministrations.

Finally, one day, as I sat beside him spooning soup into his mouth, he looked up at me, and with a sigh said rather weakly, "The stable master?"

"I'm afraid so."

"Did you love him?"

"Yes."

"That goes very hard." I found I couldn't respond, but nodded, attempting to hold back the tears that had sprung to my eyes. I thought I had cried every last tear available to me, but apparently not.

Henri pretended not to see them, instead saying, "Henri of Guise is my mortal enemy. He has killed my closest compatriots, and his new mistress happens to be Charlotte de Sauve. Why is he trying to bring you down?"

"I believe he carries a deep shame for what he has done to me in the past. By destroying my reputation, he thinks his malefactions will seem less heinous."

Henri did not ask me what Guise had done to me that was so heinous. I'm sure he could well imagine. Instead, he took my hand, and we sat together like that for a long time.

By October, Henri was well enough to rise from his bed. Our marriage, so long one of recriminations and misunderstanding, had evolved into something of an indulgent camaraderie. We played chess (he's very good, and has adapted to the new rules well,) we read to one another, and we solicited one another's opinions. One day whilst we were walking in the park, I asked him a question that had always niggled at me.

"Henri. Those beautiful sonnets you sent me early in our courtship. Were they actually from your hand?"

Henri's face reddened, and I knew the answer before he replied. "I'm afraid not, my dear. Our English friend the Earl of Oxford translated the words of his friend, that little poet who was visiting at the time. I found them rather touching and appropriate to my feelings for you."

"You are an imposter, then!" I teased him.

"Yes. An imposter. And only you see through me." We smiled upon one another and said no more about it. I found myself thinking again about M. Shakspere's play. Did the characters of Navarre and the Princess end up walking in the court garden, depleted, uninterested in one another romantically, yet somehow united for all that?

As I could now see the benefits of a child arising from our marriage, to provide a buffer between myself and the court and strengthen the kingdom of Navarre, I allowed my body to engage in marital relations with Henri. Henri's brusque workmanlike exertions, such a far cry from the tenderness and unity I had felt with Jean, were actually appreciated. I didn't want anything to happen to my body to remind me of Jean; it would have destroyed me. Having dispensed with Madame Chauderon's herbs for the occasion,

I even employed the techniques she had recommended to my mother to enhance the chances of conception.

Soon Henri was himself again. He went hunting, he participated in political debate with his fellow Huguenots, he ministered to his region, he bedded new women. Although life has taken on an outward semblance of the ordinary, my oceans of tears did not purge me of one thing.

My hatred of Catherine de Medici, King Francis III, and most particularly the Duke of Guise consumes every particle of my being. It robs me of laughter, of joy, of being fully alive. I am filled with fury at the power they wield, and my helplessness to fight them. And I am ever watchful for the moment when I will attain the key to bringing at least one of them down.

May that key be offered to me soon.

1585

11 February, 1585 - Nerac

The report on Alençon's Joyous Entry into Flanders arrived by messenger. He and his troops arrived in Flushing and were met with glorious fanfare by William of Orange. They proceeded through Bruges and Ghent for Alençon's ceremonious installation as Duke of Brabant and Count of Flanders, which was met with much celebration. I can just imagine the shine of Alençon's eyes as he accepted, finally, the accolades so long denied him.

Ghent was as far as the procession went, however, as Alençon was informed that some resistance to his presence had erupted in Antwerp, Dunkirk, and Ostend. Outraged by the circumscription of what he had been told was to be a countrywide celebration, my brother decided his best recourse would be to continue his Joyful Entry nevertheless, on the theory that once they saw his magnificent procession, the flower strewing would begin. I wish I could have been a voice in his head at that moment, saying,

"No, Alençon, this is enough. Look around at all the cheering people. You have accomplished this! You have succeeded. Our mother is proud; no need to go further."

But my brother is a sensitive man, much given to the apprehension of slights and humiliations and, in his eye, stopping at Ghent would have signaled failure of the deepest kind. Arriving in Antwerp with his troops, trumpets blaring and French flags waving, the town watched for a moment in surprise. Then they began to fire upon them with their many cannons. Alençon lost hundreds of men that day and barely got away with his own life.

This debacle, of course, lessened Alençon's position in the eyes of Bruges and Ghent; they who had just received him with flowers and song now turned their backs on him. He retreated to Flushing, whence he wrote me. He had just received a letter from our mother in which she wrote,

"Would to God you were dead. You would then not have been the cause of the death of so many brave gentlemen."

Now sick with tertian ague in addition to his wounds, Alençon left Flanders. Despite my entreaties that he allow me to come and care for him, my dear brother retreated to the court in Paris, where I dare not go.

And there he died.

14.

"Light griefs can speak; deep sorrows are dumb."

— **Seneca**

5 March, 1585 - Nérac

I feel I cannot write further about the grief that is in my heart, a double grief now that beloved Alençon is gone. It was reported to me that when Queen Elizabeth heard of his death, she donned mourning clothes and cried openly for weeks. It causes me to feel much affection for her. She's displaying the feelings I feel I must keep inside, or risk my own sanity in the feeling of them.

From a practical standpoint, however, the fact exists that with Alençon's death, there is now no heir apparent to the throne. Anjou's queen, the childlike Louise, has not conceived (and from all reports Anjou's efforts in that regard have been desultory.) She went to Spa and sought out Mme. Chauderon, but the problem was too great for even that good lady's powers. Henri and I have had no success; perhaps I spent too many years trying not to conceive. It looks very much as if Anjou and I may represent the last of the House of Valois.

In my sorrow, I can barely contemplate this state of affairs, but it seems the rest of the country can. Some argue that Henri, being connected to the throne through his Bourbon lineage, should be next in line. No one had given this much serious thought before, as Mother had so many sons it seemed she would never run out. But as they have died off, Henri's claim has become more and more credible. A great deal of strategizing is taking place amongst the Huguenots, who are determined to see Henri take the throne.

The Duke of Guise, of course, is just as determined not to let this happen. He is aware that, to Catholic France, the idea of a Huguenot sovereign is anathema. As head of the Catholic League, he sees that he may now be able to grab the glory he has been waiting for all his life. To that end, he has chosen to intensify sentiment against Henri. With his printing presses at work, he is capitalizing on the fear of Huguenots by spouting terrible lies about what life under Henri would be like, stoking fears throughout the country.

Henri could see Guise's tactics starting to work, and feel the tide of the country's opinion turning against him. It was causing him great anxiety.

I was asleep in my bed when I felt Henri's hand on my shoulder. I turned over to find him sitting on the edge of the bed in his nightclothes, gazing at me seriously.

"Henri, what is it?"

"I think we might be overlooking an opportunity."

"Can this wait 'til morning?"

"No, listen, Marguerite. You and I both have the same enemy, do we not? Henri of Guise."

"Don't tell me you're still upset about Charlotte de Sauve!"

"Please, wake up, this is serious." I yawned, sat up, and prepared to listen. "I recently learned that Guise has managed to place a traitor within our ranks."

"A traitor? Are you sure?"

"Quite sure. Twice, vitally needed funds from Queen Elizabeth have been intercepted. I have tried to learn who is leaking information about rendezvous points, but in vain. It is taking a grave toll on our ability to defend ourselves."

"I'm sorry. You spoke of an opportunity?"

"Yes, my dear. With your help, I think we could discover who the traitor is."

"Ah. Well, I'd like to be able to help, but –"

"If all goes well, it will place you in a position to have your final vengeance on Guise."

I threw my covers off, completely awake now. "What is your plan?"

"I only have the beginnings of one."

"Let me help you think it through."

We spent the entire night strategizing. By early morning, I began to see the key to my retribution lying there in the distance, waiting for me to pick it up.

3 April, 1585 – Agen

I have come alone, and I have made much show of coming alone (with the sparest of entourage) to our castle in Agen. The last time I was here, it was a rest stop on our journey to Nérac on a mission that I felt sure would come to nothing. I remember being in this very room with my ladies Rosalind, Marie, and dear departed Agatha, listening to them giggle in eager anticipation of the amusements that lay ahead. Everything felt amusing then, rich fodder for mockery and humor. How long ago that seems! How much younger I was.

As soon as I arrived, I dispatched a letter to Guise, one which Henri and I carefully concocted together.

> *Marguerite, by the Grace of God Queen of Navarre, to Henri by the Grace of God Duke of Guise, greetings and salutations.*
>
> *I have taken refuge in the castle at Agen. My husband, having fallen prey to scurrilous rumors disseminated about me by an unknown malefactor, has broken with me. The recent cruel actions by my brother and mother, whom I will never forgive, as well as the alienation of my husband's affections have driven me to understand I require protection elsewhere. I wish to discuss terms for joining forces with the Catholic League but will require additional troops to solidify my position here. If this is agreeable to you, meet me here with evidence of reinforcements at your earliest convenience. I am prepared to throw all of my support to the House of Guise.*

And now I wait.

12 April 1585 ~ Agen

He appeared on the horizon three days later. Even from a distance, I could see the number of troops under his command numbered in the thousands. Thrilled that my plan with Henri was working, but also sickened at the thought of being in his physical presence again, I took my place in the King's chambers with my counselors and nervously awaited his arrival.

The Duke of Guise was brought to me an hour later, heavily guarded by his men. He was attired in a suit of armor, which did not prevent him from adopting the new fashion of adorning himself with a large ruffle to frame his hideous features. His face looked more hawk-like than ever, and now had a long scar on his cheek, which I know he acquired from having defeated a German army at Dormans earlier this year, earning the confidence of many a Frenchman. He is now affectionately referred to by the citizens as "Scar Face." The self-satisfied gleam in his eye was unmistakable as he dashed off a perfunctory bow.

"Your Majesty. I am distressed to hear of your current circumstances, but heartened that it is within my power to provide relief." I swallowed my bile and smiled.

"Thank you, Your Grace, your kindness is appreciated. The literature that has been distributed against me has been distressing. I cannot imagine the sick and venomous mind of the monster who would conduct such a hateful vendetta."

He smiled blandly. "Shocking indeed. Of course, I fully comprehend your anger at the court. A queen of your stature should not have to endure the indignities to which you have been subjected. I am, however, surprised at this sudden turn of events. Would you care to elaborate on the reasons for your change of heart?"

I knew Guise would be too suspicious to buy my story without further explanation, and was prepared.

"Do not suppose, sir, that I align myself with the Catholic League without having given it full consideration. My private complaints are not the only reasons for supporting your claim. As a devout Catholic, it is my conviction that the Queen my mother has been entirely too lenient regarding the Huguenots. I was present for her negotiations with them at Nérac, and the concessions she offered them turned my stomach. I cannot understand how she could bend so to a cabal of heretics which, in my opinion, pose the gravest threat for overtaking the country."

"Exactly the way I see it, Your Majesty. I am heartened to hear your words."

"In addition, Monsieur, I am not unaware of the magnitude of approval lately accrued not only to the Catholic League but to you personally, whilst the crown has been much weakened by these internal wars. It appears the tide is turning, and the country is on your side."

Guise chuckled appreciatively. "It would seem so, which brings me to the question: What is it you can offer that will heighten our position?"

"I think you know, sir. Once these wars are brought to a successful conclusion, if my husband Henri still lives, my marriage with him will be annulled. If he is dead, I am free. In either scenario, I propose you take the throne of France with me as your queen."

The almost childish glee that flickered across Guise's face was instantly suppressed, and he nodded soberly.

"Myself as king. That thought has never occurred to me. It had fully been my determination to support the Cardinal of Bourbon as heir, but perhaps it is worth consideration..." He was silent for a moment, pretending to struggle with the issue whilst I pretended to believe he was struggling.

"Yes, a proposal such as that does have its advantages. A Valois would still be on the throne, providing comfort to those to whom continuity is important, whilst the House of Guise would simultaneously begin its reign. There is power in that combination, there is no doubt."

There was, of course, one issue that needed to be addressed, and I could see him calculating how best to do it. Finally, he spoke.

"There was a difficult period between the two of us several years ago, perhaps you recall. Your circumstances were much reduced, and it is possible I somewhat took advantage of your goodwill –"

I cut him off with what I hoped sounded like cool decisiveness.

"Yes, of course, I recall, sir. I'm not going to pretend it is a pleasant memory for me, but that period has been thrown into stark relief by recent much more painful circumstances. I am a woman; women must inure themselves to certain realities of life. I am also a faithful Catholic, and more importantly, I am my mother's daughter. I choose to forget past grievances, and do what must be done to survive another day."

Guise nodded, appraising me carefully. I met him eye to eye. I knew that cold detachment was the only tone I could have taken that would convince him of my sincerity. He bowed again.

"There are ten thousand troops outside, Your Majesty, at your disposal. This war is against the King of France, but it is also against the King your husband. As long as you fully understand."

"I do."

"Then you have my full protection."

I rose and offered my hand. Guise lowered his head to kiss it. I had visions of bashing in the top of his head with my scepter, but resisted the temptation.

15.

"It is a fact that if you live with lame men, you
will learn to limp."

— Plutarch

27 May, 1585 – Agen

It would be dangerous to write in French at the moment, which is why I have taken to Greek.

They're calling it The War of the Three Henris – Anjou (Henri III), my husband (Henri of Navarre), and Henri of Guise, with whom I am supposedly aligned. I feel like one of Mother's "flying squadron," and have observed those charming young ladies enough to accomplish the skill of knowing everything whilst seeming to know nothing. To that end, I am familiarizing myself as much as possible with the inner workings of the House of Guise as they use the castle at Agen for a temporary base of operations. I listen in to their meetings as I pour out goblets of wine and fuss around the room, and from what I am learning, it seems the House of Guise has gained the upper hand in many ways.

For one thing, these wars have become very expensive to the crown, and Anjou is reportedly nearly bankrupt. There was a meeting of the Estates-General at Blois two weeks ago. Most of the delegates were with the Catholic League, of which Anjou is symbolically the head, but as it was founded by Guise, everyone knows who runs it. The delegates pressured Anjou into renewing the offensive against the Huguenots, but Anjou complained that he had no money and couldn't possibly arm more forces without the necessary funds. To address the issue, he called for a vote to supply those funds. As all the members of the League are toadies for Guise, the vote was no, which cuts Anjou off at the legs.

Meanwhile, the Guise printing presses are running full time, painting Anjou as a weak and waffling mama's boy who doesn't know how to fight the Huguenots, and Guise as a strongman who will defend the supremacy of Catholicism. They mock his effeminate ways; they depict scenes of sodomy and outrageously licentious behavior within the court. They are spreading the rumor that the King is plotting to murder Guide, clearly in the hopes that they can rile up the populace to some kind of civil revolt.

At another time, this would have caused me to feel anger and even sympathy for my brother. But that was before he, at my mother's behest, ordered the death of the only man I ever loved. With new troops at my disposal, I was experiencing a surge of power unlike anything I had ever known. I had thousands of able-bodied soldiers, ready to go out on the field of battle at a word from me and fight to the death. Why not draw Anjou into battle, now, whilst he is weak? Is this not the perfect time to achieve vengeance over him and my mother?

I could just see it. Mother is comfortably behind the battle lines, recumbent in her litter in anticipation of the pleasurable activity of watching people die. Anjou is on his horse beside her, as his men take the field for what is assured to be a brilliant victory. The battle begins. It seems to go as it so often does, with valiant men, France's subjects, dying at the hands of the crown. Mother eats a peach, now slightly bored at the repetitive nature of the slaughter. She's about to give the order to return to the castle when a distant trumpet sounds. Suddenly, on the horizon – what is this impossible sight? Row after row of brilliantly caparisoned soldiers, their oiled muscles bulging, their broadswords gleaming, marching over the hill to approach the fray!

My mother sits up nervously in her litter, tossing the peach pit. Anjou's horse yanks at its reins and whinnies in fear, sensing a defeat its human masters do not yet realize.

Then, appearing on the horizon behind them, the leader of these valiant troops emerges. Who is on that shining steed, her armor glittering like Joan of Arc, riding so proudly into battle? It can't possibly be...

My mother descends from her litter and moves closer, scarcely believing the evidence before her eyes. Marguerite de Valois, called La Vengeresse by her admirers, reaches into her quiver and extracts an arrow, galloping at full speed as her men hack down the opponent, clearing the way before her. Catherine de Medici's eyes widen in alarm as this female warrior, as strong and skilled as any man, plunges toward her. Then her astonishment gives way to rage; how dare her daughter defy her in this way? Marguerite, who has always been so docile and easily manipulated. What is the meaning of this? *La Vengeresse* raises her bow and takes careful aim, thinking only of the man she loves, still loves, will always love. The Queen snarls, exposing her pointed teeth, and is about to order her daughter's immediate execution, but before she can, *La Vengeresse* releases her arrow. It jettisons through the air, faster than any arrow ever shot, knowing its target as if it were carved with this very person in mind. As perhaps it was.

"We must take action now!" I turned impatiently to Guise and Louis, a bloviating cardinal fully as lecherous as his brother. "All of this talk is well and good, but why are we waiting? We need to attack them now."

The two men looked up from their war map. "Attack who, Your Majesty?" asked Guise.

"My mother and brother."

"Attack the Louvre?"

"Why not? If not the palace itself, a significant battalion on the outskirts. I propose that I lead my troops into battle myself. I have been training with bow and arrow; we could do a great deal of damage, and the sight of me leading the charge would be utter humiliation for the crown." Guise and his brother exchanged a glance.

"Your troops are here for your protection, Your Majesty, should someone try to attack you," commented Louis.

"But surely there is value in a preemptive strike. I could –"

I didn't finish my sentence, suddenly aware of the brothers looking at me with calculating concern. My fantasy began to dissolve into thin air. Feeling the danger of the moment, I quickly retreated. "Perhaps you are right," I conceded mildly. "How foolish of me."

With piercing clarity, I had just in time recognized what was happening to me. Having spent days listening to the devious machinations of the Guise brothers, I had unknowingly become infected with their disease.

Receiving a taste of what it is to have a little power, to be a threat to other men, not only was I itching to use it but I wanted more. I wanted to become Adrienne's daughter, Christine, avenging her enemies. I wanted immediate, tangible relief from my pain, and for a moment, I had felt it. It was a heady sensation; it made the blood course through my body excitedly. I had been on the verge of throwing away my plans with Henri in the name of immediate and bloody gratification. But I was stopped cold by the following thought: *I am becoming my mother.*

It was a horrifying realization, which shook me so that it caused me to remember the whole reason I was there: I need to find out who the Huguenot traitor is.

Hate is a dangerous, seductive thing. It wills one to risk all so that one's enemies might suffer. I must resist it. As much as I would like to become an avenging warrior, my assumed role at the moment is that I am a defenseless queen caught between two warring factions. I am the wronged wife, the wronged daughter, and sister, humbled by the events of my life, and grateful for the protection of the Catholic League.

My greatest enemy is Guise himself, in the other room right now plotting the takeover of France. My day of vengeance against him will come. But only if this plan works.

3 June 1585 - Agen

The House of Guise is still clearly on the rise; there has been some kind of uprising in Paris. I received a hastily written letter from my lady Rosalind, who is living in Paris with the Duke de Biron.

> ...*Your Majesty, it is astonishing to behold! Parisians, convinced that the King is trying to sabotage Guise and name a Huguenot as the next king, have erupted into violence, even demanding the King's head! Seemingly out of nowhere, a large and well-armed militia has sprung up and are parading the streets. Not all are Parisians; many are country dwellers, who have read the pamphlets being circulated and fully believe that the King is now their enemy.*

Guise and his brother Louis, who had been in Paris, returned soon after and were giddy with jubilation. They were only too eager to relate the story to me.

"It was perfection!" gloated Guise.

"The people have spoken! The King was shitting his royal trousers!" crowed Louis. Such is the elegant phraseology often employed by the Cardinal.

The story is that Anjou, terrified of the people's militia, mustered in both the Swiss and French Guard for protection, which only inflamed the situation. Rumors went out that the heads of the Catholic League were about to be arrested, and the violence intensified. Anjou then got the misguided idea to take some kind of census - a census, in the middle of a riot! He instructed his officials to go street to street to clandestinely root out the non-Parisian militia. I can't help but wonder where Mother was when he gave that order because, of course, it went very poorly. The citizens, many of them armed, responded by putting up makeshift barricades in all the streets, and the King's troops got trapped in a few neighborhoods.

"Trapped, like rats on a sinking ship!" Cardinal Louis added helpfully.

Anjou was put into the humiliating position of having to beg for help from Guise. Guise, no doubt licking his whiskers with satisfaction, magnanimously and very publicly stepped forward to assist in the release of the royal troops. He then got up on a battlement and made an impassioned speech to the crowd, no doubt invoking God, duty, and love of country.

"They were wild with delight, Marguerite. You should have seen the worship in their eyes," said Guise.

"How I wish I could have been there!" I enthused, hating him with every fiber of my being.

"And then Louis – this is the *piece de resistance* – tell her, Louis."

Louis grabbed his tankard of ale and climbed up onto the table to demonstrate. "I got up on the battlement with him and ceremoniously offered him the crown. The crowd cheered! Yes! Take it! But my brother – we planned this – Henri humbly refused it, instead suggesting that his title should be "Lieutenant General of the Kingdom."

Henri preened his whiskers. "I didn't want to presume."

"Very noble of you," I commented. The audacity! What a pig! "Where was my brother during all of this?"

"He has fled to Chartres," responded Cardinal Louis. "Like the skulking dog he is. He knows his days are numbered."

I murmured words of congratulations, then made as if to retire to my chambers. But instead, I lingered outside the room and listened as they continued to drink and toast one another's brilliance.

"A triumph! Nothing less!"

"The look on Anjou's face as he begged for your help."

"Priceless. A moment to relish." They drank a series of toasts to God, and France, and each other, then leaned in conspiratorially, looking like two old vultures picking at an unusually tasty carcass.

"What about the funds from England?"

I edged closer to hear the response. "*En route.*"

"Our man can be trusted?"

"I have convinced him that his animosity toward the crown is more aligned with our interests than the Huguenots."

"You mean he's been bribed."

"Of course."

"Navarre knows nothing?"

"He knows he has a problem, but he has no idea of the source. He considers our man to be a trusted ally."

"Excellent. What is his name?"

Guise glanced around. I pulled further into the shadows and held my breath.

"Theodore d'Aubigne" he whispered.

D'Aubigne! I remembered him from the night of the St. Bartholomew murders, a would-be poet of rough demeanor who had a sarcastic comment for every situation, even the death of his compatriots. He was a friend of Condé's, and quite the sycophant in Henri's presence. I should have known he would be the turncoat.

I retreated to my chambers and dashed off a letter to my lady "Rosalind," telling her the name of the Huguenot noble that my Lady Agatha fancies so dearly – the very name Guise had whispered. I wrote Rosalind's name with a flourish on the envelope, sealed it *a la Medici*, and told the messenger that if anyone asked, he should say he was going to Paris. He nodded, took the letter, and headed straight for Nérac. Queen Elizabeth can breathe easily; her funds will resume their safe delivery. Of course, I did this for Henri but, remembering my darling Alençon's affection for the Queen and hers for him, it felt particularly gratifying.

But this is only the first half of my mission. The second part is going to require far more skill.

10 June 1585 – Agen

Marguerite, by the Grace of God Queen of Navarre to His Majesty Henri, by the Grace of God King of France, with deepest respect,

As you are undoubtedly aware, I have recently aligned myself with the Duke of Guise and the righteousness of the Catholic League. However, an event has occurred which has given me reason to rethink my position. Hearing of your recent setbacks and the vulnerable nature of your situation, I would like to request an audience on the neutral terrain of your choosing, away from Paris.

Though he is the head of the Catholic League and appears to enjoy the support of the greater part of the country, I view the Duke of Guise's recent despicable actions against the crown as treasonous. I do not pretend to have forgotten malefactions against me as perpetrated by yourself and my mother. However, I see now that my first loyalty is to the House of Valois, for reasons which I will enumerate when we meet. I await your response.

29 June, 1585 - Agen

My request for an audience was granted, to take place in a fortnight. During that time, I consumed six meals a day and ingested a daily herbal concoction of chasteberry, evening primrose oil, and red clover as well as other herbs and foodstuffs. Finally deeming my appearance appropriate, I set off with my troops for the castle of the Duke of Bourbon in Montluçon, midway between Agen and Chartres. When I arrived, the King and his military escort were already there in the exterior courtyard, waiting. My brother's attire was surprisingly subdued and more masculine than usual; I believe he is aware that his proclivities and those of his Mignons do not sit well with a large section of the public, who consider sodomy a mortal sin. (Watching a man be tortured and disemboweled before their eyes, however? They have no problem with that.) I felt an inadvertent pang of sympathy for him; he really had looked quite beautiful in his gowns.

Beside him stood my mother, gripping a staff. I had not seen her in some time and was shocked at her appearance. Her black hair had gone steel gray, she was crooked and gaunt, deeply bent over on her staff, and her haggard face was shadowed with age and pain. I wondered if Alençon's death had finally broken her. I thought about the rumors of her being a witch; her present appearance would certainly bolster that opinion. Descending from my coach, I approached with caution. The three of us eyed one another warily.

"Sister," said the King coolly. "You've certainly been causing a good deal of trouble lately."

"Merely trying to stay alive, brother," I responded. "People around you two seem to die so easily."

"Yet here you are," snapped my mother.

"Yes, Mother. That might seem odd to you, considering the atrocious acts you have committed against me. In fact, it was my initial intention to wreak my revenge against you by allying with the Duke of Guise."

"I'm sure it was. I'm sure it still is."

"Ah, but you see that is not true, Mother, because circumstances have recently changed."

"How have they changed?" demanded Mother.

"Perhaps you can guess from my appearance. I find that I am with child by my husband the King of Navarre, the rightful heir to the throne."

My mother gasped. Anjou examined me eagerly. "With child? Are you quite sure?"

"I am. I have not had my menses in over three months, and I have all the symptoms." I delivered this with some of the giddy excitement I had seen my sister Elizabeth express before her third pregnancy killed her.

My mother scrutinized me. "How can we be sure the King of Navarre is the father and not some commoner?" she demanded nastily. Anger surged through my body; I wanted desperately to say something hateful in response. Instead, I did something unexpected even to me.

I laughed.

My laugh rang out loud and clear. One might even call it boisterous. Mother flinched, startled. Anjou looked impressed.

"I can assure you I have only lain with my husband, Mother. We have been alone together in Nérac for the past six months, ask any of your spies. In that time, I nursed him back from a near-fatal disease and the hours we spent together allowed us to forget past malfeasances. He came to my bed many times during that period. But he soon became infatuated with another, as he is so wont to do and, in my anger, I fled to Agen. Only recently did I discover my condition. I have written to my husband and have a letter back from him expressing his joy at the news, as well as an eagerness for my return. You may read it if you care to."

I produced the letter Henri and I had carefully composed together. My brother and the Queen scrutinized it, then handed it back.

"We will have the court physician examine you," said my mother.

"I assure you, there is no need ~"

"He will examine you, or this meeting is concluded," snapped my mother.

The court physician, M. Gilet, who was so nearby it caused me to wonder further about my mother's health, stepped forward and followed me back into my carriage. Fortunately, Henri and I had foreseen this eventuality. As he was about to reach under my skirt, I stayed his hand and hissed into his ear.

"If you do not concur that I am with child, I will have your wife, Hortense, dragged from your home on Rue des Thermopyles in Montmartre. Yes, I know where you live. She will be drawn and quartered, her body will be dumped into the Seine, and no one but you and I will know what happened or why. You know I can do it; you have read about my depraved ways in the pamphlets. I am more dangerous even than they say."

Five minutes later we descended from the carriage. "She is with child," the physician concurred.

"Are you quite sure?" demanded Anjou.

"There is no doubt, Your Majesty. The child is quick."

"God be praised!" exclaimed my mother. "The House of Valois is saved!"

"Now, you understand my motive for wanting to return to home and hearth," I said. "However, I think there is value in withholding this news from Guise. I can be far more useful to our cause if he believes I am still his ally."

"Don't be silly, Margot," said Anjou. "If we tell the world that you are with child, it will entirely change the sentiment against us."

"Don't be so sure. Henri is still a Huguenot; most of the country is adamantly opposed to him."

"She's right," said my mother. Never in my life did I think I would hear my mother say those words. Adding to my delight was the fact that

Anjou looked as if he'd been slapped. His face went red, and I could see he was trying to martial his anger before me.

"It is I who decides what's right, Mother. You seem to have forgotten."

"A thousand apologies, Your Majesty," Mother said in a sarcastic voice. The chill in the air was palpable, and I decided the moment had come for the *coup de gras*.

"By the way, Eddie – you still want me to call you Eddie, don't you? You might consider this interesting - Guise and his brother Louis have plans to kill you."

The blood drained from Anjou's face. "What? That's absurd! He assisted in our escape from Paris."

"And named himself Lieutenant General, yes, I heard. He and Louis bragged about how humiliating that was for you. Such laughter that evening!" My brother's nostrils flared in anger. "I don't know his motive for helping you to escape. Perhaps he felt sorry for you. What I do know is that I overheard them, when they thought they were alone, saying the moment has come to do away with you. I'd be happy to obtain the details of your upcoming assassination if you wish."

Panic-stricken, Anjou turned to Mother.

"What shall we do?"

Now it was her turn to look annoyed. "You're the king. Think it through."

"I can't. This is shocking news!"

Mother gripped her staff with such palpable pain that her knuckles were white. "Obviously, Marguerite must go back," she ruled. "Otherwise, we will lose the advantage."

"What advantage? He's planning to kill me!"

"But he doesn't know we know that."

"I don't see how that gives us an advantage. We need a plan of our own!"

I stepped in helpfully. "Perhaps a preemptive measure? I'd be happy to facilitate that."

"You?" scoffed the King.

"Why not? Guise trusts me, odd as that may seem. Who better to catch him off guard?"

My mother narrowed her eyes at me. "This is quite the about-face, daughter. There was a time when I thought you were in love with Guise."

"That time is very much in the past."

"Why should we believe your sincerity?"

I looked Mother directly in the eye. "Because I want to see my son on the throne. Surely, you know what that is like."

She nodded almost imperceptibly. "You think you could accomplish the task?"

"I am my mother's daughter, am I not?"

My mother stared at me long and hard "You've grown up, Marguerite. I wasn't sure you ever would."

I forced a smile, then turned quickly away so that she couldn't see the tears that were starting to burn my eyes. "You must be so proud, Mother," I called over my shoulder. "I'll wait in my carriage while you two talk it over."

As I waited, I could hear the fearful silences that punctuated their bickering, and I knew that I had won.

10 July, 1585 - Paris

Charlotte de Sauve is the most accomplished member of my mother's "flying squadron." She manages to balance her many affairs expertly and was at one point mistress to both Henri and Alençon until the two men came to blows over her. She is a beautiful, talented young woman with no moral compass to hinder her decisions in life.

Recently, perhaps seeing limited possibilities for advancement with Henri, she has planted her flag on the shores of the Duke of Guise, and he's said to be quite addicted to her. But the other day she learned (from the excellent Lady Rosalind) that he's been playing her false with another, and she is utterly furious. It was therefore fairly easy to convince her to arrange a rendezvous with him at Blois. Lying in his arms, it was simplicity itself for Charlotte to relate to Guise her knowledge that the King was in such a desperate state that he was now willing to relinquish the throne to him. Delighted with the news, it was inevitable that Guise should rise from his bed the next morning, kiss her goodbye, and go to attend a council meeting. Armed with the misinformation imparted to him by his mistress, it made sense for him to respond eagerly to an invitation to meet with the King in adjacent chambers, believing his moment of victory was now at hand. This is how Henri of Guise came to enter the chambers and find himself face-to-face not with the King, but with me.

"Your Majesty. This is a surprise. Why are you not back in Agen?"

"I have business here."

Guise raised a skeptical eyebrow. "You are *persona non grata* to the court. I don't see how you could have gained ingress to the palace."

"I imagine if you thought long enough, though, you'd be able to."

Guise stared at me for a long cool minute. I could see his mind was racing. "What business is it you have come to conduct?" he inquired.

"I'm here to right a wrong, Henri. You don't mind if I call you Henri again, do you? After all, we've been so intimate with one another. Or rather, you've been intimate with me. I had no say in the matter."

The man was now on high alert. "We discussed that earlier. You took a very responsible tone about it."

"Yes. It was a tone. A very convincing tone, I would say. But the truth is, I have never in my life loathed anyone as much as I loathe you. It quite sickens me, the depth of my hatred."

The Duke's glance darted briefly to the doorway. "I must say, your acting skills have been quite impressive."

"Thank you, Henri. High praise from you."

Guise forced a rictus of a smile. "Well, I'm glad you've unburdened yourself of your resentment. I must say, Marguerite, this emotional outburst betrays an immaturity on your part that I thought you had outgrown. But no matter. As it happens I, too, have business here so if you'll excuse me~"

Guise started for the door, but at that moment an assemblage of the King's Guard, known as "The Forty-Five," appeared at both entrances to the chambers. He turned to look at me, the blood draining from his face.

"What is this all about?"

"Aside from your having repeatedly raped me? Aside from being the cause of the death of the only man I've ever loved? Aside from having made every effort to sully my reputation for all time? What is it about, you ask?"

"Please, Marguerite. In the name of our former love –"

"Don't make me laugh."

"The King will hold you responsible if I come to harm."

"The King has ordered this action."

"What action? Come, come, you can't make me believe you are in league with Anjou. Send these men away, I see no need for a theatrical display."

"This is not theatre, Henri. This is real life. This is the end of yours."

Guise stared at me for a calculating moment. Then he made a dash for the door but was stopped by the guards, who dragged him back into the room. I watched with eyes wide open as they set upon him, stabbing him numerous times until he was dead, dead, dead.

And that is what happened today to Henri, the Duke of Guise.

11 July, 1585 ~ Paris

I have had my revenge. All those months, three full years of hating a man so intensely it consumed me like a leprosy. My constant driving motivation has been "I want to see him suffer the way I have suffered." Now I have, and I keep telling myself the taste of revenge is fully as sweet as I imagined.

But the fact is I have never watched a man be set upon by forty-five men and stabbed to death until he is mere pieces on the ground. It was not exhilarating, it was sickening. I feel as though I'll never sleep again.

Once the act had been committed, my brother entered the chambers. "Is it over?" He asked with distaste, then tip-toed through the pools of blood to examine the body. Unlike Charles, my brother Anjou never actually enjoyed watching living things die. He looked down at Guise and issued a sigh.

"Well, it was him or me, wasn't it?"

"Yes, brother."

"I'm afraid his brother the Cardinal must be next."

"As you wish."

"Mother wanted to be here for this one, but she's not feeling well. She requires your presence in her chambers."

My heart sank; I was hoping for a quick escape.

Very few know of Mother's ill health; she has kept herself so private lately that no one even suspects. I did not want to see her. I nearly betrayed myself by weeping at the end of my last encounter with her. I'm not sure what overcame me, it might have been seeing her so frail, but I think more likely it was the realization that she views me, and has always viewed me, as nothing more than a means to an end; a bride for a politically advantageous marriage, a receptacle for a grandchild. When she said to me, "I see you have finally grown up, Marguerite," it broke my heart. Growing up, to her, means becoming fully as cold and vicious as she is. However, my mother had summoned me. I had to go.

She lay in bed, her appearance as shocking as if she were already a cadaver. It occurred to me she might indeed be dead as I approached, but upon hearing me she opened her eyes.

"Is it done?"

"It is."

"I advised against it."

"Did you?"

"It occurred to me you might have been lying about Guise's intentions."

"Why would I do that, when I have so much to gain by being your ally?" Mother closed her eyes and turned her head.

"You are unwell, madame," I offered, stating the obvious.

Her eyes snapped open again. "I am perfectly fine! It is a passing ague." She was quiet for a moment, then said in a voice that sounded uncharacteristically tentative, "What happens now?"

"We move forward, as we always have."

"The child. You swear to me it is real?"

"My child is as real as my love for you, Mother. Don't ever doubt that."

"So, you forgive me, then. For what happened with your – with the Equerry."

She said it as a statement, but I knew it was a question, and that I had to choke out a convincing response.

"It is not my place to forgive, Mother. God forgives. I'm sure you had your reasons."

Mother gripped my wrist, and it felt like a death grip. "I did! Marguerite, everything I do...."

"You do for us. I know."

There was a time when I believed that oft-repeated aphorism of my mother's. "Everything I do I do is for our family," she would say, usually after a particularly painful beating, or the firing of a beloved governess, and it seemed her way of saying, "Whatever it looks like, I love you." But as she gained more and more power and her actions warped more into the grotesque and cruel, I came to understand the truth about Mother; she does it to satisfy some twisted need within herself.

I felt I had to ask her one last question.

"Mother, when you had me marry Henri, what was your actual intention? Were you trying to broker a peace between the two religions, or was it a plan to lure Huguenots to Paris so that they could be killed?"

Mother looked at me with wounded eyes. "Daughter, what kind of woman would marry off her most beautiful and cherished daughter for the sole purpose of murder?"

Tears sprang to my eyes. I took her hand and was about to kiss it when, never breaking eye contact with me, her mouth slowly twisted into a malevolent smile, chilling me to the bone. I dropped her hand and backed away from her, horror-struck. She began to laugh, then broke into a coughing fit.

It has occurred to me to wonder - if my mother's early life had not been so wretched, would she have become a different person? One assumes a person does not come into this world possessed by demons – or does one? Is this why rumors of Mother being a witch have proliferated so thoroughly? Certainly, I now understand most mothers are not like her. There exist women who are kind to their children, do not use them as chess pieces, or kill their dearest loves. I have enjoyed the friendship of some warm and generous women who I honestly believe care about my welfare. I thank the Virgin that I have been allowed to know such women. I shudder to think who I would be if I had not.

Catherine de Medici's hollow choking laughter followed me, echoing down the hallway as I fled her chambers.

15 August, 1585 - Nérac

I returned to Nérac sans troops, feeling no further need for warlike pretensions. I also dispensed with the litter and rode on horseback with my spartan entourage. As we neared the castle, I could see Henri atop a battlement watching our return. He was at the gate to welcome me, anxiously taking my hand as I dismounted. "It is done," I whispered. He gave a sigh of deep relief and rushed me to a more private place so that I could relay the details.

It played out just the way we planned ~ the alliance with Guise, the feigned pregnancy, the very real murder ~ but he confessed he had been sick with anxiety. Would the pregnancy be believed? Would Charlotte de Sauve play along? Would Guise be fooled? Most of all, would Anjou be stupid enough to believe he could eliminate Guise without repercussions?

Because the repercussions have now begun on a massive scale. The city, in fact, the whole country, is enraged at Guise's assassination and hates Anjou all the more. The common man, the noble, and even some clergy are calling for the King's abdication. Today we learned Parliament has instituted criminal charges against him, that he is no longer recognized as king in several cities; his power is now limited to Blois, Tours, and the surrounding districts. A humiliating demotion! He's trying to rally support by calling a Parliament at Tours. Will anyone attend? We must wait to see what news tomorrow brings.

It's an extraordinary feeling that I, who have spent my entire life as the pawn of others, have altered the tide of history. Of course, no one must ever know I was involved in Guise's death. Huguenots will always see me as the traitorous queen who allied with the Duke of Guise. Catholics will continue to believe I am the untrustworthy wife of a Huguenot. To the pamphlet readers, I am a woman of infernal lusts who was in love with her younger brother. Such a multi-faceted personality have I!

Now, I must put it all behind me and resume a normal life. The climate has softened to the pale green of spring, much the way it was my first time here, and Henri and I have found a peace with one another that I am willing to wager is unusual in most marriages. There is no pretense. Henri continues his indiscretions, and after some slightly heated conversation, he has come to agree that he should accept mine. I shall never love again, but there are several courtiers here who seem eager to revive my spirits, and I am inclined to let them try. We have opened the chateau again to guests. We are presenting entertainments, and there is theatre, song, and dance every night. Henri still rides off to oversee one battle or another, but when he returns, we have balls, and the chateau rings with the laughter of thoughtful and witty people. We stroll the Parc de la Garenne and cruise the canal in longboats, often presenting dance pieces for the town folk that they seem to enjoy.

More keenly than ever aware of the impermanence of life, and how quickly everything can and will change, we are determined to enjoy our fleeting youth.

2 January, 1586 - Nérac

Mother is dead. She lasted longer than any of us thought she would. Guise's demise restored her spirits for a while, and the hope that I might provide a male heir caused her to catch a second breath and enter into renewed negotiations with the Huguenots, but when I announced my "miscarriage" she was filled with the blackest fury and wrote me a hate-filled diatribe accusing me of a litany of ugly things, some of which were true. After that, she launched an all-out vendetta against the Huguenots (and, presumably, me.) There was yet another cycle of war, this time more intense than before. The battles produced no tangible result, just more death and desolation, and this time Mother's health started to definitively fail. I was told she would not last the winter, and that I should come to the Louvre if I wanted to make my final goodbye. I did not go.

There was a reading of her will. Of all her enormous holdings ~ all her castles, furniture, jewels, clothing, horses ~ Mother left me nothing. So, that chapter of my life closes.

Following her death, Anjou has vacillated wildly on the direction he wishes to take to salvage his ever more tenuous hold on the throne. I'm sure he feels the vulnerability of being without his most powerful ally, however much they annoyed each other.

Today, a message arrived requesting a conference between the King of Navarre and the King of France. Not a royal command, a request; that in itself speaks volumes. Henri and I discussed it and together established the terms we would demand for the meeting to take place. The terms were met, and we knew he must go. As I walked Henri to his horse, I took his hand. He looked at me, surprised.

"You may not come back," I explained.

"There's always that chance. If I am killed ~"

"If you are killed, I will flee to another country, perhaps England. Queen Elizabeth might take pity on me as the sister of her old love and champion of her favorite playwright. I never bothered to learn their language, but I'd be willing to give it a try, although I hear England is frightfully cold and wet and their food is terrible."

Henri threw his head back and laughed. "I should have known you would have a course of action prepared!"

"But I hope you are not killed."

"Thank you. I hope so, too." He gave me a peck on the cheek and climbed upon his horse. "We haven't done so badly, have we, you and I? Given everything?"

I smiled. "Given everything, I think we've done rather well."

He gave the signal to his men, and they rode off.

14 January 1586 - Nérac

It was a fortnight of waiting, with no word from Henri, not even a message stating that he had arrived. I cursed my stupidity – another trap. I had been through this before - why didn't I talk Henri out of this meeting? I took long walks to calm myself, practiced archery, prayed endlessly, and tried not to let fear overtake me. I reflected on my sins, of which there are many, and vowed to God I would become a better person. I reconciled myself to the idea that I was now probably a widow and went to my desk to compose a letter to Queen Elizabeth.

I had just picked up my quill when there were shouts from the battlements. *What had happened? Who was dead? I rushed up to the tower, my heart pounding with dread. If it was Anjou's men, I was done for. I looked out the window.

Henri and his party appeared on the horizon. He was with his full retinue, and I could tell by the jaunty way he sat on his horse that he brought news of success. The relief that I felt almost caused me to faint. I rushed down to meet him.

Henri leapt from his horse and told me all. The negotiations with Anjou and his council at Blois had lasted eight days during which, by mutual agreement, they communicated with no one on the outside. (He apologized. I shrugged, and avowed I hadn't been worried.) The result was a focused and substantive conversation that led to an agreement; that the King of France and the King of Navarre were united by the common interest of winning France back from the fanatical Catholic League. Even though Anjou is himself Catholic, he now sees the Huguenots as his best chance for survival as king.

"He's desperate, Margot," crowed Henri. (He's taken to calling me Margot lately, too, which I rather like.) "Cardinal de Bourbon is laying claim to the throne since he is now head of the Catholic League. Anjou sees him as a credible threat."

"Bourbon? That drab old windbag? No one has ever taken him seriously."

"Believe it or not, Anjou is even less popular than Bourbon. The King's back is to the wall and he knows it. He sees he needs a public display to inspire the masses, with me by his side. I'm more popular than both of them."

"Well, that's certainly true. So, what exactly did you two decide to do?"

"We're going to march on Paris, of course. A Joyous Entry, his forces and mine together. He will publicly acknowledge me as a loyal subject and friend to Catholicism – don't laugh – and then he will declare me his heir apparent."

"Truly?"

"Truly."

"What if it's a trap? This seems like a terrible gamble."

"It's a gamble. I'm betting that it's a good one. Anyway, you know I've never been one to shy away from an interesting challenge."

Another Joyous Entry. I'm filled with foreboding and cannot expunge the thought of dearest Alençon marching into Antwerp for his Joyous Entry, fully convinced that the citizens would cheer and strew flowers at his feet, and coming instead to ruin. God forbid a similar fate meets Henri on the streets of Paris.

1586

3 February, 1586 - Nérac

The King of Navarre and the King of France (now, incredibly, the leader of just a few principalities) made their grand march into Paris with their combined troops numbering in the thousands, making an indelible impression with their pageantry, trumpets, flags, and fearsome show of force. My worries about their being shot at did not come to pass; the crowd respectfully and even with some awe watched as they made their way toward the Louvre with colors flying and music playing. Many cheered and threw the flowers that had been provided for the occasion; it seemed as if this brilliant display had had its desired effect and won the day. However, Henri wrote me the following:

> It was a triumph – all could see that the march had accomplished the goal of asserting your brother as a strong potentate who still had the support of many of his nobles and now the added strength of the Huguenot faction, with myself as his acknowledged heir to the throne. The King made his way to the throne room to receive his supplicants and sign the many papers that were awaiting him. We knew we had gained the time so desperately needed to win back the trust of the people. We breathed a sigh of relief.
>
> Surrounded by supporters and acolytes, the King began to receive the supplications of certain select citizens. A monk approached and presented him with a document for his signature. Your brother took the document from the monk, who then drew out a dagger and stabbed him, leaving a mortal wound.
>
> My dearest Marguerite, the King your brother is dead.

16.

"Being conscious of having done a wicked action leaves stings of remorse behind it, which, like an ulcer in the flesh, makes the mind smart with perpetual wounds."

— **Plutarch**

1591

12 August, 1591 - Nérac

It has been five years since my last entry into this journal. Five years since the last of my brothers died, almost six years since Mother died. During that time, it seems there has been nothing to say, because there has been nothing but endless war. There is no point in writing about war anymore; people die, there are treaties, the treaties are broken, and more people die. We at court strive to live our usual lives despite it. We laugh, we flirt, we dance, we read poetry, and sigh. I wonder sometimes if I am the only one who feels the emptiness that lies beneath it all.

I am thirty-seven years of age now. My health is good, but my first beauty is diminished; I take less and less delight in the flattery of courtiers since my mirror tells me they are lying. I read, I seek the company of those more learned than myself, I seek to improve my mind. In my experience, the mind is the only thing that stays with one relatively unchanged, or even improves during this journey that is life. And my mind is clearing about many things.

I have reconciled myself to the knowledge that I am not good. I am, however, especially these days when temptations are fewer, somewhat virtu-ous, especially for the cruel times we live in. I am reading a new philosopher, Michel de Montaigne. He opines that goodness is second nature to some; for others who wish to be good, there is virtue. To me, virtue seems like the carapace people assume after they have sinned. I am a sinner. I have mur-dered a man, or at any rate, arranged for his death and watched it happen. He was a corrupt man, but I joined him in his corruption by ending his life. Most importantly I have, by submitting to my passions, caused the death of another, much better, man. There is no atonement for that, only everlasting sorrow and the penalty I will face in the afterlife. To be good I have to con-sciously try, and it is often a battle; for too many years my heart has been corrupted by hate for the ones who have done me wrong. It is not in my nature, as it was in some members of my family, to be cruel, but bitterness comes rather more easily to me. To appease my soul, it often helps to seek the words of those more enlightened than myself.

I have been in touch with the English poet turned playwright, M. Shakspere. He has recently enjoyed a great deal of success in London, and I wrote to request another copy of the play he wrote about us, "The Work of Love is Lost." He sent it, and since I have made a study of English lately, and am now able to read much of the play. It bears only a passing resemblance to what actually occurred at court but I read it with enjoyment; happy endings appeal to me. Amusingly, the court of Navarre has become rather famous for romantic intrigue, and the timing was right for a play poking fun at our foibles. (It's always fun to poke fun at countries you know little about.)

M. Shakspere explained that he uses stories that he has heard or read about as points of departure for his tales, and though he used only my mother's name in "The Work of Love," he was interested enough by his conversation with her in Nérac all those years ago (what *did* she say to him?) to create another character in one of his more recent plays, this one involving King Henri VI of England. That character is called Margaret. She is the mother of the King and reportedly bears many of Mother's personality traits. I can only conclude that this play is not a comedy.

As I have said, the past five years have been nothing but war, yet it seems we are finally achieving Henri's desired goal of ascending the throne as the rightful king. Anjou had named him as his successor with his dying breath, but apparently dying breaths don't mean that much these days. His chief rival, the Cardinal of Bourbon put up quite a fight, but that man has unexpectedly died and, try as the other side might, there seems to be no convincing alternative: Anjou's last words will be honored, and Henri of Navarre will become King Henri IV. Everyone here is very excited.

Everyone except me.

"My lord, I would like to request a divorce," I said at breakfast. He looked up from his eggs, astonished.

"A divorce? Is this a jest? Marguerite, we have just reached the pinnacle of our ambitions."

"They were never my ambitions, dear. They were yours. I was happy to assist you with them, but now I'd like to be free to live my life. I have no desire to go back to Paris and be queen. I am not good. I fear what it might lead to."

"What utter nonsense. Of course, you'll be queen and a damned good one!"

"What about the fact that I have not produced an heir?" Henri looked uncomfortable.

"There is still time for that. Look at your mother."

"I'd rather not, if you don't mind."

"Marguerite. Be sensible."

But I am being sensible. Motherhood does not seem like a natural role for me to step into; I have not benefited from the experience of having a mother, and although I have witnessed some tender moments between many of my friends and their children, I am fairly certain those moments would come less easily for me. In addition, the memory of my sister Elizabeth's horrible death during childbirth lives within me forever.

Henri has other women to choose from, of course. His mistress, Gabrielle d'Estrées, has already borne him three children, but I don't think she's the best choice. First of all, I don't like her. She struts around the castle as if it's hers, flaunting her status as the favorite and wearing a set of gold keys in a chain around her neck, which Henri gave her and which don't open anything. Secondly, she's bloodthirsty. She enjoys war. She went onto the battlefield with Henri, seeing herself as some kind of angel of mercy no doubt, but found instead that she delighted in all the blood and gore. She came back with the most horrific accounts which she gleefully related to everyone. Thirdly, the people of France don't like her. Rumors of her behavior on the battlefield have made their way into publications, and they are calling her "The Duchess of Filth." I don't see that as a successful entrée to the throne of France.

I said all of this to Henri, of course, and he looked rather exasperated. "Well, then who in your opinion would be a good choice?"

"Why not Marie de Medici?"

"Your mother's cousin? Doesn't the thought fill you with horror?"

"Not at all. We're all related in one way or another, and she seems like a very forthright and sensible person, with a wicked sense of humor I rather enjoy."

"Why don't you marry her?" Henri grumbled.

"Now, don't be querulous. Consider, too, the fact that you owe her father the Grand Duke a great deal of money for the wars he's financed. This would be an expeditious way to repay it."

"I suppose there is that," Henri conceded.

"The Grand Duke's alignment with the Pope doesn't hurt, either. It will further solidify your claim to the throne."

"Well, well. You've thought this all out, haven't you?"

"Of course."

"I've already decided to become Catholic again, I should think that would be enough."

"Yes, I find that darkly hilarious. How do all those dead Huguenots feel, I wonder, up in their Huguenot heaven, now that their hero has agreed to become Catholic?"

"Don't jest, it's rather painful, but Paris is well worth a Mass."

The following is the plan I proposed to him: Part of my dowry (all those years ago) includes the castle at Usson. It's been almost unoccupied for years. I suggested that I be allowed to retreat to Usson and live my life peacefully. If it makes it easier for Henri, he can give some public excuse for my going there, call it a banishment perhaps, whatever pleases him and will present him most flatteringly to the public as he takes the throne.

As for me, I want to escape all these horrors and surround myself with literature, music, laughter, and peace. I should like to pretend that the world outside those castle walls doesn't exist. Perhaps I'll come to Paris for the odd baptism if God should be so good to Henri. I can be the benevolent and somewhat distant aunt to whatever issue he produces. In short, I just want to be left alone.

Henri has promised me that he will consider the idea. He's hurt, of course, but I think part of him sees the wisdom in this plan. He needs a legitimate heir.

17.

"You have power over your mind – not outside events. Dwell on the beauty of life. The happiness of your life depends upon the quality of your thoughts."

— Marcus Aurelius

1608

15 July, 1608 - Paris

Oh my, how the time hastens by without our marking it! It is fifteen years since my last entry into this book, which I have just discovered secreted in the back of a seldom-used desk, moved to a position of more prominence now that I have returned to Paris. Happy discovery! I have spent the past hours reading it over, reliving moments glorious and terrible, shaking my head at my naiveté and taking pride in the fact that I have survived events to which I quite easily might have succumbed. How shall I represent the time that constitutes the intervening years?

Henri ultimately agreed to my plan for a divorce, and I moved to the castle in Usson. I spent my time reading, (my greatest joy,) writing poetry, and entertaining friends. I designed a splendid garden that people came from far and wide to behold. Maria and her companion Françoise de Bouillon came to join me after years of self-imposed exile. (Yes, they ran away together when we were at Liege.) I have never witnessed a more long-lasting or committed love than the one between them, save possibly Adrienne and her dear Count, but there are those who deem the love between two women to be against God's teachings and often find reason to accuse them of witchcraft. Maria and Françoise found Usson the perfect escape, not only from the judgment of others but from the wars that continued to rage outside my walls.

Henri took my advice eventually and married Marie de Medici, and although she turns out to be somewhat more headstrong than I foresaw (perhaps there is a bit of Mother in her after all,) I simply dote on their youngest daughter, three-year-old golden-haired Henrietta, who calls me "Mimi" and follows me everywhere.

Marie and I have become rather good friends. She confides in me her marital woes; she was quite unprepared for Henri's serial infidelities. I don't know why ~ he's famous for them, and most of France seems to take a perverse delight in his satyr-like proclivities. They've even given him the affectionate name "The Old Spark." Interesting that they never came up with a similarly endearing nickname for me. (I jest. I'm sure they did, and I'm sure it wasn't endearing.)

Henri may be a man of many moods, but he is a good king. He brought about the signing of the Edict of Nantes, which effectively ended the wars, and since then he has brought peace and prosperity to the country, lowered taxes on the people, opened trade routes to Asia, and made peace with the Ottoman Empire. People were surprised at how quickly he accomplished all these things. I think his understanding of what was required was gained during all those years roaming around the kingdom. He met everyone, of every social class, and became acquainted with their needs. His famous phrase became that he wanted people to have "a chicken in every pot." I believe he has caused that to come to pass.

After a time, as I said, I came to Paris to live. Issues of my health, as well as the delight I take in Henri's children, caused me to move closer to the court. I have outlived all my enemies and many of my friends, I suspect (but cannot prove) because I made the decision to forego the dubious pleasure of becoming a queen of France. I have seen how power corrupts the spirit, and in the years since I renounced the throne, I have made every effort to behave in a fashion that would be the least reminiscent of my mother ~ yet, oddly, I feel her absence keenly sometimes.

This cannot be said to be the same thing as missing her.

Perhaps what I am missing most is that period of my own life when she was alive. Perhaps I also miss the constant challenge of trying to outwit her. I can't say for sure exactly what I miss, but there is a large region in my awareness that used to be occupied by her outsized disposition, that now is empty. It has taken some getting used to.

I planned for my arrival in Paris by having a chateau built on the left bank of the Seine. It's quite lovely but relatively modest; it barely occupies two city blocks. I had it built to my design by a talented artisan and friend, Jean Bullant. My rooms face the Rue de la Seine, and behind me is a fair-sized garden with a chapel in the middle of it. It has become something of a gathering spot for the artists and great thinkers of our time. I often delight in listening to the intellectual discourse and witty conversation that takes place.

Lately, however, I find society captivates me less and less. Now, I spend many of my days reflecting on times past, perhaps I am even somewhat haunted by them. It is so interesting that I found this journal today, because last night as I was preparing for bed, I heard a group of young men – not boulevardiers, but a rougher sort ~ outside my residence shouting, laughing, quarreling good-naturedly. Their raucousness was annoying at first, but then they began to sing a song I recognized, an old drinking song of unknown origin.

"When I drink of claret wine

The world, it turns and turns, my friend,

So now, my friend, here's what I drink,

Anjou or Arbois!

Let's sing and drink

And kill this bottle!

Sing and drink, my friends

To life!"

Suddenly I found myself laughing and crying at the same time. Memories came rushing back so vividly and fast that I had to catch my breath. I was again a young woman on horseback, riding through Paris with my beloved, caparisoned in men's clothing, disheveled, in danger, and incredibly happy. How very, very long ago that seems now! As if it happened to another woman.

My Jean. I often feel that I dwell with him in some alternate, kinder place where our love was allowed to flourish. I can still see him talking softly to his horse, bringing him back to health with his comforting words. I watch him managing his falcon so expertly as if he and the bird were one. I see him at the river fishing for our breakfast. And I can still hear his voice that night when we were lying so close to one another in my litter, our breaths coming fast, terrified of the enemy on the hill yet stimulated almost beyond endurance by one another's presence. His deep, gentle voice echoes within me as I recall the day that, convinced we were experiencing our final moments, I pressed him to tell me what he would remember most fondly about his life.

"This," he murmurs to me even now. "I will remember only this."

AFTERWARD

Marguerite de Valois outlived Henri by five years; in 1610, he was assassinated by a Catholic zealot. Marguerite went on to write her memoirs, upon which I relied heavily for certain portions of this book. She was the first woman to ever publish her memoirs.

Most of the historical events in this novel are true, although the dates have been massaged for storytelling purposes. Although William Shakespeare was a contemporary of Marguerite de Valois and did write "Love's Labours Lost" inspired by the court of Navarre, there is no record of his ever having traveled to France; he would have been a young boy at the time in which I placed him there. Henri, the Duke of Guise gets the full villain treatment here with, I believe, good reason, but his rape of Marguerite was invented by me (I hope.) Jean d'Aubiac was indeed the stable master, was romantically involved with Marguerite, and did meet a terrible fate at the hands of the King and Catherine de Medici. Whether he was Marguerite's One Great Love is cause for speculation; and so, I did.

ACKNOWLEDGMENTS

This book would never have been written if I hadn't spent a transformative couple of weeks at the Studio Faire Artists' Retreat in Nérac, France, run by the charming and delightful Julia and Colin Douglas Usher. One night we dined beneath the ruins of the chateau where Marguerite and Henri of Navarre resided; it was there that my fascination began.

I also wish to thank my friends and family who have read drafts of this novel, been so supportive, and made helpful comments along the way: Beth Butterfield, Gilbert Cole, Audrey Corsa, Jed Seidel, Maggie Marshall, Steve Chivers, Gin Butterfield, Jean Smart, Mary Portser, Lily Knight, Suzy Logan, Shelia Zahm, Fay Gauthier, Tim Carhart, Glynn Butterfield, Dick Butterfield, Kate Bristow, Shaw Purnell, Dakin Matthews, and Suzanne Rand Eckmann. Thanks also to Phil Swann and Michelle Hermann, for early advice.

But deepest thanks go to my husband Ron West, who allowed me to read this entire book to him aloud and made helpful suggestions, who puts up with me on a daily basis, and who always offers love, support, a laugh or two, and coffee in the morning.

ABOUT THE AUTHOR

Catherine Butterfield began her career as an actress and eventually turned to writing. She is the author of ten published plays that have been performed in the US and abroad and has written and produced for television, film, and her YouTube channel. She lives in Santa Monica with her husband and their cat, Pandita. This is her first novel.